EX LIBRIS

VINTAGE CLASSICS

THE BOOK OF FLIGHTS

J.M.G. Le Clézio was born in Nice, France, on 13 April 1940. His mother was French and his father was a Mauritian doctor of French origin and Le Clézio has dual French and Mauritian nationality. When he was eight years old his family moved to Nigeria where his father worked for the British Army. Le Clézio studied at the University College in Nice, at Bristol and London universities, and worked as a teacher at Bath Grammar School in the 1960s before travelling the world: in particular spending time in the United States, Mexico and Asia. He is a citizen of the world whose homeland is the French language. He now spends his time between France (Nice, Paris and Brittany), Mauritius and Albuquerque, New Mexico. He has published more than 40 books since he won the Renaudot Prize in 1963, aged 23, with his first novel, *Le Procès-verbal* (*The Interrogation*), and his works have been translated into 36 languages.

J.M.G. LE CLÉZIO

The Book of Flights

An Adventure Story

TRANSLATED FROM THE FRENCH BY
Simon Watson Taylor

VINTAGE BOOKS
London

Published by Vintage 2008

3 5 7 9 10 8 6 4 2

Copyright © Editions Gallimard, Paris, 1969
English translation copyright © Jonathan Cape, 1971

J.M.G. Le Clézio has asserted his right under the Copyright, Designs
and Patents Act, 1988 to be identified as the author of this work

First published in France under the title *Le Livre des Fuites* in 1969
by Editions Gallimard

First published in Great Britain in 1971 by Jonathan Cape

First published in English in the United States in 1972 by Atheneum

Vintage
Random House, 20 Vauxhall Bridge Road,
London SW1V 2SA

www.vintage-classics.info

Addresses for companies within The Random House Group Limited
can be found at: www.randomhouse.co.uk/offices.htm

The Random House Group Limited Reg. No. 954009

A CIP catalogue record for this book
is available from the British Library

ISBN 9780099530473

The Random House Group Limited supports The Forest
Stewardship Council (FSC), the leading international forest
certification organisation. All our titles that are printed on
Greenpeace approved FSC certified paper carry the FSC logo.
Our paper procurement policy can be found at:
www.rbooks.co.uk/environment

Mixed Sources

Product group from well-managed
forests and other controlled sources
www.fsc.org   Cert no. TT-COC-2139
© 1996 Forest Stewardship Council

Printed and bound in Great Britain by
CPI Bookmarque, Croydon CR0 4TD

But let us leave this city & press on.

(Marco Polo)

Can you imagine that? A great airport building in the middle of nowhere, its roof stretched flat under the sky, and on this roof a small boy sitting in an easy chair is staring straight ahead. The air is white, buoyant, there is nothing to see. Then, hours later, comes the rending noise of a jet plane taking off. The piercing screech grows louder and louder, as though a siren is revolving faster and faster at the other end of the roof. Now the noise's shrillness changes pitch, becomes a roar that bounces off the roof's square surfaces, reaches the depths of the sky and transforms it suddenly into a vast sheet of splintered glass. When the noise is so loud that nothing else can possibly exist, this long silver metal cylinder appears, gliding over the ground and lifting slowly into the air. The small boy sitting in his easy chair has not budged. He has been watching intently, with eyes that the unbearable noise has filled with tears. The metallic tube has torn itself away from the ground, is climbing, climbing. The small boy watches it calmly, he has all the time in the world. He sees the long silver fuselage charge down the concrete runway, its tyres barely skimming the surface. He sees the sky reflected in the round cabin windows. And he sees the great swept-back wings carrying the four jet pods. Blackened exhaust nozzles spout flames, wind, thunder. The small boy sitting in his easy chair is thinking of something. He is thinking that one day, suddenly, for no reason, at some

7

particular moment this long pale cylinder is going to burst apart in a single explosion, igniting a patch of gold and red on the surface of the sky, a vulgar, silent blossom of fire which remains suspended there for a few seconds before fading, sucked into the centre of thousands of black dots. While the wave of a terrible sound spreads out and reverberates in the ears.

Then the small boy gets up, and with a slow mechanical movement of arms and legs walks across the flat roof of the airport building, in the direction of a door above which is written in red letters

EXIT

and he goes down the rubber steps of the steel staircase, all the way down to the centre of the concourse. Inside the walls the elevator hums as it moves up and down; and everything is visible, as though the walls were made of glass. There are strange silent outlines to be seen: children with tired eyes, women wrapped in red overcoats, dogs, men carrying umbrellas.

In the concourse, the light is perfectly white, reflected from hundreds of mirrors. Near the main entrance there is an electric clock. Little shutters revolve in quick jerks on its square face, their numbers superseding each other at regular intervals:

15 05

15 06

15 07

15 08

15 09

15 10

15 11

Women's voices speaking close to microphones say trivial things. People sit in rows on leather settees, waiting. When anyone passes through the invisible ray the great glass doors slide back in a single motion, once, twice, ten times. Can you, can you imagine that?

Can you think about everything that happens on earth, about all these speedy secrets, these adventures, these routs and confusions, these signs, these patterns painted on the sidewalk? Have you run through these grassy fields, or along these beaches? Have you bought oranges with money, have you watched oil slicks moving around on the surface of the water in the docks? Have you read the time on sundials? Have you sung the words of stupid songs? Have you gone to the movies any evening, and watched for hours that seemed like minutes the images of a picture called *Nazarin* or else *Red River*? Have you eaten iguana in Guiana or tiger in Siberia?

> Robt BURNS
> Cigarillos
> If it's not a Robt BURNS it's not THE cigarillo

Or else:

(Wilfred Owen) It seemed that out of battle I escaped
Down some profound dull tunnel, long since scooped
Through granites which titanic wars had groined.

Or again:

(Parmenides) . . . αἰεὶ παπταίνουσα πρὸς αὐγὰς ἠελίοιο.

All words are possible, then, all names. They rain down, all these words, they disintegrate into a powdery avalanche. Belched from the volcano's mouth, they spurt into the sky, then fall again. In the quivering air, like gelatine, the sounds trace their bubble paths. Can you imagine that? The black night through which the rockets streak, and then the slabs of explosive mud, women's faces, eyes, desires that cut the flesh like gentle razor blades. Noise, noise everywhere! Where to go? Where to dive, into what void, where to bury one's head among these stone pillows? What to write on the blank sheet of paper, already blackened with every conceivable handwriting? Choose, why choose? Let all rumours run their noisy course, let impulses hustle crazily towards unknown destinations. Innumerable places, seconds beyond measure, names that string out for ever:

men!
jellyfishes!
eucalyptus!
green-eyed women!
Bengali cats!
pylons!
cities!
springs!
green plants, yellow plants!

Does all that really mean anything? I add my words, I increase the enormous hubbub by a few murmurs. I blacken a few more lines, there, to no purpose, to destroy, to say I am alive, to trace more new dots, more new strokes on the old ravaged surface. I jettison my useless ciphers, choking the insatiable holes, the wells without memory. I add a few more knots to the tangled skein, a few excrements to the pipe of the great sewer. Wherever a blank space still survives, making pure emptiness visible, quick, I write, terror, anchylosis, mad dog. These are eyes that I am putting out, clear innocent eyes that my etching needle suddenly punctures bloodily. Noise, noise, I hate you, but I am bound to you. Captured in the silo, a grain that cracks and lets it powder sift down in the middle of the motionless sea of the other grains. Letters that cover everything! Laughs, cries, groans that cover everything! Colours with lead copings! Matter with boulder limbs! Living tomb, weight which comes crashing down upon all of us, and I too am a weight, I too press heavily on the head and force it into the earth. I have everything to say, everything to say! I hear, I repeat! Echo of an echo, channel of my throat in which words stumble, channels of air, endless corridors of the world. The blind doors slam, the windows open on to other windows. Farewell was what I wanted to say. Farewell. I am speaking to the living, I am speaking to the millions of eyes, ears and mouths hidden behind the walls. They watch and wait. They come and go, they remain, they do nothing but sleep. But they are there. No one can forget them. The world has incised its war tattoos, it has painted its body and face, and now here it is, muscles taut, hands clutching weapons, eyes burning with a fever to conquer. Who is going to shoot the first arrow?

How to escape fiction?

How to escape language?

How to escape, if only a single time, if only from the word KNIFE?

One day, the person called Hogan was walking on his shadow, in the streets of the town where the harsh sun's light held sway. The town was spread over the ground, a sort of vast necropolis with its dazzling flagstones and walls, and its grillwork of streets, avenues and boulevards. It really seemed as though everything was ready, was fixed up for things to happen in this way. The layout was methodical and left nothing out of account, almost nothing. There were the concrete sidewalks with regularly repeated little patterns along the surface, the asphalt highways scorched by tyre marks, the trees standing up stiffly, the lamp-posts, the vertical buildings rising to dizzy heights, the windows, the shops full of papers and records, the noises, the fumes. A little higher up there was this swollen ceiling, neither blue nor white, the colour of absence, in which the sun's disc hung. An abstracted, anonymous expanse, an undulating desert, a sea in which the waves advanced, one behind the other, without ever changing anything.

This is what the person called Hogan was walking on: he was walking on the white sidewalk, alongside the white road, through the air brimming over with white light. Everything had been enveloped in this powder, this snow, or this salt, and the tons of grain sparkled in unison. Not a patch of colour left anywhere, nothing but this unbearable whiteness that had penetrated each corner of the town. The giant searchlight held this circle of earth in its beam, and the light particles bombarded the matter unceasingly. Each shape and object had been transformed into a tiny lamp whose incandescent filament glowed brightly in the centre of its crystal bubble. The whiteness was everywhere. Vision was blanked out. Faint lines appeared and disappeared at the angle of the walls, under the women's made-up eyes, along the scorching roofs. But the lines no sooner merged than they broke up, spread like fissures, and nothing was certain any longer. There was the line of houses squatting under the sky, the perspective of the avenues converging in the distant haze, the clouds stretched thin between the two horizons, the jet planes' vapour trails, the exhaust from the vehicles that whizzed past. Surrounded by these things, Hogan advanced, a silhouette wearing white trousers, a white shirt and espadrilles, ready to disappear at any moment, or perhaps in the process of melting gently in the surrounding heat. He advanced without a thought in his mind, his eyes fixed on the millions of sparkles in the ground, the nape of his neck bare to the sun, and under his feet there was a black shadow.

It was odd, walking on one's shadow like this, in the planet's closed atmosphere. It was odd and moving to walk on just one side of the earth, standing upright on the hard shell, looking up in the direction of the infinite. It was like arriving from the far end of the Milky Way, from Betelgeuse or Cassiopeia, encased in a platinum-coloured space suit, and beginning an exploration. From time to time one would have pressed a button and said in a slightly catarrhal voice:

'Space explorer AUGH 212 to Relay station. Space explorer AUGH 212 to Relay station.'

'Relay station to space explorer AUGH 212. Relay station to space explorer AUGH 212. Come in.'

'Space explorer AUGH 212 to Relay station. Have left point 91 and am at present walking toward point 92. Everything under control. Over.'

'Relay station to space explorer AUGH 212. Receiving you loud and clear. What do you see? Over.'

'Space explorer AUGH 212 to Relay station. Everything here is white. I am walking in a symmetrical maze. There are many objects in motion. It is very hot here. I am now approaching point 92. Over.'

'Relay station to space explorer AUGH 212. Do you notice any signs of organic life? Over.'

'Space explorer AUGH 212 to Relay station. No, none. Over and out.'

It was like walking along the bed of an ocean, too, with the thick silence of heavy bubbles rising from concealed sulphur vents, clouds of mud sliding away, fish crying out, sea urchins screeching, whale sharks grunting. And especially the invisible mass of water bearing down with its countless thousands of tons.

That's exactly how it was. Hogan was making his way through the streets of a submerged town, surrounded by the ruins of porticoes and cathedrals. He passed men and women, occasionally children, and they were strange marine creatures with flapping fins and retractile mouths. The shops and garages were gaping caverns where greedy octopuses lurked. The light circulated slowly, like a fine rain of mica dust. One could float for a long time among this debris. One could glide along currents that were alternatively warm, cold, warm. The water penetrated everywhere, sticky, acrid, it entered through the nostrils and flowed down the throat to fill the lungs, then swirled over the eyeballs, mingled with the blood and urine, and took leisurely possession of the whole body, impregnating it with its dream substance.

It entered the ears, pressing against the tympana two little air bubbles that excluded the world for ever. There were no cries, no words, and thoughts became like coral, immobile living lumps lifting superfluous fingers.

It was odd, but it was terrible too, because there was no possible end to it all. He who walks in the permanent illumination of the sun, unafraid of falling one day when the harsh rays have entered through the windows of the eyes and reached the secret chamber of the skull. He who inhabits a city of invincible whiteness. He who sees, understands and thinks the light, he who hears the light with its sounds of ceaseless rain. He who seeks, as though in the depths of a misty mirror, the fixed point of an incandescent face, the face, his face. He who is only an eye. He whose life is attached to the sun, whose soul is a slave of the heavenly body, whose desires are all forging their way toward this sole meeting place, gulf of fusion, in which everything vanishes by creating its imperceptible drop of sweat, sweat of melted granite that gleams on the forehead, sweat weighing a ton. He who ... Hogan walked in the dazzling street, in the whirlwind of bright light. He had already forgotten what colours were. Since the beginning of time the world had been thus: white. WHITE. The one thing that remained in all this snow, in all this salt, was this shadow gathered around his feet, a leaf-shaped black blob that glided silently forward.

Hogan took a step to the right; the shadow glided to the right. He took a step to the left; the shadow immediately glided to the left. He started walking faster, then slower; the shadow followed. He jumped, staggered, waved his arms; the shadow did the same. It was the only form still visible in all this light, the only creature still living, perhaps. All his intelligence, thought and strength had flowed into this blob. He had become transparent, impalpable, easy to lose, while the shadow had assumed his whole weight, his whole indefectible presence. It was the shadow that led the way, now, guiding the man's steps, it was the shadow that secured the body to the earth and prevented it from volatilizing in space.

At one moment Hogan stopped in his tracks. He stood motionless on the sidewalk, in the brightly lit street. The sun was very high in the sky, blazing fiercely. Hogan looked down toward the ground and plunged into his dense shadow. He entered the well thus opened up, as though he were closing his eyes, as though night were falling. He lowered himself into the black blob, impregnating himself with its form and power. Stretched out on the ground he sought to drink this shadow, to pump its alien life into himself. But it always broke loose without budging from the spot, rebuffing his gaze, extending the boundaries of its domain. Diligently, while the sweat trickled down his neck, his back, his loins, his legs, Hogan attempted to flee the light. He would have to go lower, still lower down. He would have to switch off fresh lamps, break fresh mirrors, in a never-ending process. The burning bodywork of passing vehicles threw off stars and sparks. He would have to crush these stars, one after the other. The light falling from the sky fragmented into millions of droplets of mercury. This dust continued to accumulate, and he would have to sweep it away as fast as it formed. Silhouettes of men and women, heavy necklaces, gold pendants, glass earrings, cut-glass chandeliers, glided around him. Each second, Hogan would have to smash all this trumpery into smithereens. But it could never be exterminated. The eyes shone white and fierce from the depths of their sockets. The teeth. The nails. The lamé dresses. The rings. The walls of the houses were heavy with the whole weight of their chalk cliffs, the flat roofs sparkled outside the field of vision. The street, the one street, always taking up where it left off, traced its phosphorescent line as far as the horizon. The plane trees rustled their leaves like rows of flames, and the windowpanes were as hermetically sealed as mirrors, simultaneously icy and boiling hot. The air crumbled into powder as it arrived, breaking like a wave, skidding along, spreading its branches of living grains. All around was a mineral hardness. Water, clouds, blue sky had ceased to exist. There was nothing but this refractory surface where lines broke up and electricity flowed in a constant stream. The noises themselves had become luminous. They described their brutal arabesques, their spirals, their circles, their ellipses. They went through the air tracing whitish scars, they wrote signs, zigzags, incomprehensible letters. The horn of a steel-clad motor coach gave a bellow, and it was a broad trail of light advancing like a crevasse. A woman, her open mouth displaying two rows of enamelled teeth, yelled: 'HI!' and immediately one could see a large star scratched roughly into the concrete of the sidewalk. A dog barked, and its call slid rapidly along the walls like a burst of tracer bullets. From the back of a shop glaring with neon and plastics an electric apparatus blared a barbarous music, and it was the tongues of fire of the drums, the burning gas of the organ, the vertical bars of the double bass, the horizontal bars of the guitar, plus, from time to time, the extraordinary confusion of magnetic particles when the human voice chimed in to yell its words.

Everything formed a drawing, a handwriting, a sign. Odours sent out their luminous signals from the top of their towers, or from where they lay buried in their secret grottoes. Hogan drew his rubber sole lightly along the ground, and at once the eddies widened their floating circles. He lit a cigarette with the white flame of a lighter, and for just a moment, at the top of his hand, this thing resembling a volcano spouted fire and lava into the sky. Each movement he made had become dangerous because it immediately unleashed a sequence of phenomena and catastrophes. He walked alongside the wall, and the concrete crackled with sparks underfoot. He brought his right hand up to his face, and on thousands of glazed panels positioned in the air a kind of dazzling S could be seen swelling its curves. He looked into the face of a young woman, and her unbearably clear eyes sent out two sharp beams which stabbed him like blades. He expelled the air from his lungs through the nostrils, a simple breath that promptly began to burn with pale smoke spirals. Nothing more was possible. Nothing more came into being, then forgot its own existence. Everywhere there was this gigantic sheet of blank paper, or this field of snow, on which the traces of fear formed a deposit. Everything had its paw, its closefisted imprint, its hoofmarks. Wrinkles, marks, stains, white wounds with lips that did not close.

One could not even think any longer. Hogan thought: ORANGE FRUIT WATER CALM SLEEP, and instantly a writing appeared in front of his eyes, inscribing in glowing outlines two concentric circles, a rain of downstrokes, a dash ending in a hook, and a grillwork that covered sky and earth. IDIOT ENOUGH ENOUGH: a flash of lightning with sharp angles, and a sun in the process of exploding slowly. DEPART CLOSE THE EYES LET'S BE OFF YES: and a host of windows opened in space, shining from all their bubble-flawed panes.

Thinking was dangerous. Walking was dangerous. Talking, breathing, touching were dangerous. From all sides, the bursts of brilliance hurled themselves into the attack, the signs with their arms full of lightning sprang up before the eyes. The immense blank page was stretched above the world like a snare, waiting for the moment when everything would be truly erased. Men, women, children, animals and trees all stirred behind these transparent skins, and the sun sent down the raking fire of all its hard, white heat. Everything was like that, there was probably nothing to be done about it. And sooner or later, presumably, one would have become just like the others, a true light signal at the corner of a crossroads, a slightly flickering lamp, hint of a star with a fraying twinkle, a star that is a prisoner of its design. One would no longer be able to say no, or close one's eyes as one went away. One would exist as a fanatical insect, all alone right in the midst of the others, and one would say, yes, yes, I love you, all the time.

Then Hogan planted himself firmly on his two feet, and tried with all his might to bend his shadow upward in the direction of the sun.

Nothing easier than pouring a little water from a bottle into a glass. Go on, try it. You'll see.

I invite you to take part in the reality entertainment. Come and see the permanent exhibition of adventures retailing the gossip that makes up the world's history. There they are. They work. They come and go for days, hours, seconds, centuries on end. They move. They possess words, gestures, books and photographs. They act upon the imperceptibly changing surface of the earth. They add, multiply. They are themselves. They are ready. There is nothing to analyse. Everywhere. Always. They are the millions of centipedes scurrying around the old overturned garbage bin. The spermatozoa, bacteria, neutrons and ions. They quiver, and this long-drawn-out shudder, this vibration, this painful fever is beyond life or death, beyond words or belief, it is fascination.

I would like to be able to write to you, as though in a letter, all that I am living through. I would like so much to be able to make you understand why I have no choice but to go away one day, without a word to anyone, without explanation. It is an action that has become necessary, and when the moment has come (I cannot say where, or when, or why) I will carry it out, just like that, simply, keeping quiet about it. Heroes are mutes, it is true, and genuinely important acts take on the appearance of the phrases carved on tombstones.

So I would like to send you a postcard, to try to tell you

about all that. On the back of the card there would be a panchromatic photograph, coated with a layer of varnish, and signed MOREAU. The photo would depict a little girl clad in rags, her skin the colour of copper, staring at you with scared eyes ringed by black lashes and eyebrows. The pupils of her eyes would be dilated, carrying a luminous reflection in their centre, and that would mean that her look was alive, for eternity perhaps.

The little girl with budding breasts would be holding her body in a clumsy pose, her head and shoulders turned in the opposite direction to her hips, and that would mean that she was ready to take flight, to disappear into nothingness.

She would bring her right hand up to her mouth, with a gesture that might have been intended to be mutinous and a bit perverse but had remained scared, a defensive gesture. As for the left hand, it would be dangling by the side of her body, at the end of a naked arm, the skin deep brown. A tinplate bracelet would have slipped down around her wrist. And the hand, with its long dirty fingers, would be closed over the coin she had been given so that the photo could be taken.

She would have been thus, appearing suddenly out of space one day, then forgotten, and all that would have remained of her would have been this fragile image, this prow-like figure sailing in the face of the unknown, affronting dangers, braving the spray that would break over her.

She would have been thus, magically multiplied in thousands of copies, stuck into the wire clips of revolving stands outside souvenir shops. Starved face, eyes circled with black, dirty locks of hair hanging loose, no thoughts knitting her brow, no throb at her temples, no prickle at the nape of her neck, red mouth half open and constantly gnawing the curled index finger of the right hand. And then shoulders motionless, body covered by torn fabric, all drained of blood and water. Paper body, paper skin, fibrous flesh tinted by chemical colouring matters. It was she and she alone who had to be found again one day, had to be taken away, setting off with her, then, along the roads that lead endlessly from falsehood toward truth.

Signed:

Walking Stick

Men and women, now. There are lots of them, of various sorts and ages, in the town's streets. They are born one day without being aware of the fact, and from that day onward they have never stopped fleeing. If one follows them as they wander around, or if one watches them through keyholes, one can see them in the process of living. Then in the evening, if one enters the post office, one can open the old dusty book and read their names slowly, all the names they have: Jacques ALLASINA. Gilbert POULAIN. Claude CHABREDIER. Florence CLAMOUSSE. Frank WIMMERS. Roland PEYETAVIN. Patricia KOBER. Milan KIK. Gérard DELPIECCHIA. Alain AGOSTINI. Walter GIORDANO. Jérôme GERASSE. Mohamed KATSAR. Alexandre PETRIKOUSKY. Yvette BOAS. Anne REBAODO. Patrick GODON. Apollonie LE BOUCHER. Monique JUNG. Genia VINCENZI. Laure AMARATO. All their names are beautiful and clear, it is fascinating to read them on the directory's much-pawed pages.

One could equally well be called HOGAN, and be a man of white race, dolichocephalic, with fair hair and round eyes. Born in Langson (Vietnam) about twenty-nine or thirty years ago. Living in a country called France, speaking, thinking, dreaming, desiring in a language called French. And that was important: if one had been called Kamol, born in Chanthaburi, or else Jésus Torre, born in Sotolito, one would have had other words, other ideas, other dreams.

One was there, inside the square traced in the muddy ground, together with the shrubs and boulders. One had eaten so much from this soil, drunk so much from these rivers. One had grown up in the middle of this jungle, one had sweated, urinated, defecated in this dust. The drains had run under the skin like veins, the grass had trembled like a tuft of hair. The sky had been there, all the time, and it was a familiar sky dappled with little wispy clouds. At night there had been many stars, and a moon that was sometimes round, sometimes hollowed out. One had performed these countless acts without thinking twice about them. One day, one had seen a fire burning in the middle of a field, on this very portion of the earth, that same day of that same year, under just such a grey cloud, twisting these twigs and gnawing this bit of rotten wood.

Another day, one had seen a young woman passing in the street, keeping to the sidewalk. She was holding a yellow plastic handbag in her right hand. And one had thought that she was the only woman in the world, as she advanced, placing one foot firmly in front of the other, moving her long naked legs, making her hips sway under the pink woollen dress, carrying before her her two breasts encased in the black nylon brassière. She was walking in a very straight line up the deserted street, and one had said:

'Miss, I wanted, I wanted to ask you something, if you don't mind, forgive me for accosting you like this, but I wanted to tell you, I.'

Lighting a cigarette, in the noisy café, and sniffing the pleasant odour emanating from the pink woollen body:

'You know, you are very beautiful, yes, it's true, you are beautiful. What's your name? Mine's Hogan, I was born in Langson (Vietnam), do you know where that is? It's on the

Chinese border. Shall we have another coffee? Listen, honey
—do you mind if I call you honey?—there's a good movie at
the Gaumont, *Shock Corridor*, I've already seen it twice.
How about it, huh?'

And it would have needed very little, an insignificant
shift to the right, a few different syllables in the name, and,
instead of saying that, one would have said:

'You filthy slut! Do you think I'm not on to your tricks?
You, you did it on purpose, I got wise to you months ago,
you're trying to kid me. Do you think I'm not on to that
cigarette-pack stunt of yours? Do you think I didn't see what
was going on? Slut, crummy bitch, and stop walking, will
you, listen to me while I'm talking to you, don't, don't
pretend you can't hear me!'

And one would have made a gesture with the arm, and at
the end of the arm the hand would be gripping the handle of
a sharp knife, and the cold blade would have penetrated the
young woman's left breast at a slight angle and she would
have said:

'Hah!'

—just once and died.

It was a particular day in this century, in a street of a
town, on this earth, under the sky, in the air, with the light
that infused everything through and through. It was about
noon, with man's constructions all around. It was raining, it
was fine, the wind was blowing, not very far from there the
sea was producing waves, black or blue vehicles were
speeding along the highway bordered with plane trees whose
trunks were painted white. Inside the concrete casemates,
the transistors were playing music, the television sets were

crammed with jerky images. In the movie house called OCEAN, at one end of the dark hall, there was a white blur on which one could see a man lying on a bed beside a naked woman with loose, flowing hair, and he was stroking the same shoulder over and over again. Their voices could be heard coming out of the wall, raucous, cavernous, sibilant. They were saying trite things,

YOU ARE BEAUTIFUL, YOU KNOW YOU
I'M SCARED SIMON
YOU'RE SCARED
YES YES
YOU'RE SCARED OF ME
NO IT'S NOT THAT I MEAN FOR A LONG TIME NOW I'VE WELL WHEN I FIRST SAW YOU I DIDN'T THINK IT WOULD TURN OUT LIKE THIS ONE DAY AND THEN YOU'RE GOING AWAY AND IT WILL BE LIKE NOTHING HAD HAPPENED YOU KNOW WHAT I MEAN

and a little farther away, at the back of the huge darkened hall, a woman was counting coins in her hand, examining them one by one in the glimmer of a pocket flashlight.

The street was full of names, everywhere. They glittered above doors, on transparent shop windows, they blazed at the back of gloomy rooms, they flashed on and off again in a never-ending sequence, they were exhibited, hanging from pasteboard placards, engraved into tinplate, painted in blood-red, stuck on to walls, on to slabs of sidewalk. Sometimes, an airplane passed across the sky, trailing a thin thread of white smoke that was supposed to be saying 'Rodeo' or 'Solex'. One could talk to these names, one could read each of these signs and answer them. It was a strange dialogue, as though with ghosts. One said, for example:

'Caltex?'

And the answer came immediately, in a bellow:

'Toledo! Toledo!'

'Minolta? Yashica Topcon?'

'Kelvinator.'

'Alcoa?'

'Breeze. Mars. Flaminaire.'

'Martini & Rossi Imported Vermouth.'

'M.G.'

'Schweppes! Indian Tonic!'

'Bar du Soleil. Snacks. Ices.'

'Eva?'

'100. 10,000. 100,000.'

'Pan Am.'

'Birley Green Spot. Mekong. Dino. Alitalia. Miami. Cook's. Ronson. Luna Park.'

'Rank Xerox! Xerox! Xerox!'

'CALOR ...'

Words, everywhere, words which men had written and which had since got rid of their authors. Cries, lonely appeals, interminable incantations travelling aimlessly along the earth's surface. So it was, today, at this hour, with this sky, this sun, these clouds. Red, or black, or white, or blue letters were affixed to the premises, they were the signatures of space and time. Impossible to wrench anything off, steal anything. They were there, and repeated stolidly, it's mine, it's mine and you can't take it, just try to take it and you'll see, try to put down your name, to move in here, to take over from me. Just try! And you'll see ...

But no one tried. People moved in all directions over the street's level surface. They were not thinking about words.

It was the same thing with cars, for example. People

27

climbed effortlessly inside the gleaming coachwork, sat down on the red upholstery, turned the ignition key, pressed their left foot down on a pedal, and pushed the lever upward. And the car moved off gently with a trembling glide, and there was no one sitting at a café terrace to look at the tyres and say:

'Why, when one comes to think of it, why does the wheel start turning like that?'

At the most, there was someone, a youngish man with a thin face and flaxen hair, reading a paper with a ballpoint pen in his right hand. Coming up behind him, it was possible to read over his shoulder:

DURING THE CREATION OF THE WORLD

There were many other things around the place. There was a young woman with a very white face, heavy eyes shining within their dark haloes, body squeezed into a white dress, legs planted firmly on the concrete ground. She was saying nothing, doing nothing. Between two fingers of her left hand, an American filter-tipped cigarette was smouldering. She was standing in front of the entrance to a bar, and from time to time she took a puff while looking across the street. Behind her, inside the bar, the sound of some piece of music vibrated mechanically. As she blinked, her gaze slid to the left. Her legs shifted slightly, bringing her body forward, then back again. She was there nonstop, like a statue of iron and silk, exhaling her perfume, breathing, her heart beating, her muscles tense, brassière fastened by a bakelite clasp pressed against the flesh of her back, her lungs filled with tobacco smoke, sweating a little under the armpits and along the loins, listening. Thoughts of a kind passed behind the eyes, fugitive images, words, mysterious impulses.

LEON MARTINE phoned yesterday evening BASTARD bastard   leave sooner get the hell out 2000 red car well well I know him   AV   yesterday   why 2000 2500 or 3000 and Kilimanjaro rendezvous and buy ham take it easy   Victor Mondolini   ah that's the coiffeur she must be 35 more perhaps no and at the Pam Pam all this lot all these things to cope with this whole parade.

But she was not the only one. Everyone thought, everyone had ideas, longings, words, and that whole lot stayed hidden inside their skulls, their bowels, even their clothes, and one could never read everything that had been written.

One would have had to understand this total language, know the meaning of this quivering of the lips, this gesture of the hand, this slight limp of the left foot, this cigarette glowing in the corner of an entryway. One would have had to understand all the words that make up the story, all the fabrics, papers, combs, wallets, leathers, metals, nylons.

→ this is what one would have had to do, to get a real idea of just where one was: stay there standing in the middle of this street without budging, and watch, hear, feel, just like that, avidly, the spectacle in the process of unfolding. Without a thought,   without a gesture,   like a signpost, silent, standing on two cast-iron legs, immobile.

Truth was lost. Scattered, winking, skipping about, truth was exploding rapidly in the cylinder heads of engines, was perforating cardboard tickets, was a shell of hard metal with tender curves, headlights with sharply focused reflections. It was the gold frame of black-lensed sunglasses, the rasping sound of stockings rubbing their scales against each other, the shimmering of wrist-watches in their cases, electricity, gas, drops of water, the bubbles enclosed in bottles of soda water, the neon trapped inside white and pink tubes.

Truth was burning away in a single pale cigarette, inside the glowing tip, and the young girl who was smoking was sitting on a bench facing the sea, suspecting nothing.

The dress she was wearing was orange with a mauve check, her legs were crossed, and she was talking to a young man, making occasional gestures with a hand whose nails were painted pink. The cigarette smouldered between the index and middle fingers of her right hand. The girl was saying:

'Yes, Léa was just coming out of Prisunic, you see, and she said to me ... '

'Yesterday?'

'No, umm, two or three days ago. I was with Manu, and she came up to me just like that. What do you think of Manu?'

'He seems to be on the level.'

'Yes, I know, it's true, he was absolutely marvellous to me once, once when I wanted to kill myself. That sounds idiotic now, but it's true. I had it all worked out. I meant to get into a bathtub filled with really hot water, and drown myself.'

'That must be a bit tricky — drowning oneself in a bathtub?'

'Not if you're really determined, like I was. And then, I'd have taken a whole lot of sleeping tablets just beforehand. I rather liked the idea of dying like that, all naked in a tub of really hot water.'

She took a puff at her cigarette, swallowed her saliva.

'And then Manu talked me out of it. He's really an incredible guy, you know, he, he really knows why he's alive. Fantastic will-power. It's he who decides everything for me.'

'Perhaps that's bad for you. basically.'

'Perhaps, yes ... '

'You go through life without any real conviction, I don't know, you seem to be sort of—detached ... '

'It's true. You know the impression I have, sometimes? It's the impression that I could quite easily fly away, if my feet were cut off I'd float up into the air, right up into the clouds, and disappear as quick as a flash.'

'So you need a fellow like Manu.'

'Perhaps, yes, basically. But sometimes I get really mad at him, you know, because I have the impression that since I've known him I'm no longer myself. That I'm lying, and that everyone else is lying, too. The point is, he does everything without hesitating a second, he is happy ... '

'Do you really think he's happy?'

'No, you're right, he's not happy, what's the word I want —contented. But I have the impression that he knows things, whereas I never know anything at all, and that really depresses me.'

She lit a fresh cigarette from the stub of the first one.

'Sometimes, you know, I get this terrific desire to go away altogether. I'd like to be as I was before, without Manu, just forget everything that happened since. But I don't know if I'm up to it. Perhaps it's too late.'

Not far away, a yellow dog with black patches was sniffing at the stale corner of a mouldy wall; a little farther away, a cigarette butt discarded on the sidewalk continued to smoulder in the breeze.

All this was happening here, in this street, at this time of this day of this century. It was the testament of this moment in time, in a way, the kind of poem that no one had ever written and that spoke of all these things. A poem, or an enumeration, that belonged to no one because everyone was part of it:

Apartment building
stone
tar
plaster
grit
cast iron
plaques
gas
water
lamp-post
household refuse
white
grey
black
earth
yellow
brown
orange peel
puddle
paper
tyre tread
engine

Over the street's tarred surface, like a frozen river, the
vehicles passed, and their tyres traced strange lines full of
little signs and crosses. The tracks met and darted apart
again, and the wheels spun frenziedly over them, pressing
their rubber suckers against the ground. The poem continued its enumeration, mechanically, as though there were
someone, somewhere, to whom it was accountable. It was
exhausting, a maddening occupation that would almost
drive a person to tear his eyes out of their sockets so as not to
see any longer. There were all these minute variations, all

these details that had to be seen before it was too late. For example, up there at the top of the totem-like steel pole, when the green light had gone out soundlessly, letting the yellow light come on, which in its turn went out soundlessly, to give way to the terrible red light. Or when the young woman standing outside the bar had taken a paper handkerchief out of her bag to dab at her nose or at a tear in her eye. When this man had appeared at the fourth-floor window of the yellow house, and had looked down. When this ambulance carrying a pregnant woman had careered down the middle of the street, sounding its bell. When this other woman, a redhead, had stepped on to the rubber platform at the entrance to the shop selling swimsuits, and the door had opened automatically in front of her, its two glass panels, on which bronze letters spelled out KAREN, swinging back with a sudden jerk. When the young girl wearing glasses had turned page 31 of her magazine and had started to look at page 32.

Town of steel and concrete, walls of glass thrusting up endlessly into the sky, city of encrusted patterns, furrowed by identical streets, with flags, stars, red glimmers, incandescent filaments inside lamps, electricity murmuring its soothing vibration while flowing through the networks of brass wire. Humming of secret mechanisms hidden in their boxes, ticktock of watches, purring of elevators rising and descending. Gasping of mopeds, popping of spark plugs, horns, horns. They all spoke their own language, told their story of crankshafts and pistons. The engines lived a chance existence, shut away inside the hoods of automobiles, exuding their odour of oil and motor fuel. The heat hovered around the engines in a permanent halo, rose from the scorching cylinder heads, spread through the streets and blended with the heat of human bodies. Town seething with life. The trolleybuses glided along on their tyres, emitting a constant groan. A number 9 trolleybus was passing, close in to the sidewalk, and its cargo of similar faces could be seen through the windows. It overtook a cyclist, it drove on over the black roadway, the tyres' broad treads flattened themselves against the hard surface with a squelching noise. The number 9 trolleybus drove on, carrying in its belly the clusters of faces inset with absolutely similar eyes. On its back, the two raised antennae ran along the electric wires, swinging from side to side, vibrating, squeaking. From time to time, a shower of sparks spurted and clacked from the tips of the antennae, and the air was suddenly filled with a peculiar sulphurous odour. The number 9 trolleybus stopped in front of a pylon which bore the legend:

ROSA BONHEUR

The brakes hissed, the doors folded back, and some people got out from the front while others clambered in at the back. That's how it was. Then the number 9 trolleybus was off again, skirting the sidewalk, carrying in its belly the cluster of whitish eggs, off toward the unknown destination. Off toward the always renewed terminus, the kind of deserted place with a dusty garden, where the trolleybus turned round slowly in its own space and then moved off again in the direction it had just come from.

And there were a whole lot of other vehicles like that. Snub-nosed buses, streetcars with battered old seats, motor coaches, trucks, taxis, metal vans that crisscrossed the town in all directions.

The town was full of these strange animals with gleaming armour, yellow eyes, and feet, hands and sexes of rubber and asbestos. They plied their particular routes, they came and went, each leading its own independent, meticulous existence. They possessed sacred territories, they confronted each other in fierce struggles, emitting nasal bellows that made the air vibrate. What did they want? What were they waiting for? Who were their gods? Inside the tightly screwed boxes, the coils and wires, the sparks, the throbbing pistons provided evidence that there was a thought process at work. Mysterious and confused thoughts that sought ceaselessly to express themselves, to modify the world. It should have been possible to know how to read the words that these movements were writing without anyone knowing that they were doing so. It would have been good to be able to guess these ideas. If one had really listened to the growling of the engines, the shrieks of the brakes, the calls of the horns, one would perhaps have heard something in the nature of a dialogue, a thought in the process of taking shape, an adventure story, a poem:

> A ladder
> resting on a balcony
> rising as high as the roof.
> There,
> leaning against the television aerial
> (smoking a Reyno cigarette),
> there is nothing.
> It is as though the sky were rusting
> and men's footsteps
> were counting the tiles.
> The iron chimney
> is smoking.
> It's nothing.
> The house has taken shape.
> Look at the mauve streets

that the ladder's summons illustrates.
Personally I deduce from this
that nothing is going to rise
from this balcony
from this exhausted population
or from these airs.
No matter:
I
smash to smithereens.

Everything begins on the day that he notices the prison. He looks around him, and sees the walls that confine him, the vertical wall surfaces that prevent him leaving. The house is a prison. The room in which he is standing is a prison. All sorts of things have been hung on the walls: pictures, plates, curios, arrows flighted with parrots' feathers, terracotta masks. But now, that's all useless. He knows why these walls are here, he has understood at last. So that he shall not escape.

Everywhere in the room, on the floor, the ceiling, there are hideous objects which are shackles. Their iron links have chains that hang down as far as the wrists, as far as the ears. All this has been devised (but by whom, precisely?) to ensure that he remembers nothing, to make him secure, to persuade him that he cannot go away. Insidiously, just like that, almost as though unintentionally, he has been made a prisoner in the centre of a room. When he entered the house he suspected nothing. He did not see what the walls and ceiling were really for. He was unobservant. He did not notice that it looked like a prison cell. There were already so many things, so many masks on the walls. He thought he could leave when he liked, without being accountable to anyone. And then the other things started arriving, the bits of canvas daubed with colours, the fragments of glass, the fabrics, the wooden and rattan furniture. He got into the habit of sitting in the chairs: certainly, it was more comfortable than sitting on the ground. The thick walls were pierced by hideous, narrow openings. Ugly, hypocritical holes which looked like nothing on earth. 'Windows, such big windows,' he had been assured. 'Look what a marvellous view they give. See, there's a tree, a short stretch of street, vehicles, the sky, clouds. And by leaning right out, it's possible to catch a glimpse of the sea. And the sun shines straight in, around two in the afternoon.' Lousy rat-trap doors! They were only there to mask the thickness of the walls, to divert attention from this solitary confinement. Now, he knows. But it is probably too late. The doors and windowpanes have been inserted to dissuade him from leaving. And the transparent pellicle where the flies will put an end to their lives! Someone or other dared make this membrane!

There are so many things to disguise the cell. Paper has been stuck on the walls, they have been given a coat of paint. The grey cement and opaque plaster have been concealed, and there, too, a membrane has been set. A pale yellow leucoma, speckled with undistinguishable blooms in an irritatingly uniform brown design! So that each day he may lose himself a little more in counting vainly the thousands of identical little spirals that are the world's ocelli. Above his head, now, he sees for the first time the white platform suspended there, so low that by stretching an arm up he could touch it: cold, hard, slightly friable when scraped by a fingernail. That's not the sky. That can't be the sky. It is a terrible lid of plaster and beams that has been clapped down on the walls, and the soaring flight of will and desire shatters against it.

Words have been projected, commonplace gestures, a language bereft of magic or hunger. A voice has said:

'More coffee? A cigarette? Here's an ashtray ... What's the

time, I wonder? What are you doing? A penny for your thoughts. You know what I'd like? A poster, yes, a big poster, there, above the divan. That would be nice, don't you think? Che Guevara, perhaps: you know, the photo where he's dead, with his mouth open and you can see his teeth gleaming. On second thoughts, no, everyone has that one. But you see what I mean, a big poster would look fine there. Cassius Clay, Mao, Baudelaire, I don't know ... '

A name has been given to everything, to each link of the chain: 'The jade statue.' 'The Lacandon bow.' 'The Khmer head.' 'The Guatemalan tapestry.' 'The moonfish.' 'The Chinese screen.' 'The Huichol picture.' 'The map of Europe.' 'The sunfish.' 'The Ibo mask.' Just so many words to smother the cry, the genuine deep cry that longed to escape from his throat:

'Air! Air! Air! Air! Air!'

He no longer sees either the sun or the moon. The electric bulb hangs from the centre of the white platform, at the end of a braided cord, shining with its evil light. When the rain starts falling, he no longer feels the water splashing on his skin, he can no longer look up into the sky with his mouth wide open and drink. He hears the drumming of the rain-drops, far away, outside, around him. But he can no longer drink. Thirst grips his throat and coats his mouth. In a corner of the wall, low down, quite near the floor, is a black pipe, and at the end of this pipe is a rusted tap. The very sources are prisoners!

Even the ground beneath his feet is no longer ground. The ground has disappeared. It has been buried beneath cinders, layers of cement, slats of glazed wood, checkered linoleums, stuffy moquettes exuding the smell of dust.

He moves forward, stumbling into pieces of furniture. Stupid cubes of wood, ugly, useless, beacons of impotence!

39

Cages which deform and arch the body. Eternal strangers which expel you and at the same moment trip you up. Benches, chairs, stools, cushions, armchairs. Sofas. They come along one by one and shove their apathetic promontories under a person's buttocks, ram his backbone against their buffers! Tables on which the meals that are served are repellent, indigestible, nauseating. Tables over which the head bends, tables for writing, high plateaux cluttered with fetishes. Buttressed on their four legs without calves, legs that never bend. Tables? They are additional ceilings.

And beds, abominable beds, soft eminences which half swallow you, then half regurgitate you, treacherous quicksands, treacherous reefs! Beds determined to stop one sleeping on the hard, gentle ground, viscous couches, eiderdowns, heaps of dead feathers, sacks of old yellow wools like the bellies of manatees! In the evening, when the hour comes (and it does not come from outside, but from within), he gives his body to this dead female, but now he knows that it is not sleep. He knows that it is this prison, as narrow as a bathtub, the hole formed by this mattress and these sheets, which keep him raised above the ground so that the current cannot carry him away. He goes to bed without hope of awakening elsewhere, without ever being able to extinguish the blinding light of his desire. And the bed keeps him level on his soft back, like a beast of burden that never ceases to be a slave, and never ceases to enslave.

It was as though a night or a great blanket of smoke had descended upon the earth and hidden the truth from his eyes. He would never see the light again. He would no longer know the meaning of the free, infinite space that stretched away outside.

Who had done that? Who had dared? Had he ever known the joy of living an uninhibited, haphazard existence? It was the hands of others, the eyes of others that had organized these labyrinths. Women's gentle hands, perhaps, and moist eyes set inside the black design of mascara-painted lashes had reigned here well before his time, and he had had no inkling of the fact. This is how, gradually, surreptitiously, the bouquets of purple flowers, the decorated vases, the lace tablecloths, the hand-painted plates had all been chosen. One by one, the objects had come from outside, they had taken possession of the place. The lampshade of plaited straw, then the chandelier with imitation crystal pendants, the silver fruit-stand, the green and blue photos, the rag dolls. He had never asked for anything. Things came in, or perhaps originated on the spot, without his having to bother his head about them. His thoughts about all this were limited to a series of awkward exclamations such as:

'The footstool, oh?'

'The porcelain statue, ah, oh!'

'Ha! The carpet!'

'The leopard skin!'

'Oh! The calabash ... '

'Oh! Ah! The big stuffed lizard! Oh!'

Flowered walls, painted walls, ramparts of wool and plastic, tons of heaped bricks ... All to conquer man, to impose frontiers on him, to suffocate him. To strap him into that terrible armour whose sharp spikes face inward. Grey, grey everywhere, grey of the whites, grey of the blazing reds, grey of the tails of birds of paradise!

Who wanted sarcophagi? Who invented pyramids in order to thrust man into the amorphous earth? Not me, I swear it wasn't me. I was born in my cell, and that's where I've spent my life. The day I decided to smash the paper wall I found out what it was concealing: my nails splintered on the stone.

And you, windows, once again. And you, windows. Snares of beauty placed upon the walls, shams, illusions; an artist of genius, a great liar, has painted them on the concrete surfaces. From the other side of the glass barrier I see rustling trees, drops of water, rays of light. I do not feel them, but I see them, clear, limpid, weightless, as though they existed only for me. I see them, so close that it would be enough to stretch out the fingers of the hand to tear away leaves, liquid drops, sparkling shafts of dust. I see them. I count the pointed blades of grass, the fibres, the grains. I see them through a magnifying glass. I see them. And they forget me.

Unbreakable snare. Outstretched snare. In their cold metal frames, the great panes of glass are immutable. It is forbidden to be in the world. It is forbidden to enter the outside world. They forget me. The delicate sounds, the colours, the odours of the earth, the little piles of trash have left me.

Windowpanes against which the birds kill themselves. Glass, sublimation of powdered rock, sand through which lightning has passed. Baked rock held rigid in its empty order.

Windowpane which swings gently on its hinges as it wards off the air. Above, below, to the right, to the left; these words apply to my home. Outside, under the sky, they are not valid. These words are the invention of the vile speculator who guesses my movements and my thoughts. He is pushing me farther and farther back. I can no longer escape. I cannot, I cannot: wish, lie, say, strike, extract my lungs from my body, float, fly, travel millions of roads, live in the sky, or at the top of a very high mountain.

I cannot even shut myself in. The house is too big for me. Even with the doors closed, the shutters barred, the bolts shot, the blinds pulled down, the portières pulled across, the heavy brocade curtains drawn, I still have too much space left, too much emptiness, too much of everything. The labyrinths lead towards the back, and my trouble is that my head is too big to go through the last door but one.

SELF-CRITICISM

Why go on like this? It really does seem a bit ridiculous. The weather is beautiful outside, today, right now, a breeze is blowing, there are clouds in the sky, waves on the sea, leaves on the trees. I can hear street noises, the clatterings, the rumblings, all the voices calling out. No one ever calls out my name. Yet how I would love just that: a woman's shrill voice suddenly yelling my name under my window, and I would lean out and talk to her, yelling back at the top of my voice. But there is never any noise on my behalf, not even one feeble toot on a horn, and that is why I am writing this novel.

I have already written thousands of words on the large, $8\frac{1}{2} \times 11$ in., sheets of white paper. I squeeze the words in tightly, pressing very hard on the ballpoint pen, and holding the paper slightly askew. On each sheet I write an average of 76 or 77 lines. At about 16 words a line, that makes 1,216 words a page. Why go on like this? It's pointless, and of no interest to anyone. Literature, in the last analysis, must be something like the ultimate possibility that presents itself of playing a game, the final chance for flight.

Since there is no choice but to hide behind words, to forget oneself behind names, the Hogans, the Caravellos, the Primas, the Khans, since there is no choice but to leave this trail behind one as one goes, all means are equally valid. All books are true. It's only a question of understanding what they are trying to say. I could have begun this in countless different ways, I could have changed each single word in each sentence, I could quite simply have made a drawing on a scrap of paper, or written down just one word, in red ink:

CIGARETTE

All the *same*, that would have been the *same* thing. I could have done nothing and stayed silent. I could have contemplated the slow sprouting of a dried bean in an earth-filled jam jar. I could have brushed my teeth and spat. It would have been the same thing. That really does seem extraordinary. Since the fragrant toothbrush contains the novel, the poem, the phrase that is already waiting, trembling, teetering on the brink of the mind, ready to pop out at any moment; since the scribbling ballpoint pen contains the novel: why should the book not contain it, too, then? And why shouldn't the book, also contain the glass of water, the toothbrush, the postage stamp and the ballpoint pen?

This is how he decided to flee. He left home one morning and walked across town until he got to a big square dotted with trees. The square, he saw, was full of people, men, women and children. The sun was already quite high in the sky, and the buses' metal surfaces reflected the light harshly.

In the square itself, there was constant movement up and down the sidewalk. Buses moved off, engines snarling, horns sounding a brief fanfare. Other buses drew up, their brakes hissing as they came to a stop. They were enormous machines, painted white and blue, with rows of windows, shiny chrome exterior fittings, headlamps and big fat tyres engraved with zigzags.

When one of these buses stopped, the crowd of men, women and children surged up to the door and they began to clamber in. The podgy faces strained upward, eyes anxious, mouths shouting. Cries blended together:

'Hey! Hey! This way!'

'Antoine!'

'The suitcase! Down there!'

'Sylvia! Sylvia!'

'Quick! Hurry up!'

'Huh! Oof! Are you coming?'

and gestures, too, windmilling arms, stamping feet.

The bus into which he had climbed had a long rectangular

body made of tinplate, tinted windowpanes, and green upholstery. He had taken a seat near the back, his canvas bag tucked between his legs, and had waited. On the other side of the window the square was flooded with white light, the trees were stirring. The idling engine gave out a regular tac-tac, tac-tac, tac-tac.

A little later, the bus began to move. There was the muffled noise of something knocking under the floor, and the engine's tac-tac went faster and faster. Now it was a continuous rumbling that rattled the bodywork and the windows.

Outside, the square began to move slowly forward, making the people still standing on the sidewalk pass in procession. The faces loomed up quite close to the windows, white smudges in which one scarcely had time to make out the eyes. Then the square revolved, displaying its trees, a newspaper kiosk, a street, houses with unlit windows.

Just now, the town was falling back at an ever-increasing speed. The rampart of houses was sliding away, taking with it its rows of openings, its cafés, its shops. He tried to read the inscriptions on the shop windows, but it was impossible. The sun's white light glared, vanished, then glared again, making one screw up one's eyes all the time. Sometimes a bump in the road lifted the bus's wheels and all the heads jerked up. The walls were still filing past. At one spot, a white billboard carried big red letters spelling out

ICA

but a patch of darkness was covering the rest, so he never found out what the message was about.

The engine grumbled. The engine sent its rapid waves along the tinplate, and it was as though the wind were blowing on a puddle. The tiny ripples spread over the

47

sheets of metal, advanced upon the windows, crept along the steel rails and lost themselves in the tyres. From there, they proceeded to flow along the roadway, brushing the asphalt imperceptibly, reaching the apartment blocks and even entering men's bodies. A young woman with black hair, walking along the side of the road, did not escape. When the bus passed close to her, roaring as it went by, she was promptly captured at the heart of this vibrating spider's web, and her hair turned quite grey.

The town was disappearing. House after house, it was falling away towards the rear, stacking up a great jumble of beige walls, dark windows, restaurants, squares, churches, shells of vehicles, arms and legs of men. Already, down there, far behind, they no longer existed. They had fallen into a deep pit, had accumulated in the town's vast sewer, alongside old rusty food-cans, threadbare tyres, rotting packing-cases, vegetable peelings, apple cores, crusts of bread, crushed oil-drums, cartons gnawed by rats. Someone had removed the stopper from the bottom of the funnel, and all the liquid was draining away, being swallowed up. Only the bus remained motionless. Sometimes, because of an obstruction or a red light, the engine stopped grumbling, and on the other side of the window a white wall stood still. Then everything started going backward again, everything went on fleeing towards the misty cavern, far, very far away.

It was strange to be here like this, a prisoner inside a sheet-metal cabin, detached from the earth, perhaps, headed for unknown places. They were passing countless streets, parks, newly built-up areas. Tunnels came rushing forward, clamped their black lids down, then opened up again at the far end with a first anticipatory streak of light.

Hours passed in this way, days. Each shape he saw through the glass, each red-roofed house, was like a year flowing backward. The engine went on grumbling and the tiny ripples covered the landscape with their millions of filaments.

Now, to the right, he saw the sea.

It appeared with brutal suddenness, between the gashes of trees and walls, a large and incomprehensibly hard slab of asphalt. Then the walls and trees closed in again, and all that remained, imprinted on the retina, was a sort of open white window that trembled as it receded.

The bus continued to devour the moving ground, roaring with its engine as it did so. Sometimes the landscape exerted more pressure from the left, and all the passengers leaned towards the right. At other times the opposite happened. Seated facing the great sheet of glass across the front, the driver turned the steering wheel, changed gears, pushed down on the pedals with his feet; all that could be seen of him was his broad back, the nape of his neck, his head topped by a grubby cap, and a pair of hairy arms connecting him with the steering wheel. The mountains, houses and clumps of trees rushed straight at him, at a dizzy speed, but at the last moment they miraculously split apart, slid along the sides of the hull and finally vanished. The bus was something like a bubble made of steel and glass, rising interminably through forests of seaweed. One day, perhaps, it would reach the surface and burst in the face of the sun. A bubble that had emerged from the ooze at a depth of more than 26,000 feet and was making its way toward free air.

They had been travelling for days and days. For months now they had been digging this tunnel through the earth. And always there were houses, beige walls, gardens, trees in the wind. Sometimes it was a little village that passed by, its concrete platform crowded with people. Their faces, almost brushing against the surface of the bus, wore fixed expressions that were no sooner seen than forgotten. A man wearing a beret, a fat woman with sunken eyes, a thin, grey-haired woman, a woman wearing glasses, a young boy smoking a cigarette, a policeman with his mouth open, but what he was saying was inaudible inside the bus. A series of snapshots fluttering back, carried away by the wind.

In the sky, clouds built up, changed shape, becoming successively fish, snake, squirrel, woman's breasts, castle, face of Christ, giant amoeba.

They were motionless, immensely motionless. The thousands of possible gestures were leaking out of them at high speed, gestures that spurted out and spread themselves around the world, transformed into eddies whirling in opposite directions. The bus was the great central engine which actuated the world. Inside its tinplate shell, the machine grumbled without a stop, transmitting its energy to the cables and cogs. It was the engine that made the clouds sweep forward, that tugged the trees and hurled them towards the rear, that shook the mountains with little tremors. It was the engine that made the sea teeter in sudden glints, in the depths of the gaps torn in walls and fields.

Inside the bus, they remained unaware of all this. They were all asleep, heads lolling against the seats' headrests, mouths nudged open by the constant jolting. They were being carried at great speed toward other places, toward unknown places where they could once again lead motionless lives. They were dreaming of towns, perhaps, of mirror-like cities, of gardens and fountains. With private rooms presided over by a jabbering television set. With movie theatres, cars, churches. Carlin, for example, over there: tomorrow, his wife would be waiting for him. She would cover the table with the plastic cloth that had a design of red flowers. She would serve him a piece of boiled beef with potatoes. She would not forget the bottle of wine, or the grapes. Or take Raiberti, over there. When he arrived, he would go straight to the Hotel Terminus and have a shave. Then he would go to the office of the Société Franco, to complete arrangements for the delivery of the engine he had bought. Sitting in front of him, Monique Bréguet. Her friend Françoise was awaiting her at number 15b in the rue Papacino. A little farther up the bus, to the right: Mohamed Boudiaf, on his way to seek work in a shipyard. The little black case, at his feet, contained some clothes, a hunk of stale bread and some cheese, letters, a transistor radio, and, hidden in a pile of socks, his wallet containing his work permit, 250 francs, and a photo of his family taken in front of his house in Algeria. But none of this was particularly important, no, it was all common knowledge.

As for him, he did not budge. He just sat there, in the green-upholstered lounge seat, his hands resting on the metal rail in front of him. He looked through the window, and the pupils of his eyes jerked with the effort of following the landscape's movements. He stared eagerly at everything, as though he had never expected to see again these palm trees, these cypresses, these houses with shutters, these hills of red earth, these tufts of grass. He studied these patches of shade, these clearings, he tried to decipher these outspread signs. It was a book, it was an unfolded newspaper telling an interminable story. Of course, a choice had to be made; impossible to see everything. An eye had to be kept open for the appearance of unusual shapes, the rumpled landscape of telegraph poles, the sea's dazzling flashes. Suddenly, the whitish block of a house loomed up from nowhere, and the eye was obliged to watch it arrive, sliding crazily along on its side, like a crab; it grew, it passed by, proffering its pitted face with distended holes through which it was possible to catch a brief glimpse of human forms lurking in the shadows, a table, a dog, a net curtain flapping in the breeze. He entered the unknown home, penetrated into the hollow house through its orifices. Then the gale carried it far away, and he was back in his seat again, sitting there, a prisoner of the metal hull. A tunnel appeared, swooped down on them like a locomotive. He was swallowed up inside the mountain, beating against the hard rock with all his strength. A vast plain opened up on the other side of the mountain, and he had to spread himself immediately over the whole expanse of ploughed fields. Then it was a service station that loomed up, a sort of white temple standing in the centre of a concrete arena. He saw it all rushing at him: the red letters inscribed on white flags, ESSO, ESSO, ESSO, the platforms, the glittering pumps, the open garages in which vehicles lay weltering in pools of oil. Some men in blue overalls were standing on the ramp, gazing stolidly at the road.

They were truly in flight, hurrying away as though some catastrophe had just taken place nearby and was about to overwhelm the country. They did not know that. No one did. Men, women, trees, rocks, clouds, no one knew that. It would happen soon, in a few minutes perhaps. A flash of unbearably bright lightning would cross the sky, and the earth would be transformed into a volcano. An electric blur would cover the horizon, expanding, moving forward over the mountains and the sea. There would be no sound, just a silent blast that would flatten everything, and a wave of heat that would melt the television aerials and dry up the rivers. Then everybody would be dead.

The bus went still faster. Its metal plates creaked from the effort. It was shaken by all the obstacles that swooped down upon it. It went as fast as the sun hanging motionless in the sky. The tyres scorched over the rough surface, the roadway flowed away between the wheels like a waterfall.

There were bridges, level crossings, tunnels, crossroads, wide bends when everything leaned to one side. There were steep downgrades, there were hills that tilted the roof upward and crushed the bodies against the green seat-backs. The engine's grumbling continued endlessly, and at the front of the hull, facing the onrushing movement, the driver gripped the steering wheel with all his strength.

Where were they going? What was going to appear, one day, at the far end of the road? What new town, what plain? What nameless river, what sea?

He was there, motionless between these two movements, checked between these two doors, the one through which everything entered, and the other through which everything fled away. He raked the earth's contours with his body, he rubbed himself against all the protuberances, sank into all the hollows. That's what getting to know the world meant. Across each country men had constructed these channels of tar and cobbles to break up the forests and mountains. The bus crossed fields, rivers, hills. The road had no ending. Originating in the central point where the catastrophe had taken place, the road went straight ahead, splitting into two, doubling back on itself, climbing, dipping. It had been born one day, in the centre of the dazzling crater, and since that moment it had had no rest. Sometimes it struck against a steep mountain and had to start climbing in a series of hairpin bends. Then there was a pass, some snow around, grey clouds overhead, and it started crawling down the other side. At other times it plunged into great expanses of tall grasses, making a beeline for the horizon. During the day the puddle-flecked road shimmered in the heat. At night it spurted from the black depths, full of luminous signs that moved. The bus floated upon the road like a boat, carrying its cargo of sleeping humanity.

He was still looking out of the window. He watched the ground slide away along the sides of the bus, and his mind was a blank. Not everything moved at the same speed. First, nearest the window, were the embankments, springing forward so fast that one did not even notice them. The concrete poles, too, rapid, darting toward the rear like propeller blades. The low, sagging telegraph wires undulating with a vertical movement. After that, the houses, the fields, the walls. But they were still apparitions, openings, winks of the eye. White face, red face, pile of stones, white face, tree, tree, tree, white face, yellow face, pile of stones. A little farther away, the houses lumbered forward like huge trucks, like huge boats. The beige-coloured blocks floated above the trees, then veered aside, and became heavy, laden rafts as the current carried them away. The tops of the trees thrashed around, drooped, made their little leaves sparkle. Occasionally, a branch, higher than the others, stretched up and passed across the sky like the arm of a drowning man. Still farther away, the motionless hills, with their cubes of houses, their patches of fields. After that, the landscape was no longer motionless: it retreated. Enormous blocks of mountains, cliffs, reservoirs of the sea, capes, black islands. Their slow movement twisted the earth, ripped the forests and headlands. Lastly, overhead, in the sky, the clouds altered their shapes completely as they merged, then drew apart again.

The cumulative effect was one of dizziness. All these superimposed movements that were destroying the landscape were heavy, painful, tragic, filling the eyes and creating a hollow feeling in the pit of the stomach. The grumbling of the engine went on and on, constructing its own silence out of all its multiple waves that swarmed all over you.

The world crumbled, very quickly and very slowly at the same time. And each departing thing stripped the back of your mind of an idea. Each uprooted tree fleeing towards the rear was a vanished word. Each house proffered for a single second, then spurned, was a desire. Each face of a man or a woman that had appeared in front of the window, and been repudiated in the same instant, was a strange mutilation, the abolition of a very tender, much beloved word.

He went on looking out of the window, lost for words. Some were off in a flash, BOOK, CAT, CIGARETTE, the time it took two or three concrete poles to fall back. Others flew by interminably, WALL, IDEOLOGY, LOVE, INNOCENCE, while the black mountain slid forward, leaned, pitched forward, and gradually sank into the earth. There were tattered cloud-ideas which disappeared mysteriously: they hovered in the sky like great birds, then, circle after circle of them, melted into space. And there were ant-ideas which swarmed among the tufts of grass, and which were crushed in millions by the headlong flight. Each mile he became more impoverished. Dumbness entered his body. Perhaps it was the engine's noise, its regular throbbing that was sending waves through him.

Trees toppled, carrying clusters of figures, 10,000s, 200,000s, 1,000,000s. Gaping garages in which whole books were sound asleep, philosophical treatises, scientific textbooks. Fallow fields where dictionaries had made their home. Streams full of poems. Barns stacked with politics, vats brimming with sport, lakes of songs and movies, railroad tracks of love. It was all going away, but that was perfectly all right.

In addition, he lost gestures, motions of the right hand towards cigarette packs, of the left hand towards brass cigarette lighters. Winkings of eyelids, shivers at the base of the neck, swallowings. He lost consciousness. The names emerged from him and fled, GÉRARD, ANDRÉ, SÉBASTIEN, RIEUX, DUNAN, SONIA, CLAIRE, JANE, MARIGOLD, GABRIELLE, LAURE ...

> (Her face bent forward, Laure watched. Her made-up eyes blinked lightly, the moist pupils changing colour, becoming green, then blue, then golden. Locks of hair tumbled over her forehead, etc.)

He lost names of streets, avenues, boulevards. He lost mile upon mile of sidewalks, bread-smells, soap-smells. He lost dogs, pigeons, fleas. It was all going away, coming out of him. Soon, there would be nothing left. The bus would be an empty torpedo, flying towards its target, toward combustion.

At one moment, so as to remember, he had wanted to light a cigarette. But he had hardly exhaled the first cloud of smoke before the driver had half turned his head and shouted something like:

'... smoking, you down there!'

And he had had to crush the glowing tip under the sole of his shoe.

That is what it was, then, the solitude of movement. Something had been broken, a cord, or a chain, and now one was rushing forward. Fear, perhaps, the ancient mask that covered people's faces. The sun was very high in the sky, directing its merciless heat on to the metal roof. It was the sun that one was fleeing in this way, it was the light of unbearable truth. One was fleeing the glaringly white town, the eternally straight walls, the sound of footsteps, the traffic noises, the pangs of knowledge. One was going away so as not to see some woman, some child any longer, so as not to have to listen to any more café conversations, so as not to have to answer, ever again:

'Very well, thank you, and you?'

Crushed, rejected, trampled under foot, that vile town. Covered with cinders, with old papers. Forgotten, the open sewer awash with putrescence. The town's grave had been dug, then manure had been piled high on top of it. The steel bus sped through the country, and its wheels crushed armies of slugs. Already, perhaps, down there, very far behind now, the explosion destined to wipe out everything in four seconds had suddenly sent up its immense column of fire.

Those who are motionless on the wandering earth: the voyagers.

Those who flee over the motionless earth: the stay-at-homes.

But those who flee over the wandering earth, and those who are motionless on the motionless earth: what should *they* be called?

SELF-CRITICISM

Was it really worth while writing all that, just like that?
I mean, where was the necessity, the urgency of this book? It
might have been much better to wait a few years, perhaps,
thinking quietly about it and saying nothing. A novel! A
novel! I'm genuinely beginning to detest these threadbare
little accounts, these tricks of the trade, these redundancies.
A novel? An adventure, supposedly. But that's exactly what
it isn't! All these efforts at co-ordination, all this machinery —
this playacting — for what? Just so as to grind out yet another
story. Hopeless dishonesty of the person who doesn't dare
say 'I'. Clumsiness of the person who flaunts his nettle-rash
and his inflammation of the bladder and then tries to
camouflage them so that no one will know that it is he who is
the sufferer! Sickly, shifty-eyed creature! One tries to
intercept his glance, hoping to pass through the windows
of his eyes, to enter his being. At the last moment one finds
oneself staring at a mask, a mask with empty eye-sockets.

If only it were a work of imagination in the style of
Swift, or Jules Verne. Even Conrad would be better than
nothing. But no, he doesn't even try to make up a story. He
presents you with the bag from his daily hunting expedition.
Tittle-tattle he has picked up indiscriminately, tag ends of
notebooks, newspaper clippings, sob stories. Stendhal,
Dostoievsky, Joyce, etc.! Liars, all of them, liars! And
André Gide! And Proust! Little effeminate geniuses,

crammed with culture, intolerably smug, watching themselves live and for ever churning out the same old tale! All of them in love with suffering, adept at talking about it, happy to be themselves. 'I write for future generations.' What twaddle! Do you know where these future generations are? In the grey classrooms of high schools, woolgathering in front of an open textbook, grinning and nudging one another every time the word 'woman' or the word 'love' crops up!

Create reality! Invent reality! As though it were possible! Horde of ants, that has stockpiled its culture in precious tomes! Horde of monkeys, that deserves the gang of charlatans that leads it! And if all this were even funny. But no, it's quite serious, done with a great deal of enthusiasm, accompanied by endless meditation. Perhaps it is the language of mankind, but language stripped of all its music and clamour. These kinds of mischievous insects not only dare to exist, in the name of logic; they have even decided to take blank sheets of paper and write stories on them. Why? To entertain? To help them flee far away? No, to stick fast, rather, to smear the world with their lime, and then sneak off. Yes, just that: to save your own sneaking little life, and to hell with the others!

No masks are barred. What one says, of course, is — I'm an analyst. I reveal human character. I go in for psychopathology, I provide others with the keys to consciousness. Psychology! Does it really exist? As if the human spirit could be reduced to a few gestures, a few words. There is also, needless to say, the study of passion. You know: how the life together of a man and a woman suddenly acquires fresh meaning, by means of this great contest. The next step was to invent the love story. Which, it seems, is eternal. That is the only true novel form: the handsome young man meets the beautiful girl, resulting, successively, in:

1. Love at first sight.
2. Crystallization.
3. Union.
4. Breakup.

Extraordinary, isn't it? The idea that those things really happen. But people are happy. They have the impression that that's how things were with them, and they are delighted to come across things they recognize. Don't start talking to them about the adventure of a glass with a toothbrush, or about a ruttish encounter between a turkey-cock and a turkey-hen. Don't try to tell them what goes on inside a tree. They couldn't care less. They will turn the pages, looking for that spicy bit where the girl with red hair, after having sipped drinks and made conversation, unclasps her brassière and offers her two pointed breasts to her lover's kisses.

Novels that mumble, novels that drivel away like old women. Novels without adventures, written by people without a past! Novels written like one plays billiards ... Novels written in the first person, but the author is very far away, hidden behind his great walls of paper. Psychological novels, romantic novels, cloak-and-dagger novels, realistic novels, saga novels, satirical novels, detective novels, science-fiction novels, new novels, verse novels, essay-novels, novel-novels! All of them designed specially for human beings, knowing their failings, flattering their cowardice, purring gently along with them. Never novels about the hereafter, never novels for rebirth, or for survival!

Novels about people:

Written by women:

'Lucie is a young woman of thirty. Etc.'

Written by men:

'Carlos has gone through the war without ever getting caught up in it. Now that it is over, what should he do? What future awaits him? Is it Beatrice, his wife, in whom he has lost all faith? Etc.'

And along comes a thirty-year-old woman, and a man called Carlos, who buy the book, and promptly say:

'How well put. That's me all over.'

Pleased that there was nothing to be surprised about.

So what have *I* got to say, then? Carlos, Hogan, Lucie, aren't they the same thing? Don't *I* talk about *problems*, too? Am I writing for human beings, or for flies?

The Book of Flights, fine. But, in fleeing, shouldn't I turn round from time to time, just a quick glance, merely to see whether I'm not perhaps going too fast, whether people are still following me? Hmm?

Meanwhile ... They had crossed chains of mountains, wide rivers, grey plains, and now there was this big town sprawling along the edge of the sea. A town made of concrete, flat, white, with straight streets crossing at right angles. It was in Italy, or Jugoslavia, or else Turkey. It was 1912, or else 1967, or 1999. No way of knowing. An unreal town, perhaps, simply a mirage in the vast desert.

Young Man strolled through its streets, without knowing where he was going. He followed the maze of streets, keeping to the sidewalks except when crossing over. He studied the faces of all these unknown people. He passed under dark archways where beggars were squatting. Brightly coloured photos were on display outside an open-fronted shop. They were pictures of the Bosphorus, the Acropolis, or else the Isle of Krk. Young Man bought a few photos and wrote on the back:

Best wishes

Y. M.

Then he mailed them.

The sun was directly overhead, its rays scorching the flat surfaces. The town hummed, rustled, exploded in all directions. Young Man began to feel tired. He looked around for somewhere to sit down. But it was the town centre, where no one ever thought of sitting down. Young girls with black hair and black eyes passed close by him without seeing him. Bald men, sweating in their nylon shirts, strode along rapidly. There was the same strange dizziness in the air here as a little while ago, back there; an odd sort of whirlwind was dancing like a top, flinging the human bodies backward. The vacuum zone in the centre of the whirlwind was moving slowly forward. Soon it would surely be on top of him, and he would feel all the tiny legs crawling over his body, all the mandibles gnawing at him. Something had to be done. This is what he did.

He went down to the sea. It was there, on the left, down there, about half a mile away. He walked very quickly, keeping to the edge of the sidewalk, avoiding the human torrent streaming back up. When he reached the promenade he saw the great expanse of grey and blue and all the sparkling waves. It was the sea. He looked at it as though for the first time, or as though someone had just drowned in it. The horizon was still in the same place, a faint line blurred with mist.

Young Man sat down on the concrete parapet. He put his beach bag at his feet, lit a cigarette and started looking.

What he saw was quite extraordinary: perhaps man's dominion reached no farther than this point. Men had smoothed the earth's surface, had ploughed it and made it fertile, they had hidden it behind walls and under layers of tar. But the earth came to a halt here, along the coast, hesitating. And there began the domain of liquidity, of blueness. Everything was blue. Not a dull, washed-out blue like the blue one sees in the sky or in paintings. But a deep blue, a living blue, which breathed, expanded, became lost in its own depths. An unknown, absolute blue without the least hint of pink or violet or green.

Young Man shifted position, to face squarely into the blue,

not wanting to see anything else any more. At first it was difficult. There were various distractions: the shouting of people, the screeching of cars, the rasping of the surf. The solution was to concentrate one's whole attention on the colour, without noticing the waves' undulations or the sparkling lights along them. Then suddenly the sea ceased to exist. There was no more swell or foam. Above all, there was no more earth. One had slipped into the bath of colour, one was floating in it, stretched out flat, a wafer-thin skin blended with the surface. Then one could look upward, and everything was blue.

Young Man sank into the astonishing colour, and remained there for some minutes. Then a cloud passed by, a car hooted, an orange floated, and the colour vanished abruptly from the sea.

At the end of the promenade there was a pebble beach and a jetty. He went over and sat down there, to look once more at the demarcation line between sky and sea. A wall, an absolute wall that went deep under the water and held the world up.

Then he looked at the outline of the coast, gulfs, capes and peninsulas stretching as far as the horizon. It was a pre-historic coast, full of the ancient remains of the age of squids and savage animals. Dirty water gushed out of the rotted bones, out of the black, slime-covered vertebrae, out of the seaweed-entwined skulls. There, too, one could sink in and disappear into the thickness of time. A curious weary sigh was rising slowly from the swirling waters, a breath laden with heavy odours. The town was leaking into the water through the mouths of all the sewers. All the excrements were slithering along the pipes, sliding down the sea's long slope. Without a doubt, one was just a part of that moving mass, a black turd pushed forward by the water's gulp, on toward fabulous countries ... But when will the earth be *dry* at last? When will this basin, this froth-filled tub, be drained? One day, perhaps ... One day the sun will blaze down at last upon a great desert, and the clouds will no longer be made of water but of sand, dust and ash. And secret caverns will appear, all black from the thousands of centuries spent far from the reach of day.

While waiting for this to happen, Young Man retreated from the scene. He turned his back on the sea and walked in the direction of a big dusty square where some pine trees clustered in the centre of the asphalt. He sat on a bench, there, in the shade, and saw all these people whom he did not know. He tried to remember each one of them, and to do that he took a notebook out of his blue bag, and with a ball-point pen wrote down descriptions of everyone who passed by:

> Little girl with a Band-Aid on each knee.
> Man looking like Hemingway.
> Man with wine stain on thigh.
> Woman suffering from tuberculosis.
> Man in shorts, scratching his genitals as he walks.
> 3 women of various ages wearing 3 identical hats.
> A group of romanies, dressed predictably and wearing dark glasses.
> Girl with bare midriff.
> Girl with FLORIDA written across her bosom.
> Man with squashed face.
> Little girl throwing a box up into the air.
> Woman with target between breasts.
> Little girl with an aquiline nose.
> Man with dark glasses tucked into the collar of his blue jersey.

Little girl crying out Ahoua Aho Ahoua.

Ice-cream cart pushed by an old man and an old woman.

Human cork.

Girl wearing green slacks, with the head of a doll protruding from a pocket.

Woman with a very long nose accompanied by a son with identical nose.

Little girl with rings round her eyes.

Two young women with mascaraed eyes.

Small boy blowing into a harmonica.

Two girls pass by, one chewing bubble gum, the other singing 'No matter who no matter why'.

Mother and daughter, each with an inflamed boil on the leg.

It was inexhaustible. One could settle down there, day and night, with one's notebook and one's ballpoint pen, and do nothing but write, write, write.

On the ground, people's feet came and went endlessly. That, too, was something new. Young Man studied the concrete surface over which the feet were moving. The shoes all had their own way of treading on the ground. Some came cracking down hard, heel first. Others progressed more slowly, twisting very slightly at each step. There were women's sandals with stiletto heels which left tiny half-moon imprints behind them. There were fraying espadrilles, sneakers, tennis shoes with perforated uppers. There were scuffed clogs, there were beaten-up old loafers from which the big toes emerged. There were naked feet, the toenails black with grime. All that, moving, moving to and fro, never stopping.

Suddenly, Young Man detected a sound that he had never

heard before: a low, disturbed noise, a sort of deep rasping that drowned all the other sounds. It rose unrhythmically from the ground, reverberated, fell like spadefuls of sand, smouldered into powder. It moved forward, too, but over the same spot. A rubbing sound, an endless CRRR, CRRR that seized you and gradually buried you. It was the sound of shuffling feet, the soft, listless, terrible sound of feet in the process of walking. Impossible to forget that sound. Suddenly, the earth, the sky, and even the sea, far away down there, began to ring with this sound of footsteps, and everything became a path for these feet.

Town of iron and concrete, I no longer want you. I reject you. Town of valves, town of garages and sheds, I have frequented you long enough. The eternal streets hide the earth, the walls are grey screens, so are the posters and the windows. The glaring cars glide along on their tyres. It is the modern world.

The people who hammer the hard ground with their heels, in rhythm, have no idea what they are doing. But I have. Which is why I am leaving.

A habitat arranged in groups, but at the same time split up, multiplied, annihilated. Black throng that repudiates itself, herd with movements that cancel each other out: the town reverberates; the town speaks; the town writhes; the town eats, drinks, fornicates, dies. The roofs are grey: that is where the raindrops strike. Piles of dust lie in the angles of the walls. Calcined trees sprout through the surface of asphalt deserts. Starved dogs roam around, and cats. At night, rats dart between the wheels of the parked vehicles. Town filled with the odours of food, smoke, vomit. There are people who were born in the town, and died there. Surely the earth is one vast town from which escape is impossible? Surely the streets plunge under the surfaces of seas, misty boulevards stretch-ng to infinity, peripheral rings rising and dipping, beyond imagination? Escape? Where to? Avenue number 8. Detour. Endless expressway leading to yet more blocks, roofs, streets ... Town with a visible skeleton, monster infested by minute parasites that quietly gorge themselves with blood. And then town in ruins too, pathetic walls sticking up, defying the sky's emptiness. Town, the great infinite town, is perhaps simply the invention of man's fear. Not a refuge, nor a secret cell, but a cluster of harpoons with old shreds of skin fluttering from their barbs, pointed constantly towards the distant body of the sky's enormous whale.

That town is the one I am in. It is my time, my space. How could it not be? I am there, this day, this hour, I and the town's millions of inhabitants. I no longer know what was there before this slab of concrete, before these fake mountains that are hollow and riddled with openings. I am no longer in a position to know. One moment, throughout the universe, this kingdom happened; like a book, just like an open book in which the words describe a self-sufficient scheme of knowledge that no one can really understand but that no one can really remain unaware of, either. One never knows what one is doing. One does it, that's all. It's the same with the town. It is there; either one is in it, or one isn't in it. If one isn't, that's another story. But when one is, there's basically no means of realizing the fact. One is a townsman, and from the depths of one's casemate one gazes at the sun and the sky. It is the town that is the object of one's hatred. But one hates it with insults welling up from one's innermost being, with other roofs, other sidewalks. One longs to kill it in one's soul; and suddenly one's soul is this black limousine gliding to the sound of its hot engine along the white streets.

Town? Woman, all woman. She stretches out her hand and it is an intersection of radiating streets. Her made-up face is an inhabited house, her body a department store. So that's what it is. Everything is there: drains, streams, noisy roadways, streetlamps, winking lights, reservoirs, public gardens, fountains, depots; curious names that are her own:

Groin Street
Avenue of the Five Senses
Boulevard of the Femoral Arteries
Vena Cava Street
Ministry of Breasts
Pubic Garden
Kneecaps & Co.
Larynx
Suburbs of the Anus
Sex District
Occipital Lobe Grand Theatre

It is she, my town, my town that is all woman. Now do you understand why I visit her so assiduously?

I am walking. I move through the town, and my feet slap the tough ground. Silence has closed around me. I walk on the horizontal ground and hear nothing. The silence has swollen horribly in my head, has pressed against me with all its strength. I advance without knowing where I am going, the world has suddenly been emptied of its sounds. The ground is hard, flat. The walls are high. The roofs are not visible. The sky is an immense, deserted esplanade. Around me, the movements of fast cars, the itineraries of people. From behind my glass screen I can see them, unobtrusive, humble. But I hear nothing. I walk like a deaf man, enclosed within my peaceful bubble. People cry out and I hear nothing. Cars spurt forward with roaring engines, jet aircraft fly through the clouds, and I hear nothing. Well, I do hear them in a way, I register the rumblings and the horn blasts. My ears vibrate with noises. But it is inside my head that I am deaf. All these ruthless, earsplitting sounds are around me. I can see them all, really, just as they are, large dark splotches bearing down on me, pack of mad dogs, circular waves radiating from the sun, arrows, thick patterns. But inside my head, as I walk, nothing. I have no sooner registered them than they are forgotten, gone without even leaving a scar. Or else I am under water, 3,000 fathoms deep, in a world of slime that quivers and swirls into sluggish clouds under my feet.

No, I hear nothing. Silence is in my head. I do still hear something, but it is so hard and so terrible that it thrusts me even farther into silence, it hurls me yet more light-years away from a free existence: it is the sound of my footsteps. One, two, one, two, one, two, dull blows of heels on the sidewalk's concrete, blows as though I was driving nails in with my feet. Plodding of my footsteps, alone, in rhythm, tenaciously, alone, quite alone. I walk over myself and bury myself. The noise of my heels echoes through the world, it is just as though I were hastening, knowing that escape was necessary, along a deserted corridor reigned over by a silence that was tubular.

It is this silence which abstracts me. It is because of this silence that I am no longer there; silence dense as an ocean in front of which one sits and stares. Silence of cast iron, of ferro-concrete, silence of a lake of mud. I should never have thought such a thing possible: to be in the midst of so much noise, so much matter and light, and hear nothing. Balls of wax thrust into the auditory canal, balls of calm water. Screen of unbreakable glass that has been raised without my knowledge, isolating me. I shall never be able to re-experience the music, the long, complex music of anonymous cacophonies.

But I am mistaken: I do hear them. The bus brushes the sidewalk as it passes, and I feel myself engulfed by the piercing shriek of its engine. It scrapes the ground, spreading out like a volley of sharp flints. It zigzags, it spits from the machine gun's barrel, and its bullets ricochet explosively from the walls, smash into human flesh and open up little stars of blood. The heavy machine gun fires upon the crowd, while a peculiar grey-blue cloud spreads out, acrid, deadly, the cloud of mortal dust, the dangerous fog which penetrates through the pores of the skin and disintegrates life.

Or else, the aircraft crosses the blue sky, heavy silver bird bombarding the earth with its din.

Or else, the subterranean cries of television sets, the music of radios, the jolting kicks of jukeboxes at the back of dim cafés.

Or else, the human voices, the brief little yelps going on and on in a universal chorus.

The barking of dogs.

In the trees, the screeching of birds.

On the smooth rails, the black tumult, sweating oil and sending out sparks, that heralds the approaching train.

Hubbub, outbursts, confusion of languages, clicks, tick-tock, slitherings, jets of steam, uncoilings, fluids, muffled rhythms, luminous rhythms, tremolos, castings, births, hiccups, gongs, gargles, deep vibrations, scratchings, and then, flight, so many ways of fleeing.

I hear everything. I register everything. But I am there, slightly withdrawn, late perhaps, or a tenth of a second fast, and nothing is true any longer. EVERYTHING IS AT STAKE. In my body reigns a desert that has no parallel anywhere in the world. In the centre of my head there is a boundless ocean. What is that? What does that mean? I am at the centre of events, practically invisible. Suppose I don't really exist at all? Suppose I am nothing but a node, the interference point of sound waves? Or alternatively, is this all a dream that I am dreaming?

The world surges, never-endingly, from my head, like rays, like a gentle mechanical sound filled with the whirring of springs and caroming of cogwheels of a wristwatch. I am mad, I am right, I am alone, I hear, but I am deaf, I see, but far, always, elsewhere than myself, without myself.

And the sound of my footsteps at the back of my skull inflates, swells up, fills everything in me that is inexhaustibly, painfully HOLLOWED OUT.

A café waiter in blue
sets a glass of beer
on a cardboard disc in
the centre of a red table

To walk in the sun

The calm vase of flowers

Nothing can really affect me any longer. Everything that
happens, happens very far away, as though in another world.
I am seated, facing eternity perhaps. Accidents, passions,
desires, dreads, I contain them all, they all shift around, grow
lively, carry on their struggle. While I look on. I *create*. And
the familiar spectacle that results cannot become tedious,
being BEGOTTEN.

I WALK ON THIS FLAT LAND
WITH NEVER ANY PURPOSE

There was another way of fleeing. I will tell you about it. One evening, around ten, Young Man Hogan found himself in a strange part of town, a different town. The night was pitch-black, and he instinctively made his way towards the places where there was some light. He walked at a fairly brisk pace, swinging his arms. The night became less black as he approached the district of bright lights: the sky gradually took on a reddish hue, as though there had been a volcano over there, or at least a big blaze.

Y. M. paused a moment to look at the lights. At the end of the street, there, they were shining with fierce flashes, launching their appeals, blinking on and off unwaveringly. They were crazy stars, motionless on the frontages of bars and stores, blood-red planets, green comets, nebulas, suns with paws. He had never seen anything like it. Under the night's dark blanket, all these lights danced, trembling in the humid air, changing colour, stretching and contracting their convulsive rays.

For a moment he was scared and wanted to turn back. He looked behind him. Over there, in the opposite direction, the town disappeared into the night. One could see the streets outlined dimly by streetlamps, and the headlights of the vehicles gliding along them. But over there, too, danger awaited. Peculiar animals made of steel prowled the ravines, their wings glittering savagely, a disquieting gleam in their eyes. When they turned their backs, two red points lit up and sped into the distance. Hereabouts, mechanical life held sway. In vanishing below the horizon, the sun had left the field free to all these little lights, and now they were gnawing away, gnawing away tirelessly. The night was made of steel. The town had been overlaid with hard sheeting, had unsheathed its razors, was lying in wait. In the depths of the sky, there were no mirrors, and in place of the sun a great bleeding hole gaped where perhaps a molar had been wrenched out. The sea had probably emptied, leaving the hollow of its basin rimmed by a dizzy precipice. The earth itself had disappeared, had ceased to be solid. One was on an unknown planet, Jupiter, or Neptune, a planet made of gases trailing in layers above each other.

In the great monoliths of houses, the skylights were blocked up. The people had shut themselves up in their grottoes, because they were frightened, or else because they did not want to see. In the hermetically sealed boxes of their apartments, they were sitting under electric lamps, they were watching screens from which waves of blue light flowed. Here and there, in enormous temples, people were sitting in rows of armchairs. On the far wall, facing them, a dazzling blur. It was *The Savage Eye*, or *The Little Soldier*, or else *Woman of the Dunes*. But that was of no importance, because what the people had come to see was not stories or images, but light, simply light.

Y. M. lit a cigarette with his lighter, and walked towards the place where all the flashes were coming from. It was a very long street, its sidewalks jammed with people and lined with cars. Entering the street, Y. M. had to screw up his eyes because the light was so intense. He stopped a moment, to look at the neon signs. They were everywhere, on walls, above shop windows, at the backs of shops, and even suspended above the street.

76

Some of them were static, burning intensely like suns in the centre of vague haloes. Others flashed on and off, endlessly. Or moved. There were red ones which cast their stark scarlet rays straight ahead of them. White ones striping the night, blue ones going round and round. Sharp-angled signs wrote strange names, like flashes of lightning travelling through clouds. The letters gesticulated above doors, revolved, formed themselves, then erased themselves. In the centre of a huge white design undulating like a carpet, a word continually appeared and disappeared: RONSON. Above an empty department store, a red-and-green arrow advanced, streamlined point foremost. Then it touched a circle, and in an explosion of gold the word WALLACH was spelled out in black. As well as all these letters there were crosses, triangles, circles which never stopped radiating outward, spirals of fire, zigzags, dots, bubbles, explosions. The whole lot talked at once, emitted mute cries, underlined, exhibited, spat. There was no peace. One was inside an erupting volcano, caught up in the gouts of magma, or in the centre of an electric storm. The neon tubes crackled in the air, the light flickered like rising fumes. Y. M. advanced slowly down the street, changing colour, his eyes full of sparks. There was no pity. At one moment, he stopped under the KELVINATOR that opened and closed its red letters. He looked at the trembling street, and at a very big sign right at the end of it, on which COCA-COLA swam in the centre of a star that turned from red to white to black. It was towards this sign that he made his way.

He ended up at an intersection where the frenzy of the lights was at its height. Here, hundreds of words called out in all directions; but they were false alarms. Behind the flamboyant letters there was nothing but a maze of tubes and wires. The windows of the building lit up harshly, the façades became red. It would have been easy to stay a long time, here too, reading everything that was written all around. With a little effort, it would have been possible to write a poem with these words, a poem composed of fugitive letters, unfinished sentences, chaotic thoughts. One could have set one's words up, riveted them to the walls of houses, and launched one's appeals. One could have written something like:

S S SI SI SIL SIL SILEN SILEN SILENCE SILENCE

DEATH

HELP ME HELP ME HELP ME

PLEASE
LOVE ME

ap ap ap ap ap ap

APPEAR!

Or else one could have drawn things, with all those electric bulbs and neon tubes. An immense heart in the process of beating, clamped to the sixth floor of a building, and then, along the whole length of the street, a gigantic woman with green eyes that lit up and blinked on and off, with a candy-pink body, with breasts that heaved with each breath she took, a great woman floating on a blue-and-mauve carpet, holding in her right hand a cigarette with a wisp of smoke rising from its glowing tip.

That, all that, was madness, perhaps. Somewhere in the world, in the middle of the night, there was this node of throbbing lights. The appeals were desperate because they were getting nowhere. There was no path opening up behind the words, only walls and plate-glass windows. Everywhere, one came up against these impenetrable barricades. The cold flames danced in the night, leaped up mechanically, and it was all meaningless. This roaring, this extraordinary and beautiful explosion, echoed around the earth, but it was for nothing. The objects had sped far away, their steel doors shut tight. The crazy words repeated to you, tirelessly, 'Eat!', 'Drink!', 'Smoke!', 'Come here!', 'Love!', and nothing was ever offered. Here was the dizziness of empty space, here was the vortex filled with great eddies of light. There was no language. There were no signs, no colours. There was no day. Only night, nothing but night, absence.

Around Y. M., people came and went. Couples strolled by, lit by the strange glimmers. Men passed quickly, tight little groups talking as they strode along. On the roadway the cars followed each other in an endless stream, their side-panels and tops reflecting broken light patterns, their fenders loaded down with headlamps, winking lights, red warnings.

Y. M. entered a bar, and drank a glass of beer at the counter. This place, too, was decorated with neon tubes: green, white and pink stripes. There were some people in the room, drinking. On the walls, great sheets of mirror glass reflected the light. Even the glass that Y. M. was holding in his hand was luminous, as though carved out of a diamond, and the beer was the colour of gold. Y. M. lit a cigarette, and for a moment the lighter's flame was a spark, the centre of the universe with its countless galaxies. He looked outside. Near the entrance door were two pinball machines and a jukebox. The jukebox was sparkling with all its might; on top, it sported a sort of glass crest inside which one could see halos of colours, iridescent patterns, concentric circles all swimming around. Music with a heavy pulse mingled with the flashes of light as it boomed from the apparatus, then settled over the people in the room. Each drumbeat was a hovering sheet of electricity, and beneath it the rapid sparks of the guitar sputtered up to the ceiling. In front of the jukebox, a girl was standing, swaying her hips in rhythm with the music. She was gripping the warm cabinet's raised rim with both hands, staring at the sort of iridescent mouths that were opening and shutting inside the glass crest ... Beside the jukebox, the two pinball machines gleamed. Green electric lights flashed on and off on their glass indicator-panels. On one of these was depicted a girl in a bikini, whose eyes suddenly blazed, for no apparent reason, like gun barrels. Two men were standing around one of the machines. One of them was playing, his body shaken by spasms. The other was watching him playing, without saying anything. From time to time this second man would take a coin from his pocket and place it on the glass table-top, with a deliberate gesture of the hand. Each time the coin disappeared into the machine's slot he placed another coin on the glass. And his eyes glittered like those of the girl in the bikini.

Y. M. could see two women in front of a bookshop on the other side of the street. They were standing there on the sidewalk, one beside the other, waiting. They were both very young, they were beautiful, and they looked highly respectable. Wearing lovely costumes, gold and silver jewellery. They had intelligent, refined features, innocent eyes, smartly styled hair. From time to time, they spoke to each other and laughed, one could hear their high-pitched voices burst into the laughter of young girls who have scarcely attained puberty. Delicate hands, delicate smiles, graceful, supple bodies. Their movements were full of elegance, as they crossed their long legs, tugged at the shoulder-straps of their handbags, played with a necklace or a bracelet. Faces full of grace and modesty, necks set haughtily, aloof expressions. The light from the shop windows enveloped them, carried them in its halo, made them almost transparent. And when a man passed, some portly gentleman with a protruding stomach and bald pate, his breath reeking of cigars and wine, they tilted their heads a little to one side, and without a word, with their eyes alone, offered themselves for sale.

Y. M. left the bar and started walking again. Suddenly, this is what he saw: passing in the night, a mulatto woman wearing a metallic dress, gliding haughtily through the crowd, like an armoured car. Her long, lithe body, moulded by the steel-coloured dress, cast reflections. She turned her head, and Y. M. saw her brown face, her coal-black eyes, her thick hair drawn back from her brow. She crossed the street and stopped to light a cigarette. Y. M. walked toward her very quickly, his eyes focused on her alone as he got closer and closer to the shining silhouette. She was so tall that she towered above the crowd as she stood there, moving her long arms to choose a cigarette and make a small flame spurt from her butane lighter. When Y. M. came up beside her, he was surprised to see that she really was very tall, six feet three inches probably; her muscular body was squeezed inside the tight dress covered with little metal scales. When she saw Y. M. she stopped smoking for a moment and studied him with those black eyes in which the whites gleamed harshly. Then, without saying a word, she was on her way again, moving with a long stride, swinging her arms alongside her hips. The heels of her shoes rapped the ground, the scales of her dress clinked together. Y. M. walked by her side, without saying a word either.

He glided along, attached to the mulatto woman's body, drawn along by the rhythmic movement of her legs, by the sway of her hips, by the supple oscillation of the nape of her neck. She kept her mouth closed, breathed silently through her nostrils, and from time to time brought the cigarette up to her lips to inhale some smoke. Reflected lights from the shop windows flowed over her black skin, over her thick tresses, bounced back off the steel of her coat of mail. People stepped aside as she, as he, approached, voices fell silent. It was like walking beside a machine, sharing the violence of its regular movement, while the engine turns soundlessly, while the hood breaks the air's obscure resistance with its chrome-plated muzzle. A machine become woman, with an unknown system of gears, a dangerous body, an invincible rhythm. She advanced up the street, in the night, without unnecessary gestures, without swerving an inch from her path. At one moment the mulatto woman stopped at a traffic intersection; she waited there for a second, staring straight ahead. Then she was off again, drawing Y. M. along with her. The walk might last for hours, days. The woman's body was capable of moving forward across miles of town, crossing asphalt streets, passing bridges, tunnels, barbed-wire frontiers. Then continuing under the sun, and the metal dress would glitter with a thousand sparkles, like an airplane. In the rain, and the water would stream down the coppery cheeks, drip from the hair made of some plastic substance. The body was capable of crossing oceans like a submarine, or crossing cloud-filled spaces like a nickel-plated rocket. It would grow cold in the frost, it would burn in the desert heat. Nothing could ever graze this sleek skin, pierce this iron shell. The woman would always be triumphant, walking the streets at night, swinging her long naked arms, holding her brown head high, staring unblinkingly with her bright eyes. Y. M. walked beside her for a long time, without looking at her. Then he slid inside her, melted into her body, inhabiting the machine with the metal fuselage, moving his legs forward inside her own, breathing with her lungs, looking at the crowd with two eyes like searchlights.

Later, he entered an empty bar and sat down with her at a table. On the walls of the bar, the mirror panels were lit by the reflections of the metal dress and the copper skin. She spoke with a funny sort of husky voice that vibrated deep in her throat. Each time she had finished speaking, she looked at him for a few seconds, then turned her head away and stared at the entrance door. They discussed matters rapidly, like the words written in red and blue letters on the fronts of buildings.

'What are you drinking?'
'You got money?'
'Yes.'
'How much?'
'Here, look.'
'O.K.'
'So?'
'Rum and coke.'
'Cuba Libre.'
'What?'
'That's called a Cuba Libre.'
'Don't know.'
'It's true.'
'What's your name?'
'Young Man.'
'What?'
'Young, Man.'
'That's not a *name*.'

'It's what people call me.'

'Hmm.'

'And you?'

'What?'

'What's your name?'

'Ricky.'

'Ricky?'

'Yes.'

'Where are you from?'

'Tobago.'

'Been here long?'

'Two years. And you?'

'Got here this evening.'

'Staying here?'

'No.'

'Where you going?'

'Maybe Tobago.'

'Oh yes?'

'Or somewhere else, maybe.'

'Yes, oh yes.'

'And you?'

'What?'

'You going to stay here?'

'Don't know. Might go to London.'

'Yes?'

'Work as a dancer. You know the Six Bells?'

'No.'

'It's a nightclub.'

'Ah.'

Later, the mulatto woman got up and left the bar. They walked side by side in the street, stretching their legs and swinging their arms. They passed through streets of yellow light, vanished into holes of darkness. The cold air struck their faces, swirled round the metal dress. People in front of them continued to draw aside. Then the woman entered a house without even glancing behind her. She climbed steep flights of stairs, lifting her long black legs very high. At the second floor, she opened the door of a room and went in. Through the drawn curtains a red glow infiltrated the room, then died away. At regular intervals the glow lit up a bed with white sheets on it, a table, a few chairs, and a cracked washbasin with dulled brass taps. Without saying anything, she sat on the bed, and Y. M. sat down beside her. They spoke a few more words, in metallic voices, and Y. M. brought out some money. The woman counted the notes and tucked them under the mattress.

From then on, everything became mechanical. The dress covered with thousands of little scales slid down the brown body and crumpled, clinking, at the foot of the bed. In the room, with the red light blinking on and off in an indeterminable rhythm, there was no longer a man, nor a mulatto woman. There was a sort of whirlwind, a wrestling match, which traced great horizontal movements. There was a desire to kill, perhaps, to crush the world, to trample the crowd underfoot; nameless things receded at tremendous speed, mountains of time, and space, and thoughts. The copper-coloured skin vibrated under the tremors of the engine, the belly hollowed itself, the hands opened and closed, the long legs pressed downward with all their strength. The air was dense with floating dust, particles of iron filings, no doubt, the odours of motor fuel and household gas. And the breaths came in ever quicker pants, raking the walls of the room, filling the world with their efforts. Hhhh-Hhhh. Hhhh-Hhhh. Hhhh-Hhhh. Without words: the whirlwind became hollow, it must have tunnelled right through the earth by now, vertiginous channel through which the red-hot lava would be flowing. The flight is desperate. It is gathering momentum in every sense, every direction, by every possible means. He lights a cigarette with his red-and-yellow flame: he flees. He takes up a book called *A Nose for Trouble, The Tragedians, Lord of the Flies*. He flees. Moving gently forward over the path of black dust, listening to the whistle of the cold wind: he flees. He thinks of the infinite number of years that separate him from his budding image: he flees. He eats day-old breadcrumbs from the hollow of his hand: he flees. Seated in the dentist's reclining chair, he contemplates his tooth, as though the steel needle were eating away the only tooth in his head. He is fleeing, don't you understand, he is fleeing. The path is explosive, its eternally winding course covers the surface of the earth. It is soaring through the sky, too, like the darting midges, or else fixed solidly, like a B52 jet engine. It passes through the depths of the sea, on the snout of a shark, silent, prompt, effective.

Rape is tragic, because it is the outcome of a pursuit. In the room there, on the white bed, the enemy has been overtaken and vanquished. Its body has been hammered, broken with blows. Its loathsome autonomy, and that of all women, has been destroyed for a few seconds' duration. Now the machine ceases to advance. It is ticking over, has stopped vibrating, is grinding to a halt. Somewhere among the rumpled sheets, so far away that it seems like miles, floats the head of the mulatto woman. She is not looking. She has no desire to see anything, disdainful, indifferent, bronze mask, with fibrous tresses. And suddenly, while the man works away furiously, the long arm reaches out, the hand gropes around the table to the right of the bed and returns holding a cigarette. The distant head starts smoking calmly, puffing grey smoke-rings up toward the ceiling, and it is not of the least importance if, lower down, on her body, the engine has been ripped out and the parts dismantled.

Ten minutes after he had climbed the stairs, Y. M. went down again and found himself in the street once more. He wanted to light a cigarette, but noticed he had lost his lighter. So he decided to play at asking people.

'Do you have a light, please?'

Just to see what they would answer.

DIARY OF IMPONDERABLES

May 30th, 1967

Column of ants advancing along the centre of a long furrow.
Two black ants dragging a straw along.

Gipsies.

Hedgehog.

To be sitting on a bench, in the sun, with the town spread out at one's feet, and wait.

The earth and the sky are born of the gods' saliva.

And now, a few insults:

Slob! Cocksucker! Chiseller! Fourflusher! Stumblebum!
Peasant! Monster! Imbecile! Pig! Moron! Slut! Lout!
Guttersnipe! Fatso! Clodhopper! Peanut! Gargoyle! Skin-
flint! Greedyguts! Boob! Torpedo! Blackguard! Creep!
Sawn-off runt! Blockhead! Pimp! Son of a bitch! Swine!
Squitty asshole! Shitface! Snot-nose! Mushmouth! Drivel-
ling idiot! Lunatic! Buffoon! Hobo! Beachcomber! Sourpuss!
Quack! Scoundrel! Yellowbelly! Birdbrain! Shylock! Yahoo!
Punk! Dinge! Nitwit! Uncle Tom! Chicken! Dirty rat!
Hairy ape! Squealer! Road hog! Freak! Bumpkin! Hooker!
Finagler! Old bag! Bastard! Prick-teaser! Hustler! Floozy!
Tramp! Scrubber! Double-crosser! Human wreck! Traitor!
Stinker! Bully! Gallows bird! Drizzle puss! Chucklehead!
Drunk! Lush! Dope fiend! Gorilla! Twerp! Slowpoke!
Backbiter! Assassin! Fanatic! Unfeeling brute! Dodo!
Nonentity! Oaf! Nincompoop! Boss-eyed monster! Slug!
Meatball! Numskull! Fag! Pansy! Blimp! Crackpot!
Butterfingers! Sissy! Profiteer! Barbarian! Jigaboo! Coon!
Nigger! Chink! Jap! Limey! Frog! Eytie! Blowhard!
Blatherskite! Spik! Shine! Smart aleck! Schmo! Jew boy!
Goon! Malingerer! Judas! Screwball! Creeping Jesus!
Foreigner! Con-man! Egghead! Paid hack! Dauber! Prig!
Pain in the ass! Snob! Sucker! Fathead! Zombie! Dumb
jerk! Idle layabout! Black marketeer! Holy Joe! Tightwad!

Bourgeois! Loan shark! Skunk! Dumbbell! Boozehound!
Heel! Crapper! Peeping Tom! Snake in the grass! Dirty
Commie! Ugly mug! Louse! Crank! Gimpy! Schizophrenic!
Trollop! Whore! Ogre! Epileptic! Fascist! Gigolo!
Dumb Dora! Syphilitic! Jailbait! Hippie! Stalinist! Pro-
curess! Manic depressive! Neurotic! Hysteric! Sap! Cuc-
kold! Kaffir! Boogie! Stoolpigeon! Sodomite! Heathen!
Cheapskate! Stuffed shirt! Roughneck! Brat! Parasite!
Sponger! Cadger! Fop! Wanker! Grifter! Beefbrain! Softy!
Hayseed! Dogmatist! Reactionary! Capitalist! Imperialist!
Liar! Hypocrite! Old fogy! Crumb-bum! Prude! Oddball!
Drip! Slave driver! Drudge! Shyster! Bimbo! Phony!
White trash! Pussy-chaser! Bigot! Fink! Brown-noser!
Dimwit! Pickpocket! Fleabag! Panhandler! Schnorrer!
Bohunk! Greaseball! Shamus! Croaker! Pulpit-pounder!
Chowderhead! Lunkhead! Pantywaist! Pollack! Skivvy!
Bullshit artist! Cutthroat! Rubberneck! Scrounger! Cow!
Shrew! Flatfoot! Gunsel! Dumb cluck! Fat frump! Blabber-
mouth! Wise guy! Fuddy-duddy! Spook! Pirate! Anarchist!
Jawsmith! Armchair warrior! Puppet! Toady! Kook! Cream-
puff! Carper! Cockney! Fraidy-cat! Deadbeat! Wobblie!
Proletarian! Goofball! Blubber-face! Bloodsucker! Flim-
flammer! Turncoat! Atheist! Heretic! Fairy! Clip artist!
Bonehead! Hag! Bindle stiff! Clown! Rapscallion! Beanpole!
Funk! Sad sack! Queen! Bluenose! Hermaphrodite!
Nympho! Cootie! Penny pincher! Beatnik! Square! Maoist!
Troglodyte! Kibitzer! Grundy! Boche! Kraut! Fritz!
Jerry! Sawbones! Charlatan! Gunfodder! Casanova! Madam!
Sneak! Two-timer! Donkey! Scandalmonger! Weary Willie!
Potbelly! Moneygrubber! Balloon! Slowcoach! Humbug!
Mongrel! Gringo! Nip! Yankee! Redneck! Canuck! High-
brow! Slum-rat! Dipso! City slicker! Gook! Racist!
Twat! Schlimazel! Street Arab! Gollywog! Tub-thumper!

Sky pilot! Gink! Little squirt! Urchin! Whippersnapper!
Freeloader! Clip-joint operator! Shill! Dummkopf! Pisspot!
Turd! Crowbait! Skunk! Schnook! Dude! Tourist! Mother-
fucker! Gash-hound! Milksop! Greasy grind! Wino!
Abortion! Tomcat! Peewee! Fartface! Busybody! Mouth-
piece! Stooge! Crackpot! Wog! Pusher! Cokie! Finger man!
Blackleg! Skid Rower! Snowbird! Pinko! Lunatic! Cannibal!
Bat-ears! Foetus! Lummox! Crone! Horse doctor! Meatball!
Hash slinger! Pothead! Cretin! Fruit! Shrimp! Geek!
Junkie! Cardsharper! Plater! Tapeworm! Stick-in-the-mud!
Mafioso! Mobster! Jughead! Jelly bean! Al Capone!
Tigress! Meanie! Plug-ugly! Pettifogger! Sponger! Wop!
Nazi! Sunday driver! Gasbag! Broad! Heel! Martian!
Half-wit! Don Juan! Pushover! Swellhead! Spendthrift!
Tattletale! Momma's pet! Slag! Left-wing intellectual!
Coward! Yes-man! Bedbug! Spermatozoon! Lickspittle!
Frankenstein! Cadaver! Witchdoctor! Succubus! Vandal!
Plagiarist! Freethinker! Devil's advocate! Front man!
Pigmy! Riffraff! Mongoloid! Adventuress! Sheeny! Dike!
Goody-goody! Calamity Jane! Sob sister! Randy bitch!
Pariah! Jesuit! Painted hussy! Mucker! Poof! Harridan!
Chippy! Sow! Whoremonger! Bum! Nut case! Liar! Liar!
Liar! etc.!

(Dear Ricky)

Savagery of the relationships between people. Here, everyone is on the make, all of them doing their damndest to take someone else by surprise, to relieve this man of his property, to enjoy that girl's flesh. There is no gentleness, there are only pleasures. Eyes which already devour the easy prey offered them, eyes which seek out the chink in the armour, the weak point, the little patch of pale skin into which the nails can sink and bring blood spurting out. Spying eyes, fierce eyes, sharp eyes which loathe and wound. A look which passes summary judgment, a knowing look, one which wants, not to understand, but to keep at a distance, to consume at a distance. A kind of tentacle, eye-sucker clamped to the intellect's stomach. The world is not pure. The world is free, roamed by wild animals, inhabited by greedy, hate-filled monsters. Loneliness, indifference: hatred.

The young woman wearing a fur coat crosses the room, and she is weighed in the flesh like any hunk of meat.

The man enters the restaurant, stands under the light from the white ceiling; and the woman's glance, flickering over him for a fraction of a second, is harsher than this light. It indicates indifference, terrible indifference, rapid evaluation, contempt, rejection.

The three girls entering the store are squeezed into nylon

92

dresses that look too new. A woman is standing on the steps outside the entrance, young, pregnant, her belly swollen, a sleeping baby in her arms. And she raises her wide, brown face with its narrow eyes, holds out her hand. The three girls in their too-tight nylon dresses dart a glance at her, then burst out laughing. And their glances have anticipated their mouths' laughter.

Among the endless streets, with their horizons that are constantly opening out, then closing in again, like series of sliding doors, he who is walking without going anywhere advances into the devouring jungle. He leaves scraps of his skin, fragments of his flesh on the thorns and the hooks. There is no emptiness more empty than this abundance, there is no cruelty more cruel than this security, everywhere.

Sheets of metal, iron-panelled doors, sidewalks, walls, safes, tin roofs, hardness everywhere, impenetrable surfaces.

The hand cannot pass through, the hand of thought.

The havens are false, they lie.

The skin is hypocritical, only cold steel can pierce it.

The face with familiar features,

hair
forehead
eye   eye
nose
mouth
chin

is a mask of plaster and tinplate, it never says anything. There is nothing more dead than this living person. There is nothing that radiates greater silence.

Play performed for the other person, game for nothing, game that is not gentle, game played to win, and never to lose.

Carapaces, breastplates, skins, costumes, habits, words, gestures, ideas; exclusive games. I mean, as far as I'm concerned I've had enough. Played enough. Pretended long enough to believe in the game, spent enough time closing my eyes, mouth, nose, ears. Had enough of being sold out, enough of buying up.

I mean, why shouldn't they make me a present of a double defeat, one day, without reason, just like that, in a restaurant with white strip lighting? My own defeat, and someone else's?

Why shouldn't they give me the gift of a weakness, one day, without necessity, so that I may take it and make it mine?

Let me look through his shattered windowpane, this scandalous breach through which vicious strength disappears and scatters, let me see the reverse, the interior, life's red hollow, the fissure, the ball of fear and love, pain that has spread, yes, perhaps, the hidden number of the domino which no longer wants to win the game.

> Far away from unkindness
> far away, very far away.
> Far away from vice, unhappiness, hatred,
> Carry me far away
> very far away
> far away
> on board ships
> on board iron aircraft
> along tracks of thunder.
> I want to be set down far away,
> so far away, in a country so foreign
> that I can no longer recognize myself.

Far away
in the country of the far away
of the huge, of the burning, of the vibrating
of the distant far away.

That's what I need to do, then: devour landscapes. Like
someone who could never be sated with earth, with life, or
with women, who would always need more of all these. It's
not a matter of understanding, or of analysing. No, it's a
matter of turning oneself into an engine, into a monster of hot
metal, pulling its weight towards something unknown. I
move forward, quickly, quicker still, exerting every effort, I
propel myself along the unknown road, I move, I traverse
the air, I fly as straight as an arrow toward other regions
which will open up in their turn. There is no end to the
doors. I hear nothing. Hear what? Stop where? Languages
pullulate, faces surge up and then are shattered. Understand
what? There is nothing to understand, nothing at all. There
are no chains of events, no reasons. Got to keep moving at
all costs. Scamper across the thorny fields, hurry down the
slopes of hills, run beneath the sun's rays, strike the earth
with the soles of the feet. I devour landscapes, like that, and
then people, too, and young women's lips, old men's hands,
I gnaw children's backs. Everything that presents itself
changes incessantly. I draw my body out taut across space.
It is necessary to start breeding. I cover the sequences of
miles. It is necessary to start measuring. It is I who sets the
course, eating it up as I do so. A river? I throw a bridge. A
mountain? I bore a tunnel. A sea? I drink and drink. I would
like to have maps, a lot of maps. I spread them out and I read
the names of towns and villages, the lines of roads, the
numbers of meridians. I change the time of day: 10.30, 0.25,
2.10, 4.44, 23.00. I read all the dots, all the crosses, the

contours of the coasts. Capes, islets, sierras, alluvial plains, deserts, subtropical forests, ice caps, névés, tundras. I look at all the countries that are mine, all the rivers that flow for me. I look at this painted mask that is the face of my earth. I take possession, as though from the top of a tower. I am at home everywhere. I devour my territories, I masticate them slowly, and the juice trickles slowly down my throat. Earth containing plants, earth containing lagoons and fjords, earth full of red, humid, acrid earth in which millions of worms wriggle. With my mouth, with my hands and their splitting nails, with my feet, with my eyes, nostrils, ears, with all the adventurous holes of my body, I take possession. I urinate upon it in a never-ending stream. Like someone who has not eaten for centuries, I swallow tons of earth: everything that grows on its surface slips into me. Houses, trees, birds, cacti, dense crowds, twinkling cities, I eat, I eat! My hunger is not one that can easily be satisfied! I need towns of six million inhabitants with fleshy faces, I need forests through which one hacks one's way, month after month, through all that wood, all those leaves. I advance quickly, preoccupied as a black-beetle, for what I take I do not return.

Flee, never stop fleeing. Be off, leave this place, this time scale, this skin, this thought process. Extract myself from the world, renounce my possessions, reject my words and my ideas, and go away. Leave, for what, for whom? Find another world, inhabit another town, get to know other women, other men, live under another sky? No, not that, I could not truthfully claim that. The chains are everywhere. The town, the crowd, the familiar faces are everywhere. Those are not the things that have got to be left behind. What is the point of a slight geographical displacement, a little slide to the right, or to the left? Flee, that is to say, betray one's heritage, vomit up what one has digested through the centuries. Flee: flee flight itself, deny oneself even the ultimate pleasure of negation. Enter into oneself, dissolve, evaporate in the fire of consciousness, be reduced to ashes, promptly, inexorably.

First of all, pulverize one's name, one's mask. Remove the cardboard and plaster carapace, take off *one's makeup*.

The fine cutis scarcely veils the bones. A single abrasion, the shuddering of a vehicle's metal casing, for example, would be enough to burst the fragile envelope and send its contents gushing out, flowing on and on until they had filled forbidden space. That is the truth. Not what is true, not what brings forms together for the glory of a new name, but what succeeds in drawing aside painfully the theatre's two grey curtains.

Behind them is the magical scene, behind them, unknown to anyone, the scene of passion and bright light. It glitters, this vast hall lined with infinite mirrors. Hall one does not enter. Cathedral of glass and steel, a sort of giant ship, vibrating, sinking into the water's mass. It is here. I shall not set foot in this place. I do not want to set foot in it. I simply want to see it, as though with a backward glance, because this glance is the sole link between my flight and reality.

I speed away from this unknown place at thousands of miles an hour. I am launched like a torpedo in the direction of another magnetic objective which will soon destroy me. And life's light-show continues to speed away from me, irremediably; quickly, so quickly. It recedes, it disappears into the black gulf, well of hatred, crater, it grows smaller and smaller, vanishes, leaves me, exists no longer.

Am I really in full flight? Or is the world perhaps rotting away under my tread, a kind of slimy sand closing its mouth over my footprints?

I am fleeing from you, earth, so as to get to know you

better. I am leaning towards you, disc cracked with fissures, as the sun stands directly overhead. Here and there, foothills, faults, gorges, steep cliffs. Dotted around, a tree, a fern, a plant with dusty leaves. And a splintered boulder, a single splintered boulder, pointing its sharp tip upward. Signs, perhaps, scripts, ancient hieroglyphs engraved in the hard crust. Wrinkles, very finely etched crow's-feet, cracks, too, that have spread over the fragile glass surface. Deep holes that the wind has plugged up, but whose channel must surely plunge deep inside the earth, as far as its seething centre, perhaps. Miniatures, tiny faces painted on medallions, surrounded by rose-bushes, thistledown, limb joints, broken metatarsals strewing the ground after a storm of hands and feet has rained down.

Decorative flourishes, minute scars left by thousands of whirlwinds. The air has passed over this ground, the rain has often flowed in these valleys. What has been put down in print, there? What is marked on this slab? The names of the dead, perhaps, and the spiral-shaped imprints of the living. Signatures, too. The days' dates, and the hours' figures, the years' numbers, 1002, 1515, 1940, 1967, 2001, 36628. The phases of the moon, the winds and tides, the solar eruptions. The number of leaves on all the trees, of scales on all the snakes, of legs on all the centipedes. Fish-bones without number, ancient vestiges, leftovers from the feast, crumbs, all crumbs! This is my realm, my prison. I shall never leave it. But I want to count the grains of sand and give a name to each one, for this is the only way of filling the dizzy emptiness of my flight.

I no longer want to know. What good would it do me? I simply want to measure the space that separates me from the starting point. I want to be an integral part of my fall, I want to become part of the force that is urging me on.

I am a railroad car. Beneath my wheels, the cold rails are stretched out tight, let me conjure a spark from the heat of my onward rush. The sinister sound of the air, as it strikes, is my silence. Motion is my tranquil truth. The trees flickering by, along my flanks, the singing in the ears caused by the tunnels' air-pockets, the flashes of darkness and light slap me ceaselessly. This whirlwind is my thought process. By the time each silhouette appears, it is already wrapped in the darkness. In the endless motion, the earth breathes, it moves, it has tentacles and jaws. It gapes, yawns, snaps shut again, moves away, buttresses itself, crouches for a spring, strikes, sways, melts, burst, into flames.

Beckenham Junction, Mont-de-Marsan, Ventimiglia, Trieste, Constantinople.

Reality smokes. Reality wears makeup. The earth is soft, and the thousands of ships with sparkling breastplates, made to last a century, are slowly sucked under. I, too, am a castaway of the earth, at least I think I am.

Farther still, later still. There were more and more towns, more and more people walking in the streets, in the sun. There were the oil-streaked waters of harbours, there were shanties, and big marketplaces smelling of fruit and garbage. There were ravenous dogs with protruding ribs, their rumps scarred with kicks, competing with small children for the possession of scraps of rotting food. There were mumbling beggars with glazed eyes, slaves dripping with sweat, flies, lizards, black rats, hard-eyed policemen, three-months-pregnant prostitutes, dark lanes with lines of washing dripping overhead, old jalopies. There were stocky men with brown faces and deep-set eyes, who remained sitting for hours at the edge of the sidewalks. There were women with long black hair, gleaming eyes, wide mouths, who strolled along the streets on shapely legs, laughing, talking loudly in drawling voices. Their heavy-breasted bodies were clad in light linen fabrics, and patches of copper-coloured flesh could be glimpsed through the tears in their blouses and dresses.

Above all, there was the sun. The white-hot searchlight always trained on the earth, sending out an endless wave of heat. From every direction, it could be seen blazing in the depths of the empty sky. High up above the roofs and terraces, it darted its rays, it hovered, almost motionless; or else it plunged earthward with terrifying speed, boring a hole through space, passing through infinity in a second, already illuminating with a great splash of yellow its chosen point of impact in the universe.

Above the towns, the treetops, the napes of men's necks, there was always this indestructible white disc. Even after closing one's eyes, one went on seeing it, stationary, a blind blob pressed against the retina, swimming in a bath of blood.

Young Man H. had been travelling for days in the direction of the sun. For years, now, he had been walking, looking straight ahead, guided by the white disc from which light gushed out in spouts. He had been born like that, perhaps, and the first image he had seen had been this one: through the window suddenly flung open, against the grey wall, the immense eye, the crazed eye plunging its pitiless gaze into the depths of his pupils. It was an appeal, and at the same time a threat, an implacable judgment that had condemned him in advance. There was no way of resisting. At night, when the eye was no longer there, one could sleep. But when one wrenched one's lids open in the morning, the eye was back again, ominous as ever.

Sitting on a stone, facing the road, Y. M. H. wrote a poem to the sun on a sheet of paper. It was:

> Here is S
> Mortal face
> with high forehead marked by 4 wrinkles
> with eyes that see
> with vertical nose pierced by 2 holes
> wrinkles in his cheeks
> and around his smiling mouth
> Baby's countenance
> Face!
> Forehead!
> Eyes!

Mouth!

Baby!

The world is flat and never wants to be anyone.

Then he hid the message under the stone and went away. It was that day that he began to cross the desert.

Just outside the town, he saw this ochre wasteland stretching out to the horizon, these black mountains, these dried-up bushes, this naked sky, and, in the middle of all that, the road going straight ahead. He began walking along the road, his steps following the tracks of the truck wheels. He did not walk very fast, because of the heat, and the blue bag slung from his shoulder banged against his hip. From time to time, there was a pile of stones by the side of the road, and he could see the sharp points glinting in the sun. He could hear nothing. To the left and to the right, the sand dunes absorbed all sounds within their hillocks. The road was flat. Y. M. H. walked for several hours, without stopping, his head and shoulders burnt by the sun. Once, when he felt thirsty, he took a lemon out of his bag and started chewing it, as he walked along. He listened to the odd sounds the bitter needles made inside his mouth. A little later, he looked around and saw the town very far away, dancing between the dunes. It was rather like a spangled dress stretched tight over a woman's belly, but the woman was invisible. All that could be seen were the diamonds and the cheap flashy jewellery that leaped up and down, very far away, in the haze of rosy dust.

He lit a cigarette and smoked as he walked. But the smoke of the tobacco mingled with his saliva and formed a mucilage inside his mouth that made breathing difficult. He had to throw it away without finishing it; the burning stub fell in the sand and lay there smouldering.

Fine dust spurted up from the ground at each step, forming a little cloud that rose into the air. The tracks left by the truck tyres made hard depressions in the road's surface, straight lines that came together, then veered apart again. People had once passed that way, heavy machines filled with men and raising clouds of sand as they crossed the desert. Y. M. H. studied the tracks that slipped away under his feet; they had imprinted signs in the sand, series of Zs and Xs, and sometimes Ws. The soles of his shoes crushed them at regular intervals with a little dry noise, and on the road behind him there were these oval marks striped with symmetrical bars, which signified that a man had walked that way.

The sun had gradually climbed into the sky; now it was right above his head, suspended there like an electric light bulb. The ground was dry and sparkling, the tiny grains of sand had lost their shadows. The silence and the light weighed down upon the plateau, and it became an effort to remain standing. The only way was to press forward, head held high, back stiffened, hands dangling at the end of the arms, resisting with all one's might. If one lowered the head, or began to count one's footsteps, one ran the risk, after a few minutes, of falling flat on the hard sand.

Y. M. H. halted. He urinated at the side of the road, watching the yellow puddle that the sand drank up thirstily. Then he looked around him. As far as the eye could see, there was nothing. The town's trinkets had disappeared, a moment since, behind the dunes. The sand flowed away in all directions, swallowing itself up. Great congealed waves waited. Farther away, at the end of the visible road, the outlines of the black mountains remained unaltered, neither nearer nor more distant. The path pursued its unswerving line straight ahead, receding towards the horizon. Bushes continued to poke out of the ground: roots of a sort pointing skyward, blackened claws, old calcined branches. Fire had swept the earth, no doubt. A scorching flame had descended from the sun, one day, and consumed everything. Trees, lakes, rivers, soft ground, everything had vanished in the blazing mass, everything had melted. And today there remained nothing but these ashes, these twisted fragments, this vitrified surface covering the stone ground. Everything glittered, everything gleamed in the sun; that was because flames still lurked inside the grains of dust. They wanted to burn the world to a cinder, evaporate the last drop of water, destroy the last living flesh. The empty sand was covered with cruel mouths that wanted to drink and go on drinking. The razor-edged stones were dizzy crevasses that drew you into them, seizing your legs, tearing strips from your skin. And over there in the distance, the dunes were slowly raising their walls, reducing gradually the size of the amphitheatre through which the man was moving, closing the prison of their circle. It was like having fallen into the ant lion's pit, one day, without hope of escape. In the centre, the soft-bellied insect waits for its prey to grow tired and slip into its jaws. It was like being an ant imprisoned in a sandpit dug out of the beach by an eleven-year-old boy.

The road had begun to climb. It went up steeply toward the sky, a thin vertical stroke drawn on the stone wall. With constricted throat, Y. M. H. began scaling the cliff, leaning his whole body forward. Sweat poured down his back and his face, and his legs stumbled violently against the ground, as though they had been worn away up to the knee-caps. In the silence, he could hear the rasping of his breath, a sort of deafening kchch kchch like a locomotive. At the top of the dust-clogged cliff was the sky's wall, a veritable sheet of steel dominating the earth. And somewhere in the metal lid there was this drop of molten matter, this blast-furnace mouth blowing its blinding heat. He, a man of tender skin and liquid blood, was the prisoner of this iron landscape. The world wanted him destroyed, no doubt about that, had already condemned him to death. It was useless to walk quickly, stub his toes against stones, raise little clouds of dust with his feet. The sand went faster than he did, swirling to and fro on the same spot, like the sea. The little square grains rolled over each other, covered the road, filtered into his body through his mouth and nostrils. The sky set its steel dome turning round and round, and the furnace's gaping mouth blew and blew. He walked under the volcano's crater while the scorching breath beat down upon his head and penetrated his spinal column. An icy fire that numbed the fibres of his muscles and blanked out his thoughts.

The heat hung heavy and thick, like layer upon layer of curtains. The air had stopped being light: now it was oscillating over the whole surface of the desert, a block of turbid gelatine that made movement difficult. Y. M. H. was no longer walking; rather, he was swimming, his body straining forward with the effort, his arms opening and closing, his legs threshing against the distant ground. On the horizon the black mountains trembled like seaweed-covered reefs. Y. M. H. tried not to lose sight of them. The jagged peaks drifted behind the white haze, became double, stood out clearly, were swallowed up again. First, they rose several miles high, as though someone were breathing very hard; then they sank back, deflated, into the ocean of sand. The world was sick with fever. The world was dying of thirst and exhaustion. The world was stupefied by heat, its perspiration was streaming under its armpits in long ribbons of mica. Gold, there was gold everywhere, nuggets as big as eggs, gleaming in the middle of the grey dust. The wheels of the trucks, sinking into the road surface as they passed, had left behind grooves of powdered gold that sparkled in the sunlight.

Y. M. H. looked at all these riches spread over the sand; they pleaded with him to stop, to have a drink and fall asleep. So he sat down at the edge of the track, stretched his legs out and took the water bottle out of his bag. It held something over three pints. The first water supply point was a two days' walk away. It was there that the trucks filled their tanks.

Y. M. H. took a gulp, then a second, then a third. The water filled his mouth and made a raucous sound as it went down his throat. Y. M. H. squinted through the neck of the bottle to gauge the level of the water, then damped his handkerchief and wiped his face, neck, chest and arms. He recorked the water bottle and put it back in his bag. He felt the need for a smoke, lit a cigarette, and smoked it, sitting on the ground. When he had finished, he extinguished the butt by poking it into the sand. His mouth hurt him. He took out the water bottle once more and swallowed another mouthful. The bag also contained some biscuits, some hard-boiled eggs, a can of corned beef, some oranges and lemons. With his knife, he peeled an orange and ate it slowly. After that, he started walking again.

About two o'clock that afternoon, he heard the sound of an engine. It was a truck, lumbering toward him in a cloud of dust. He watched it grow larger and larger on the road. When the truck stopped in front of him, Y. M. H. noticed that the driver was a swarthy man with sharp features. Sitting beside him was a fat red-haired man wearing a T-shirt, a turkish towel knotted round his neck. The driver looked at him without saying anything, but the fat red-haired man climbed down from the truck and walked up to him. He burst out laughing, then said to him in English:

'O.K., buddy, what gives?'

'I'm walking,' said Y. M. H.

'On *foot*?'

'Yes.'

The fat red-haired man dabbed at his face with a corner of his towel.

'You crazy or something? This heat will roast the hide off you.'

'Do you happen to have a little water?' said Y. M. H.

'Not a drop,' answered the man. 'Apart from what's in there!' He gestured towards the truck's engine, laughing.

'Is it far?'

'What?'

'The water depot.'

'Supply point 100?'

'Yes.'

'Forty or fifty miles!' said the man.

'Yes, that would be about it.'

'You have enough water?'

'Yes, I've got some in my bag.'

The red-haired man was mystified.

'Say — is this a bet, or something?'

'Sort of,' said Y. M. H.

'Because, goddamn it, man, this sun will burn you to a cinder.'

'I'm used to heat.'

'Too bad we're on an outward trip, today,' said the red-haired man, 'otherwise I'd have given you a lift.'

'That's all right,' said Y. M. H. 'I like walking.'

'All the same,' repeated the other, 'this sun will burn you to a cinder, that's for sure!' Then he climbed back into the truck's cab, and shouted 'Good luck!' The driver looked at him without saying anything, and let in the clutch. Y. M. H. closed his eyes because of the dust. He heard the sound of the engine grow fainter as the truck vanished into the distance; then everything was the same as it had been before. On the road, now, two fresh tyre marks stretched straight ahead.

The sun was lower down, now, and to the right. It leaned against Y. M. H.'s body, digging its fist into his flank to make him fall. Little by little, thirst once more descended upon the desert's plateau, spattering the sand with millions of droplets of quicksilver. To resist this new thirst, Y. M. H. tried to concentrate his mind. He closed his mouth and made an effort to think about something else. But nothing stirred in his head. Only the water flowed, the river of water, leaping, clear, murmuring, the quick-fingered water running down his body, entering his eyes and nostrils. It made a peculiar noise, like a woman's voice, close to his ear, it swirled around his feet, throwing him off balance. Y. M. H. tried to eat a lemon, but had to spit it out again right away, because it tasted salty. Inside the bag slung from his shoulder, the water bottle was a dead weight. Y. M. H. shifted the bag's position. Looking at the sky, he suddenly saw that it had become black. Then white again, but with great rippling circles. The circles were vultures wheeling around the sun. The vultures disappeared, to be replaced by checkers painted on the great slab of marble, huge black and white squares ready to be played on. On the board, the pieces moved around incredibly rapidly, winning dozens of games every minute. They were scarcely lined up before they started rushing at each other again, banging into each other, forming fighting combinations, wiping the other side out in the wink of an eye. Then the squares scattered, giving way to the grille of a crossword puzzle, and here, too, words flashed, drove each other away, clustered, were erased. They were all very long words, like Catalepsy, Thunderbird, Superrequeteriquísimo and Anticonstitutionally. The grille faded away, and suddenly the whole sky was covered with linked words, long sentences full of semicolons and inverted commas. For the space of a few seconds, there was this gigantic sheet of paper on which were written sentences that moved forward jerkily, changing their meaning, modifying their construction, altering completely as they advanced. It was beautiful, so beautiful that nothing like that had ever been read anywhere, and yet it was impossible to decipher the writing. It was all about death, or pity, or the incredible secrets that are hidden somewhere, at one of the farthest points of time. It was about water, too, about vast lakes floating just above the mountains, lakes shimmering under the cold wind. For a split second, Y. M. H., by screwing up his eyes, managed to read the writing, but it vanished with lightning speed and he could not be sure. It seemed to go like this: *There's no reason to be afraid. No, there's no reason to be afraid. There's no reason to be afraid. There's no reason to be afraid. No. No, there's no reason to be afraid. No, there's no reason to be afraid.*

At nightfall, Young Man Hogan chose a spot, by the side of the road, where he could sleep. He settled himself under the shelter of a dune, and ate, sitting in the sand. Then he drank for the second time that day: four or five gulps of water. His mouth and throat were so dry that he could not swallow. Shadow rapidly spread across the desert. Y. M. H. lit a cigarette and watched the night fill the sky. The stars came out one after the other, shining steadily in the depths of the blackness. After a moment, the moon rose, white, with little designs etched in its centre. Out there, too, there was a desert, no doubt, with great plains of sand and silence, endless silence. Since he was still thirsty, Y. M. H. ate an orange while he gazed at the moon.

Thirteen centuries before, Hsüan-Tsang had seen the same thing, after the first day, the second day, the third day of walking. He had eaten a fruit, just like that, while looking at the moon. His companion had turned to him, and had said to him in a voice pitched low because of the silence:

'Master, when shall we reach our goal?'

And since Hsüan-Tsang did not answer and continued to gaze at the moon:

'Master, are we near?'

Hsüan-Tsang had answered:

'No, we still have many days' march ahead of us.'

'Master, I am afraid of the unknown,' pursued the companion.

'There is no unknown,' said Hsüan-Tsang.

'I am afraid of the silence, O Master!'

'There is no true silence,' said Hsüan-Tsang.

'Why do you say that, O Master? Is it not the unknown, here? Is it not silent?'

And he added:

'Master, I am afraid of dying before reaching the goal.'

Hsüan-Tsang, without taking his eyes off the moon, answered simply:

'It is not the unknown, since it is the path of the Buddha. It is not silent, since we have the word of the Buddha. Why should you be afraid to die, since it is the life of the Buddha?'

Then his companion no longer dared say anything. He burrowed into the sand, his teeth chattering, and gazed eagerly at Hsüan-Tsang, who went on gazing at the moon.

On the following day, the sun was back in the same position again, and Young Man Hogan continued walking. He had drunk the last remaining drop of water an hour before. The water bottle, stowed in the blue bag that dangled from his shoulder, weighed almost nothing. Y. M. H. looked at the black mountains. They seemed to be closer now, great peaks that ripped the sky's white sheet. Over there, at the foot of the mountains, was water.

He had already been walking for hours along the sand track. His feet came down regularly one in front of the other, sending up little clouds of dust. The dunes stretched as far as the eye could see, motionless, on either side of the track. Even the calcined bushes had petered out by now. Nothing was left but the dazzling sand with its millions of tiny broken grains, and dry, striated stones that crumbled away in layers. Occasionally, there was a sprinkling of bone fragments and broken seashells beside the track; or empty, rust-gnawed cans that had once contained beer. No one. No trucks passed. No humans walked. No aircraft ever appeared in the immense sky. The insects and the lizards were all dead, the snakes had migrated to another continent. The nothingness was so great that it could not even be called solitude any longer. It was like walking on top of oneself, crawling eternally over the same bit of ground at the bottom of a crevasse. It was like being spreadeagled on the ground, without respite, or being fastened down on an esplanade in the middle of a desert of automobiles. It was like floating on the ocean, thousands of miles from land, while tiny waves sweep forward in ripples. The very idea of solitude had vanished from the surface of the earth; it had been swallowed up by the sand, gulped like water. Everything had been instantly filled to the brim; the sky had been stretched taut, an invincible ceiling harder than steel. The black mountains reared up, the dunes were frozen in mid-movement; the line of the horizon lay close to the sky, a thin black thread that never ceased to contain, to retain. And above, the sun was a glowing dot, nothing but a dot. It would have been impossible to add a single thing more: this was a world crammed full to overflowing, a world with a bulging bag, standing guard against intruders. There was no room for anyone. The crowd had jammed itself into the car in its hermetically sealed tunnel lining, and the doors had closed upon them. Each element of the desert weighed a ton, pressed violently downward. The heat in the air was as thick as mud, and the air itself so hard that it would have needed an axe to cut through it. The ground was an enormous crushed rock, and the road streaked to the horizon, like a wall or a dike.

Everything reverberated, everything vibrated, was full. It was all the same scene, presumably: the same city crowd, neon flashes, carapaces of automobiles. Today they were wearing different masks, indulging different violences. But it was still the same place from which flight was necessary, desperately necessary, in order to breathe freely once again.

Noticing the buttress supporting the far horizon, Y. M. H. identified it as his body, his body which had already overtaken him. He identified two or three ideas of his in full flight, over there, across the expanse of sand. He heard his

words as they made off up the road, words of his now
stretching their ellipses round the sun. No one would ever
reach the goal. No one would ever find anything to drink,
not even a puddle of stagnant water at the bottom of a hole,
not even a gob of spittle.

It took him a little time to realize that he was lost. He was
walking in the tyre tracks left behind by the trucks, staring
straight ahead of him at the cruel landscape. And it gradually
dawned on him that he was no longer going in the same
direction as before. He looked for the black mountains:
they were behind him now, distant, inaccessible, floating
above the dunes. Not only that, but *they had changed shape.*
Y. M. H. stopped a moment, his feet sinking into the sand.
He swivelled round and looked back along the trail. There,
across the desert, ran the tyre tracks, and, superimposed on
them, the hollow ridges left by the soles of his shoes. The
road must have forked, a while back, and Y. M. H. had
taken the right-hand path without noticing. Under the
sun's heat, everything was equal, silent, consumed by fear.
Emptiness encompassed the earth, and the sky was absent,
lacking depth. Nothing spoke. There were no signs. At the
zenith, the bright hole swarmed with light, hurled its white
darts. There were no clouds. It was just as easy to go in any
direction. It made no difference at all.

Y. M. H. began retracing his steps. Then he stopped
again. He looked for the mountains, and they were there,
appearing and disappearing at every corner of the horizon.
The black peaks rose from the river of sand for a few
seconds, then sank again. They had become a gigantic
shark swimming in the distance, circling its prey. It was
slowly closing in on the lost traveller, forcing him to zigzag, to
flee blindly. At the last moment it would rear up right in
front of him, would swoop, its jaws wide open.

Y. M. H. turned round once more, and thought he saw the black summits far away across the sand, between two dunes. He set off again along the trail, his eyes burning, his feet slapping the hard sand at an ever-increasing tempo. He stumbled up to the top of a hillock, so that he could see as far as possible. But his gaze seeped away on the surface of crumbled stone, his gaze slid straight over the burning sand, meeting nothing on the way.

Without understanding what he was doing, Y. M. H. simply followed his nose, in a strange kind of stupor. He walked for a long time in the red sand, gasping. He saw the ground rise and breathe like a wave. He saw the dunes slide over each other, great billows with foaming crests. The sky itself had become a sheet of sand, had grown dry, hard, filled with hatred. The sun, haloed with dust, glided through this leaden sea. It was an endless road fragmenting itself across the world, pulling forward with all the force of its emptiness. Y. M. H. looked down at his feet, and noticed that the tyre tracks had vanished. There was nothing left but sand, a heap of smooth sand into which the soles of his shoes sank with a crunching sound. Y. M. H. rummaged in his bag for the empty water bottle, brought its neck to his lips, and tried to suck out one last drop. Something wet touched his cracked lips and evaporated before reaching his throat. Everything was dry, here, utterly waterless. The sky, the sun, the earth, the stones were all dying of thirst, but an immense thirst, a thirst so intense that it would have needed all the Mississippi, the Nile and the Vistula to slake it. The grains of sand were no longer soft: they were cruel needles lying in wait, from the depths of their heat, for the tiniest drop of water, urine or blood, so that they might drink at last. The sky was an unbearable blue, the blue of thirst, and the sun blazed fiercely, the full force of its violent heat straining, like a jaguar's tongue, towards the earth.

Y. M. H. moved forward more and more rapidly, his eyes dim from sheer fatigue. Ever since he had left the trail, the sand had been making its way into his clothes and shoes, and after a time he took the shoes off and started walking barefoot. The fine powder also entered his mouth, scorched his gums and throat, parched his glands. He would surely fall soon, for the first time, face down in the sand, and the black circles floating round the sun would swoop down upon the world.

On the afternoon of the eighth day, Hsüan-Tsang was plodding on, absolutely alone in the middle of the desert. His companion had slipped away, one night, without saying a word for fear of his master's reproaches. When Hsüan-Tsang had seen that he was now alone, he had understood that his disciple had not had the courage to continue, had been unable to endure such sufferings and had preferred to regain China. Perhaps he would reach his home safe and sound? He had absconded with half the supply of water and half the rice and other rations. Hsüan-Tsang had understood, too, that the Buddha had need of him and no one else, having left him alone, like this, in the middle of the desert. And this thought had helped him to carry on.

He advanced westward, without ever stopping. His robe was reduced to tatters by now, and the sun burnt his emaciated body. His face was the colour of brick, and his eyes had been so fretted by light glare and sandy dust that they were quite gummed up with tears. The sand had gradually rasped the skin from his feet, so that they oozed blood on to the track as he walked. Sometimes the pain was so agonizing that he sat down on the ground, groaning, and wrapped his feet in bits of cloth torn from his clothing. His right hand was bleeding, too, from gripping the stick that rested on his shoulder and that had the bundle of provisions dangling from its tip. Hsüan-Tsang walked straight ahead, over the sizzling sand, under the empty sky. It was a long time since he had placed his parched lips to the aperture of the calabash and drunk the last gulp of water. He had been saving up that last drop for days, without daring to think about it, but finally his thirst had become too strong for him; now there was none left, none in the whole wide world. He walked over the sheet of motionless sand, leaning forward, butting the wall of heat with his forehead. Each time he placed one foot in front of the other, a peculiar noise came from his throat, a sort of rrhan! rrhan! of pain and effort. His head, too, was filled with emptiness, an unbearable emptiness. The faces of mankind had disappeared. Words, their long sweet-sounding words, had vanished across the sands. Silence weighed upon the world like a stony haze. A long rosy-hued grey cloud rising from the grains of sand and swelling the air.

Hsüan-Tsang was moving forward over the surface of an unknown planet. It was always the same wall that he had to batter down with his body, with his arms, with his flayed feet, the same vertical rampart that closed the world and made it impermeable. On the other side there was nothing, an abyss, a hole of black shadow, perhaps, which would swallow him up. Or perhaps there was no other side.

The desert was endless, a trap of dry stone which never released from its grip those who ventured into it. Hsüan-Tsang advanced westward, and the sun sank slowly in front of him, throwing his wavering shadow behind him. When he fell for the first time, Hsüan-Tsang was filled with astonishment. With the help of his stick, he got to his feet immediately and set off again.

Then he fell a second time, a third and fourth time, again and again. Until he understood at last that his legs could no longer carry him: then he felt an icy weight moving down towards his heart. He looked at the ivory-coloured sky and the earth's crust. The wall was no longer receding; now it stretched from one end of the desert to the other, calm, gigantic. Hsüan-Tsang no longer battered it down. He only managed to make part of it crumble away, opening up an ever narrower breach in the mud bricks, dislodging little bits of rubble with increasing difficulty. Finally, Hsüan-Tsang fell more heavily than before. His chest thudded against the hard ground, and his bones cracked. For long minutes he struggled vainly to get to his feet. There was a terrible weight on his shoulders, on the back of his neck, a weight that was crushing him against the sand. The rosy mist thickened over the desert and turned grey, then black.

Hsüan-Tsang, blind by now, groped for his stick, got hold of it and hoisted himself to his knees. Since he could no longer walk, he started crawling on his hands and knees, watching the black gulf that covered the desert. He longed to speak aloud, to beseech the Buddha's help, or else to let out a cry so loud that it would reach the lands of the West. But his throat was like a thousand-year-old tree, and words could no longer travel through it. He longed to concentrate his thoughts on something, on water, on wind, on the sound of the wind in the filaos, on the singing of birds. But his brain was like a ten-thousand-year-old stone, and nothing came. There were only these bright images that flashed across it and then flickered out: images of frantic running, of streams of lava, or of blood, images which swept him away with them across the sand's swell. Flights of birds of prey scattered shreds of his skin through space, long-maned chestnut horses dragged his bones in the dust along an unknown road. There were sounds, too, muffled sounds of a subterranean music vibrating through the air. It was the wind, no doubt, making the dunes sing, or perhaps it was the army of the desert's women with their long piercing sobs. And these supernatural voices drew him towards them, forced his bleeding body to continue wriggling across the sand, westward, always westward. Thanks to them, thanks to the wild horses galloping towards the horizon, Hsüan-Tsang advanced. He crawled, day and night, anchored to his stick, his eyes closed by congealed tears, scarcely breathing, his legs transformed into bleeding stumps. Hsüan-Tsang had become the colour of the sand, cruel and hard as the sand, empty as the sky and the sun.

Hsüan-Tsang was a patch of the desert, nothing but a tiny patch of the desert slithering forward along the path of the wind, stretched thin and taut in the song of the subterranean women, westward, westward, toward *water*.

When the truck passed close to him he did not even hear it. When the fat red-haired man forced the neck of the bottle between his teeth he drank for minutes, hours, years on end, maybe. Then he retched. The truck lurched along in a cloud of dust, and his head banged against the metal floor, but he felt nothing.

All this happened in Libya, or else in the Gobi desert, in the year 630, 1966, something like that.

I want to flee in time and in space. I want to flee in the depths of my consciousness, flee in thought and in word. I want to map out my route, then erase it, like this, time and time again. I want to break what I have created, so as to create other things, so as to break them in their turn. It is this movement which is the true movement of my life: creating, and breaking. I want to imagine, so as to obliterate the image immediately. I want to desire, the better to scatter my desire to the four winds. When I am one, I am all. And my system, my *counter*-system, consists also in breaking each rupture as soon as it has been achieved. No possible truth exists, but nor does any doubt either. Everything open closes again suddenly, and this stoppage is the source of thousands of resurrections. Revolution without profit, anarchy without satisfaction, unhappiness without promised happiness. I want to glide on other people's rails, I want to be movement, movement that goes, that makes no progress, that simply counts the milestones.

When a frontier opens up, it is a new frontier that appears. When a word is pronounced it becomes a different word. I say *woman*, that is to say *statue*, that is to say *octopus*, that is to say *wheel*. I say Transvaal, that is to say Jupiter. Yin, that is to say Yang. I say nothing. I say that, this, that. I want to take a leap forward. Who has spread out these fields? Who has raised these mountains? Who has sculpted this sea? Surfaces that are always solid, surfaces enjoyed, then forsaken, inexhaustible surfaces.

One day, movement possessed me, and its exaltation shows no signs of abating yet. My motor pulls me along, and there are always new miles ahead of me. My voice has stretched me over my reasonable route, and there are always new languages ahead of me. I batter down doors. I break windows. I thrust back walls, like someone dying in bed. And I can never forget.

THE WORLD IS MODERN RAPTURE OF MECHANISMS
OF ELECTRICITY
OF AUTOMATONS

Modern world: rapture of metals and glass walls.
Pale are the walls
Pale
the broad concrete brows
facing the ocean of sound and light.
It is war, calm war
being fought with wielded lines and curves.
War between plastics and linoleum
between neon nylon and dralon®
The war of savage mouths.
Today
the armies have burrowed inside the walls
beneath their hard boots the ground shakes
and the air quivers.
They are modern
They are called
SUBSIDIZED BUILDING PROJECT, AUTOROUTE DU
SUD

TURNPIKE, TORRE DE AMERICA LATINA
HIKARÍ TRAIN
KODAMÁ TRAIN
MAFEKING SEMENT MAATSKAPPIJ BEPERCK
Those really are their names.
They boast these extraordinary retractile names
They have fingernails, hooks, knives and fists
They have silver breastplates
Wide white blocks and black bars against the sky
From their throats emerge the mysterious cries
FISSURE FISSURE
LIGHTNING FLASH
(Prrfuitt-clack!
BOM! BODOM!)
Highways bridges parking lots
Snowy buildings
Deserts, o deserts!
They strike, and their staggering blows
arouse a sweet rapture.
They tear asunder
opening wounds that do not bleed but smile with pleasure.
They crush beneath their four black tyres
and trace on the skin the path's secret
the spirit of the war against death
all the zigzags of the century unconscious of its identity.

I am fleeing. I am scurrying off like a rat. I am hurrying
down the steep slopes, toiling up the hills, stumbling over
the pebbles, scratching myself on the brambles. I am
fleeing. I am trickling away mechanically, and each particle
that detaches itself follows the same route through space. The
sparkling drop of liquid falls like molten lead, splashes on to
the ground, explodes into powder, bubbles, droplets.

Noiselessly. Effortlessly. Without cries, words, gestures. My flight is the sliding of an avalanche, my flight is a slow flow of lava, or else the lightning's white fracture, so rapid that it remains a black crack on an immense chalk-coloured wall surface, an imperishable photograph.

I am fleeing forward, backward, upward, downward, inward. I am abandoning tons of memories, just like that, leaving them behind me without the least regret. I am passing through whole series of settings, high cardboard walls on which are painted life's falsehoods as seen by mankind:

fields of green grass swept by the wind
houses with closed shutters
white towns under the sun
coils of magical lights
deserted streets

parks, gardens, jungles, swamps over which a thin vapour hovers, cafés filled with legs and hands, temples, iron towers, twenty-storey hotels padded with felt, express-ways along which blind vehicles hurtle, hospitals, rivers, pebble beaches, black cliffs where birds are perched, etcetera.

I am floating. I am swimming backward. I am the pro-peller-driven boat, and the helicopter with the blades that can decapitate. I am the fierce bird descending the staircase of the air, I am the fish with transparent wings. I am the flight of flies, the zigzag of nervous mosquitoes. I am the succulent plant, imprisoned in its red vase, which will never burst into flower. I am idiotic movement, heavy vibration, the gesticula-tion of desire, the moment of thirst, of copulation, of speech. I am the unfurling, then the contraction. The muscle, and at the end of the arm with its bulging veins there is the fist tightened round the pistol spitting a bullet that pierces the throat. I am the heat of the sun, the slow progress of sweat-drops over the curve of the loins. The young woman's back arches, while her hand touches the tips of her toes and paints the nails a pearly hue. The drowned girl's hair floats in the ever-flowing water, coils of seaweed, herbs of forgetfulness.

I am he who strides forward without knowing where he is going. The earth is small, all paths are short, one always arrives somewhere. The boundless sea is scarcely as wide as a lake, one can see shores, shores everywhere. In the far horizon, lost in the mist, languishes the thin black strip shaped like a fish's back. That is where I come from, that is where I am going. There are trees, there, giant grasses, thickets inhabited by insects. There are rivers that wind gently down, eating away their bends. There are hollows of shadow, splashes of mud, dances of rain, rocks, plains of snow. As for me, I pass over all these things, arduously, clumsily. I recognize each fold of the ground, now, I can make out the tracks of my own footsteps preceding me.

I have no thirst for what is new, remain impervious to virgin lands. No, I am not obsessed by novelty. I have a hankering for this place that I shall recognize as having always been mine although I did not know it. To choose a territory with care and passion: I would like nothing better than that the voyage should serve to find, to inherit. I would so much like the movement to stop, so that I might become involved in a different movement, that movement, resembling the unfolding of a beautiful story, which carries me happily onward from one point in my life to the next.

Signed:

John Traveller

This is what Ben said to me one day, as he sat in front of a plate of spaghetti with tomato sauce, in a garden where the company also included his mother and an army of ants: 'You know, I'd do absolutely anything to achieve self-expression. If someone said to me, go on, make some jam, I'd try to achieve self-expression through jam-making.'

While drinking tea, in the stifling heat, Locke Rush was speaking of Zen. The Master of Ryutaku-ji had taught him this: to create silence in oneself, to empty oneself totally, to be no longer anything at all. Then I showed him the garden, all those things, the millions of little leaves that look at you all the time, that are impossible to forget. Locke Rush was displeased: he did not like thinking about little leaves.

SELF-CRITICISM

It is true: there are no limits any longer. Everything breaks free, splits into parts, speeds off in all directions. After starting to open doors of flight, after liberating one's mind, or one's hands ... Just how far can one let oneself be carried away? When I lie on my bed, in the dark, my head resting on a pillow, ideas surge up endlessly, explode, trail a fiery wake. I want to stop. I want to grasp. But it is impossible. Perhaps I have not come far enough, then? No alternative but to begin again, try to capture the sense of an idea, a half-idea. Where will that idea carry me? Toward what knowledge of the future, toward what revolt, toward what resolve? Can anything be more wretched than writing for one's own pleasure? Writing so as to re-read oneself in a glow of self-satisfaction, playing tricks with words, playing tricks with memory, allusions: eyes, that is what must be liquidated, once and for all! Who cares about my mother, my life, my birth, my gastric troubles! Acting so sincere! What nonsense! Discussing contemporary problems, sneering alongside the hyenas, showing off in front of a row of happily grinning mouths! What a life! Or else, lying: lying by concealing one's faults, volunteering ten slight failings so as to conceal a single shameful defect ... And style, that stupidity called style. The mechanism that immediately allays any twinge of doubt as one turns the dog-eared page. Ah yes, that's him, that's him all right, that's just his touch.

We were expecting him to turn up there, he hasn't let us down. Ha! I can see a guideline, I can perceive a deeper purpose in the work. What is that musty odour? Philosophy, no doubt. Quick now, the label: Gothic novel, propaganda movie, Western, surrealism, theatre of the absurd. And when, by chance, a small door, no, not even that, a fanlight is opened, allowing a little substance to leak out: why, what's that? Oh no, that's not his at all, that's terrible, that's not a bit like him! What's that supposed to be about?

Books, caverns of resounding echoes. And you, iron collars that strangle me, straitjackets that make me gasp for breath. Decorations everywhere: flourishes, clusters, baroque foliage, all disguising the rock at the centre. The real action is taking place in the background, very far away. The one who plays, the one who refuses, the one who betrays. The one who hopes, who lives on thin air, on purity, on distance: eager eyes can never have too many magnifying glasses through which to view him.

Everything that I write, I cross out. Everything that I seize brutally and smear on to paper, with ink uglier than glue, the whole lot is repudiated, simultaneously, by some-one other than myself: a hidden phantom who shakes his head and makes endless denials. Confess! Confess! I switch on the third-degree lamp and shine it straight into the face of the accused. I shake him by the shoulders, punch him in the mouth, whisper to him what he is required to say, and give him another punch for good measure. The world would rejoice if he said yes. But he shakes his head, refusing silently.

Do you know what? Books should never again have names.

Everyone should work, with ant-like concentration, on a single great tome which would be the dictionary of the world, and should contain nothing but songs. Alternatively, everything should be burned at regular intervals, on fixed dates. Every twentieth year would be proclaimed extermination year. Paintings, movies, museums, cathedrals, houses, temples, barracks, archives, bibles, clothes, prisons, hospitals, airplanes, factories, farm crops, everything would end up as pulp, ashes, muddy liquids. No more statues, no more medals, no more telephone directories, no more war memorials, no more exegeses.

How to go in every direction? How to obliterate one's tracks as one advances? What mask to assume, what false nose, what base thought, what spurious existence? To deceive others is to get to know oneself, and vice versa.

It is not sufficient to hurl abuse at literature. That must be done with something other than words. Abandon one's conscious self, disappear into the world. Become a Martian. Reappear on earth one day and enter a big restaurant, watch the people moving about between the tables, and say:

*zkpptqlnph!

Which would mean, roughly:

'How comical to see all these erect creatures suddenly fold themselves in two and sit down on their backsides!'

But how to become a Martian?

I must forget myself. I must lose my name. I must become smaller, even smaller, so small that no one will ever notice me. I must learn to walk along the flagstones, surrounded by scurrying ants, toward the reeking mountain where a full garbage can points its peak at the sun. I must learn to make marks and notches. I must halt the theory-machine, the beautiful, clinking, chrome-pistoned machine that turns out an endless stream of theorems. There are so many figures of rhetoric, systems, postulates, Q.E.D.s, machines:

machines for living
machines for walking
anti-war machines
love-making machines
machines for forgetting death.

Everyone has his own kind of machine, so what's the use? There are those who think Cadillac and those who think Volkswagen.

One day I shall hope to find the girl who is like this:

PROPERTY : SHE SEES AN APPLE
AND SHE THINKS THAT THE FRUIT
BELONGS TO HER BY RIGHTS
   SHE PICKS IT UP FROM THE STALL
AND EATS IT
WITHOUT THINKING
THAT THE FRUIT HAS BEEN GROWN POLISHED
   BOUGHT
    THAT IT COST MONEY
THAT IT IS FOR SALE

Farther still, later still. Days spent in railway trains are long, days racing backward at full speed, and there are great piles of towns and mountains stacked up on the horizon. Roads have no ends, they never come to an end. The great dusty avenues that sweep forward in a straight line are deserted. The wind blows hard on the plains, the sun in the centre of the blue sky is pitiless. Crushed dogs litter the roadside, and carcasses of cows are surrounded by gorging vultures.

The red truck with SATCO written on the side roars along the road at full speed, and Y. M. Hogan is sitting at the back, under the tarpaulin cover. He watches things as they go by. Sometimes he sees great empty intersections, with men sitting on the ground, waiting. The plains stretch out to the end of the world, the mountains are motionless, with filaments of cloud strung between their peaks. Rivers send their tainted waters rushing downward in their channels, telegraph poles bristle.

Occasionally, one becomes acquainted with large gas stations, pagodas made of grubby cement, all alone in the middle of space. Under the overhanging roof, the green and yellow pumps with broken dial-glasses vibrate stridently while the red liquid descends into the tank. One urinates into a blocked-up toilet, washes one's hands under a cold tap, combs one's hair in front of a greasy mirror, and gulps down a bottle of iced soda water that has a sulphurous tang. At a pinch, one may pass a few words with the driver, from the opposite side of the concrete platform, while gazing idly at the dusty road, the wooden notice boards, the sun, the tin shacks. People always say more or less the same thing:

'How far to Habbaniyah?'

'How many hours will it take to reach the frontier?'

'Know of anyone who's going to Rohtak?'

'To get to Cuttack, is it necessary to pass through Raipur?' And then the ports also contained wooden boats that carried you over the sea for two days and nights. Y. M. Hogan was sitting on the deck, watching the mass of black water that swelled and subsided ceaselessly. He could see, in the distance, the land's thin belt with little lights twinkling along it. Then he slept, stretched out on the deck, in the shelter of a coil of rope, and the engine conveyed its vibrations to his body, shook him, punched him with thousands of tiny fists.

Around midnight, he woke up covered in sweat and went down to the lower deck for a drink of water. He groped his way towards the rusty drum which served as a water container, and scooped up in the hollow of his hand some of the black water: it tasted of gasoline. Cockroaches scuttled out of his way, their armoured wings giving off peculiar red reflections. Near the companionway, a sailor was sitting with his back to the bulkhead, his eyes closed. He was humming, in his throat, an interminable wordless song consisting entirely of nasals.

Mmmmmnn, mmmm, mmmnnn, mmmm, mmmm ...

When Y. M. Hogan passed in front of him, the sailor opened his eyes for a second, revealing a disquietingly steel-like glint in the pupils. Y. M. Hogan climbed on deck again, and smoked another cigarette while contemplating the motion of the sea as it swelled and subsided.

He was not going anywhere. He was suspended in time, somewhere between two centuries, expecting nothing. He was floating on invisible waves, borne along by the wooden hull, not very far from the shore's thin belt, at random. Anyone who knows anything should say his piece now. Anyone who has revelatons to make should make them now. This is the moment, this is exactly the right moment.

But perhaps there is nothing to say, nothing to reveal? Perhaps the only thing that is genuine is this pendulum movement, this monotonous sliding over the surface of the Amazon, this truck turned boat, this boat turned airplane, this airplane turned raft. The engine throbs, from an indeterminate point in space. Sometimes ahead, reverberating from somewhere on the far side of the capes and peninsulas. Sometimes pushing from behind, slapping at the water as though with two mechanical feet. The engine slips away on each side, burrows into the close-knit water, floats very high in the air. Or else the entire earth is fitted with its own engine; vibrating slowly, the earth vanishes into space, sailing broadside on, letting itself drift along its yielding roadway towards incomprehensible places.

When the sun appeared in the east, and rose some way above the horizon, Y. M. Hogan woke up. He went forward and watched the extraordinary, insignificant landscape from the bows. He watched how the sky became red, pushing back the patches of darkness little by little. He watched the flat sea, and the sharp-edged waves which skimmed over it like rows of razor blades. The coast was always there, on the left, a thin grey-green belt dotted with huts and beaches. The ship's bows sliced through the series of razor blades, one after the other, with a sort of crunching sound. In the stern, the engine thrashed away, and amidships the funnel sent out puffs of smoke. They would soon be arriving, in three or four hours, perhaps; there were various signs to this effect, the limpidity of the air, the neat disposition of the green trees along the coast, and so on. The sea has different smells in the morning and in the evening. This was certainly the moment to think about something. Y. M. Hogan thought:

Thoughts by Y. M. Hogan
on board the old tub *Kistna*
off Vishakhapatnam
6. 10 a.m.

'Perhaps I should stop. Yes, perhaps it would be best if I stopped, I really don't know. Perhaps it would be best if I did that: when the boat arrives, I'll stop. I'll walk along the docks with my bag on my back, I'll go and drink a cup of tea in the marketplace. I'll be in the shade. I'll live in a house, in the shade. I'll have some sandals with soles made from a truck tyre, a pair of white trousers, and a cotton shirt without buttons. I could live in the village, I would eat rice and dried fish, I would drink iced tea. I would wait. The years would pass, and I would at last play a part in one of those years. Never outside, any more. Never far away, any more. I would learn people's names by heart, remember the location of all the lanes. I'd get to know all the dogs. Maybe I'd have a wife and children, and friends, and all those people would say memorable things to me. Or else I would write a very long poem, a few words each day, a poem that would be very beautiful and that would at last mean something. One day, I'd write: today, conscience is clearer and more sensitive. On another day, the sun is a red wheel in the sky. The following day, the sun is a black spiral in the red sky. The day after that, the sun is a coin. And then, the sun is an egg. There might be some days when I could at last write uninteresting things, such as, for example, after three months: the sky is a swift colour since one cannot see it. Or else profound things, such as: the state of *lobha* and the state of *dosa* are always accompanied by *moha*, since *moha* is the original root of all evil. Those are the sort of things I could write if I decided to stop. And every evening, too, I could stroll down to the beach and watch the boats in the act of floating. Sometimes I would go on to the beach early in the morning, to watch this boat arrive, this very one from which I would have disembarked. It would be a strange life, a really incredible life. The boat will soon arrive. The boat is crossing the river Styx. I would never have thought that the river Styx was so muddy and so wide. I would never have thought that the Acheron was like that. When I arrive, I shall walk on the beach, I shall bathe, and then I shall stop. Perhaps. If I have enough money, if there is a place for me. I shall stop. I shall stop.'

That's what Y. M. Hogan was thinking, standing in the bows. Since a gull passed just at that moment, skimming the water, he added:

P.S. 'I never knew that gulls' wings were transparent. If you look closely at a gull flying above the sea, you will notice that its wings are *blue*.'

At night-time, boats move forward secretly. When day comes, everything explodes. This is how Young M. Hogan was thrown out by a town. He had arrived there after days and months of travelling. At the end of the deserted roads, the railroad tracks, the sandy trails, at the end of the wakes left by boats, there was this city of more than two million inhabitants, with squat houses, broad symmetrical avenues in which thousands of vehicles agglutinated, vast squares laid out with artificial lawns, gleaming white eighteen-storey buildings, thick crowds with mechanical feet.

Young M. Hogan had been wandering through this enormous town for a very long time, but it rejected him.

He had arrived there, gliding, like an airplane, or else speeding in a stifling bus.

Little by little, the countryside had been strangled in the grip of concrete-surfaced houses, waste ground, shanty towns. The white cubes had squeezed together more tightly, had piled on top of each other, and at each new accretion the weight on his mind grew heavier still. Buildings had sprouted from the grass, shiny automobiles had appeared, resplendent with enormous radiator grilles. Human faces had loomed up, suddenly, from nowhere, brown faces with inquisitive eyes. More and more women and children had appeared; soon, Young M. Hogan could no longer count their feet and their hands. He was obliged to calculate them by tens, and even then so rapidly that mistakes were quite possible.

The heat was suffocating. In the bright light the cubes

of anguish multiplied endlessly, white boxes with tin roofs, walls pierced by windows without panes. The noises grew gradually louder, cries, snarls, rasping breaths all casting their frightening nets. All that, without a stop, marching past, swelling the ranks, until there is no grass left, no more hills or rivers, nothing but town, town, town.

Young M. Hogan was hurled into the furnace. Everything around him was burning, trembling with heat, blistering. It was like walking through the desert, but this time the thirst was no longer the same. It was no longer water that one yearned for, or the flesh of a lemon. There was no longer a water bottle in the bag to combat this thirst: what was needed now was oblivion and calm, with closed eyes.

At about two in the afternoon, Young M. Hogan was walking along a street called Païtaï. It stretched in an absolutely straight line from one end of the earth to the other, a river of asphalt and cement bordered by houses. Neither the beginning nor the end of the road was visible. On the horizon the lines all met, lines of windows, lines of vehicles and sidewalks, lines of sky. There was this point of infinity where everything was mingled, this point of silence and death. Young M. Hogan walked toward it.

It was hot. In the sky, the clouds were very low, little balls of tow gliding gently along. The cars followed each other without interruption along the road's concrete river, and people were wafted away in the cabins of scorching metal. The noise was continuous, too, and violent. It growled from all the motors, from all the horns, from all the mouths and from all the feet. The crowd swayed in front of Young M. Hogan, pranced, stamped the ground. In the faces, the inquisitive eyes darted to and fro, and the mouths smoked, chewed gum, spat. Children ran around, darting in and out

of the traffic. Above all, though, there were walls: walls
that repulsed violently, that crushed, that were white.
Sweating profusely, Young M. Hogan forged on, keeping
close to the walls and avoiding the crowds. Each time he
passed a door, a vibrating machine blew hot, odorous air
into his face. The shop windows had steel shutters covered
with red signs and exclamation marks. The neon tubes
crackled in the sun, and the electric music howled.

Young M. Hogan walked for a long time along that street,
without finding its end. Over there, at the opposite end of
the earth, there was this blanket of haze, compounded of
gas and light, into which the road plunged. It would certainly
have taken him days to get there. The cars' shells sped along
the roadway, fled towards the vanishing point. Perhaps
they would never come back ...

Young M. Hogan changed streets. He took a different one,
and then a different one again. And they all went straight
ahead, laden with cars and insects, for all eternity. Sometimes there was a bridge straddling a canal, or a main drain.
Sometimes one caught sight of a white tower, a building
floating nonchalantly high above the others. Or else a kind of
cement-work fountain from which the water spurted in
plumes. But the road skirted the obstacle and went on its way.
It was a meadow of stones, a beach of gigantic pebbles, and
each boulder was eroded, hollowed, inhabited by colonies of
grubs. Taxis passed, horns honking, their drivers leaning
out to yell at pedestrians. Grey buses with glassless windows
careered along, a few inches from the curb, their cutouts
screeching. Motor-tricycles jolted along with crab-like
movements. Occasionally, an airplane crossed the sky
ponderously, covering the town with its shadow, with its
thunder.

Young M. Hogan had been living in this town for years.

Maybe he had been born there. He had worked in a real estate agency, in a newspaper office. He had suffocated between walls, he had breathed in the vapours of gasoline, he had listened to the purring of air conditioners. He had taken trips in boats with roaring motors, he had eaten in restaurants illuminated by strips of yellow and pink neon, where a jukebox blared out 'Evergreen', or 'Maï Ruchag' or 'La Raspa'. He had talked with men: Wallace, Chayat, Jing Jai, F. W. Hord. With women: Suri, Janpen, Doktor, Laura D. He had slept in all sorts of rooms, lightless concrete cells where the air was a solid block of foulness, air-conditioned rooms with blue carpets, and windows opening on to swimming pools, rooms with wooden walls through which the air filtered gently and where red cockroaches paraded up and down.

He had done all that very quickly, almost without being aware of it.

And, little by little, the town was driving him away.

It applied imperceptible pressure on him, cornered him with its walls, exhausted him with its volcanic rumbles, drove him mad with its straight roads stretching farther than the eye could see. Through the centre of the town, the wide river flowed ceaselessly, carrying branches along with it, and the corpses of dogs. This was a hint to him to get out, a move to dump him back in the sea.

One day, Young M. Hogan arrived at a place that was the avenue of evil. It was a street just like the others, straight and broad, packed with crawling cars, lined with identical white cubes. But in the centre of the cubes, towards their base, were series of openings, rather like the mouths of caves. No one to be seen in front of the closed doors. But when Young M. Hogan walked through one, it was as though he had suddenly closed his eyes. An icy blast struck his face, and he was bathed in a black-red glow. He groped his way forward, feeling moist bodies press themselves against him, clutch at him. The room was very big, and cardboard stalactites hung from the ceiling. In the centre was a big red blob illuminating a band that was playing jazz. He heard nothing, he saw nothing. He was cold. He sat at a table and started drinking beer. Nothing was going on, in this black room: some women in glittering dresses crossed the floor slowly. A black soldier was dancing. The alcoves contained peculiar kinds of motionless human bundles. The music shrieked from every direction, without finding the exit. Young M. Hogan stayed there several hours, drinking beer. Then he left. Outside, the sunlight was still whiter, the heat more scorching. Young M. Hogan entered the next grotto, then another, then many others. It was the same every time. Bodies pressed against him, fondled him, drew him towards a table. A young girl looked at him through the black coal that covered her eyes. She drank beer and spoke in a lilting voice. The strident music echoed round the cave, among the muffled, ponderous blows that made the floor shake. An American soldier leaned over to him, across the table, and started a sentence that gradually tailed away. While speaking, the man knocked over a glass of beer, the liquid ran over the table, very quickly, although it was possible to follow each detail of its route, and dripped on to the ground. The music raised its head, its shoulders, and projected them endlessly towards the ceiling. Young M. Hogan dug an elbow into the soldier's stomach. The girl with coal-black eyes opened her lips and began laughing. This revealed two gold teeth, and Young M. Hogan asked her about them. She said that she had been beaten up. She said that she had had a motorcycle accident. She said it was all the dentist's fault. She said nothing. Young M. Hogan had no more money.

He asked for some from the American soldier, who handed him a few bills. Everyone was dead drunk. The music penetrated the beer glasses, fused with the bubbles, shattered the glasses into fragments, flowed down the throat. At the back of the cave, a Negro in a grey suit was banging a drum, but it could not be heard. The electric guitar was scratching away, but that could not be heard either. All that could be heard was the traffic noises, the vibrations of the light, the busy clicking of feet on cement. They were underground, yes, they had descended the long tube of a well-boring, and now they were moving about in the world's belly. Above their heads, the town was seething, for no reason at all, simply for the sake of making a noise. Young M. Hogan gave a cigarette to the girl with the gold teeth, and offered one to the American soldier who was falling asleep, his head on the table in the puddle of beer. Then he wanted to say something. But the din drowned his words. So he cupped his hands round his mouth and, leaning in the direction of the girl's ear, shouted:

'I DON'T UNDERSTAND!'

The girl yelled:

'WHAT?'

He took another breath and yelled:

'THAT! I DON'T UNDERSTAND! WHY! EVERYTHING IS SO! SILENT!'

The girl yelled:

'SO WHAT?'

'SO SILENT!'

The girl thought he was joking, and began to laugh.

'NO!' yelled Young M. Hogan. And after a pause:

'IT'S TRUE! THERE'S LOTS OF NOISE! BUT NO ONE! EVER SAYS ANYTHING.'

He took a sip of beer to clear his throat.

'WHY IS EVERYONE! SILENT! INSIDE! I DON'T UNDERSTAND!'

The girl laughed, flashing her gold teeth, and yelled:

'THAT! DOESN'T MEAN ANYTHING!'

Young M. Hogan yelled into her ear:

'AND THE TOWN! I DON'T UNDERSTAND! WHY ALL THESE PEOPLE! ARE TOGETHER! THE OTHER DAY! I CLIMBED! TO THE TOP OF A BUILDING! TO SEE! AND I DON'T UNDERSTAND! WHY! ALL THESE PEOPLE ARE HERE! I MEAN! WHAT KEEPS THEM HERE! WHAT DO THEY DO! WHY ARE THERE! ALL THESE BLOCKHOUSES! AND THESE CARS! AND THESE BARS! HERE RATHER THAN SOMEWHERE ELSE! HERE! AND NO ONE! WANTS TO TELL ME! THE PEOPLE SAY NOTHING! NOTHING SAYS NOTHING! THE STREETS SAY NOTHING! EVERYTHING IS CLOSED! THERE IS NO EXPLA! NO EXPLANATION! ONE NEVER MANAGES! TO FIND OUT!'

The girl made a loud-hailer out of her hands:

'WHY DO YOU WANT! TO KNOW?'

'BECAUSE! IT INTERESTS ME!'

Young M. Hogan gulped some beer straight from the bottle.

'I'D LIKE TO KNOW! WHY THE PEOPLE! ARE HERE! I DON'T UNDERSTAND! HOW THEY MANAGE! NEVER TO SAY ANYTHING! IT'S AS THOUGH! THEY WERE MADE OF WOOD! THEY ARE ALL! THEY ARE ALL EXTERIOR! NO WAY! OF KNOWING WHAT GOES ON! INSIDE THEM!'

The girl brought her lips forward. Her eyes were two lumps of coal.

'NOTHING!'

'NOT TRUE! OTHERWISE! THEY WOULDN'T STAY! TOGETHER!'

Then:

'WHAT KEEPS THEM! TOGETHER?'

It was good to yell like that, across the uproar of the music. It was like standing on top of a mountain, and calling out to a woman standing on top of the mountain opposite.

'I DON'T UNDERSTAND! WHAT'S MEANT BY THE WORD COUNTRY!'

'I DON'T KNOW!'

'WHY! DON'T THE PEOPLE EVER SPEAK?'

'NOTHING TO SAY!'

'THEY ARE HIDING!'

'THEY ARE SCARED!'

'SCARED OF WHAT?'

'DON'T KNOW!'

'DON'T YOU CARE?'

'NO! ALL THIS YELLING! IS MAKING ME TIRED!'

'DO YOU WANT! SOME BEER?'

'YES!'

'TELL ME! WHY THE PEOPLE! NEVER SPEAK!'

Young M. Hogan yelled one last time:

'I DON'T UNDERSTAND! WHY! WHEN ALL THE NOISES! HAVE BEEN TAKEN AWAY! EVERYTHING BE-COMES! SO SILENT! THERE IS NOTHING! UNDERNEATH! PEOPLE LIVE LIKE THAT! TOGETHER! THEY DON'T KNOW WHY! THEY DON'T WANT! TO KNOW! WHY! THEY SAY NOTHING! THEY ARE! RIGID! THEY ARE! TONGUE-TIED! THE CARS! SAY NOTHING! EITHER! THIS SILENCE! HURTS ME! IMPOSSIBLE! TO HEAR A WORD! THERE IS! NO ONE! NEVER ANYONE! I DON'T UNDERSTAND.'

His voice stopped yelling. He lurched to his feet, and stumbled toward the exit, through the noise and the crowd. The girl with coal-black eyes hung on to his arm, and to-gether they entered the other still bigger cave in that street which sagged under the weight of sunlight. There, there was no longer even time to ask questions. The important thing was to walk quickly and watch out, because from all sides the street was massing its walls for offensive action against him.

Perhaps the answer was this: a floating island, on the water's muddy mass, in the centre of the stream, in the stifling heat, and on this island the trees and plants grow in wild profusion. The huge leaves with upturned edges, the flowers giving off pungent odours, the roots thrust into the red earth, the outstretched branches, the broken branches, the soft dust filling up the hollows, the boulders, the fossils buried five feet deep, the haze that rises slowly from the ground, around three in the afternoon, when the sun in the centre of the sky scorches fiercely.

Across the surface of the island, almost everywhere, the trails of tiny animals, the paths of insects and floating seeds, the passages of the wind, cool, warm, cold. It is an occupied speck of the earth, a speck like millions of others that are scarcely similar, scarcely different. In the centre of the brown river the island floats indolently, as though resting on a suspension of hundreds of silent, flexible springs. A bed, perhaps, a big double bed with very white sheets, containing a man and a woman, naked and asleep. A love bed, a platform on which two frenzied bodies sweat and gasp as they grapple. Or else a deathbed, hard and cold, driving its rows of sharpened needles into the flesh of an old woman.

That, then, is the speck of land that is to be visited, for one day, as though by a god descended to inspect his creatures. The disembarking traveller must study this island's green blob for a long moment, examine each feature of this compact shape in the middle of its river, attempt to possess the landscape of this place, buy it, allow himself to be seduced by it. After which, there is no reason to hesitate. The river's movement carries you peacefully toward the bank, the invisible winch hauls you in, gently.

The river goes on flowing downward, and its long gliding indifference hollows a path through the arid earth. It comes from the mountains somewhere to the north, and flows toward the sea, somewhere to the south. It is long. It is peaceful. It possesses no intelligence, and its power means nothing more nor less than this: to flow.

The river's bulging, opaque mass sweeps along within it bits of earth, tree trunks, corpses, bubbles. The river descends, calm, free of hatred, free of desire, for ever deepening and broadening its frothy-banked channel.

And, without budging, the island proceeds upstream, wedging its stem into the centre of the water, just like that, easily, but painfully too, like a submarine trying unsuccessfully to dive. The sheer weight of solitude is here, in the obstinate isolation of this block of earth, this ancient mountain that the water has reduced to the present lump of mud and trees. One slides slowly into this ancient body, one assumes its ovoid shape, one stretches out on its liquid mass, and one fights against the movement that descends purposelessly, mindlessly. The waves part continually to follow the contour of the island's flanks, creating a series of eddies in the process.

It was exactly like the eye of a cyclops, or the centre of an extinct volcano, or the stranded carcass of an enormous black-boned whale. One approached the monster, gliding along in the flat-bottomed boat, pushing the water-lilies' plates aside, one after the other. One followed the current's curved path, skating silently over the flow of mercury that reflected the sky. One descended. The heat vibrated between the reeds, there were birds, and passages of wind, cool, cold, warm. In the centre of its aquatic prison, the island's bulging mass was perfectly still. Imperceptible shivers went through it in all directions, the trails of constantly oozed, constantly absorbed drops of water. The rasping of brambles, the scratchings of bushes and great trees, all these grids, dotted lines, prickles, heads of hair, advancing rapidly, extending their ramifications indefinitely over the earth. And then fading away immediately, shrouded once more in silence and shadow.

This was life, the island of life, with countless tastes and stinks; there was really nothing to be said about it. The best thing would have been to concentrate, smoke a cigarette, take a ballpoint pen, and write down on a bit of paper a few words and figures:

KOH PEIN' TUA
ME PING
18° 50 N.
99° 02 E.

to be followed, on the same bit of paper, by the words:

beauty
heat
dirty water flowing
and
cries of birds
and
water lilies
and

reflections of the sun
black-bellied insects
snakes
empty sky
cries of horned toads
beauty
beauty

while thinking, at each word, death, death, death. There was so much beauty on this island, so much tranquillity and sweetness everywhere here. Where was this place? Why had all these trees taken root here, why had they grown tall here, aged here?

One was on board the ship, now, drifting aimlessly. Paths crisscrossed the sand in every direction, bearing footprints that led to secret places. Signs had been planted there, no matter how, to deceive you, to make you believe that life existed, that it was in full swing somewhere. One was forging ahead. One was walking up the path, passing ceaselessly through the wall of heat. To left and right, the leaves of the trees were attached to their twigs like labels. Yes, that was it, labels bearing nothing but an eye that watched you. Impossible to forget anything. Danger was intensely present, invisible, inaudible. Nothing but the cries of fantastic birds, the droning of insects, the quick flight of stiff-necked lizards, and the enveloping water, the water tightening its leaden sheath. The sun, too, but no one raised his head to look at it.

Beneath him, the patches of shadow moved imperceptibly. They crept over the ground's dull surface, spread out, extended their transparent membranes. And it was a little as though a wind had blown continually in the same direction, flattening the blades of grass side by side. No one noticed this. From somewhere beyond the river the night was advancing, and no one paid attention to it. The moon emerged from a thornbush and stretched like a bubble, no one ever gave it a thought. All this happened mechanically, hour after hour, day after day, and it might just as well have been happening on a strange planet.

But, on the island itself, certain things were becoming clearer. There was a village, now, a village like any other village, its streets lined with identical little houses, cubes of white concrete pierced by the holes of two windows and a door. In front of each cube was a little garden of flowers and foliage, and above each door a name was written. The successive names were all different, WARAPHOL, T. E. SIMMONS, CLARKE, BRUCKER, NIELS, YOUNG, HOKEDO, and all said exactly the same thing. It was a camp, a neat, prosperous labyrinth. Streets radiated in straight lines from the centre of the floating island, sandy corridors flanked by white cubes, along which one progressed noiselessly. One advanced as though imprisoned within a bubble at the bottom of the sea, floating through the vestiges of a forgotten city. One did not stop. Where could one stop? It was an endless duplication of the same blocks of concrete, the same empty sockets of windows, the same doors, the same bunches of red and gold flowers, the same names written on the wooden plaques, MATTHEWS, AH SONG, DORIAN, as though it had always been the same word written in black letters, in the middle of the spectacle of beauty, of silence and of life with its delicate movements: DESTINY, DESTINY, I. M. DESTINY, DESTINY & CO., DESTINY, GEORGE F. DESTINY. So there was no choice but to go on walking along the narrow streets, peering into the depths of the empty houses in the hope of seeing an image, a face, a hand.

Dust settled on the petals of the red and gold flowers,

the patches of shadow wandered over the ground, heat was ever present. The island was as big as a continent, one could spend years exploring it at leisure.

Faces without noses, hands without fingers, fingers without nails, eyes without lids, ears torn off, mouths without lips or teeth, feet cut off, legs cut off, arms cut off, stumps, bodies pitted, ruined, obliterated, earth-coloured, and the patches of shadow had settled on them, continuing a snail-like progress from left to right.

They said nothing. They were standing stock-still in the sun, or else squatting in the sand, waiting. There was no kind of fear in their faces; age and youthfulness mingled, poverty, stupidity, impotence. The inhabitants, the island's only inhabitants, had gathered together in a sandy sort of plaza, in front of a tin shack. They were talking in low voices, without looking at one another. They were there, for no compelling reason, prisoners of the river's circle, prisoners of the odours of the hyacinths, the red and gold flowers, the houses' concrete cubes. Perhaps they no longer had names; they were the property of MEREDITH, DRAD, KOHLER, DELACOUR and the others who had bought the wooden plaques so that they could have their names engraved on them.

Something had brought them together there, something incomprehensible, a disease wearing a leonine mask, and displaying swollen hands with fingers that were rotting away painlessly. That must have happened a very long time ago, and now no one remembered anything any longer. The labyrinth with its white cubes was ready, each dim cabin awaited its body, each earthenware bowl awaited its mouth. It had really been very simple. All that was necessary was to cross the river. On the island, the masses of green foliage, the nodes of twigs and leaves, the flowers, the raucous cries

148

of birds were ready, too. They had set their traps of beauty and delight, they had opened their mouths to the intoxicating fumes, they had offered their silence and their peace; and human beings had decided to start living there. They had been there, now, for something like eternity. They worked. They had passions, loves, children. They talked. They ate. In the evening, they drank a little, then fell asleep. They fetched water from the river, they cooked their meals over log fires, they smoked the American cigarettes that people gave them. From time to time they went into the big white house, and people gave them injections, made tests. That was all quite easy, no one was afraid. From time to time, too, they stopped because people were approaching them on the sandy path, a man dressed all in nylon, and a young woman with long hair and a sun-tanned body. The young woman was walking awkwardly because of her high heels, and the young man was wearing dark glasses. He came to a halt, there in the sun, gripped the young woman by the arm, and said in a low voice:

' ... And that one over there, did you see?'

'Ghastly, yes, absolutely ghastly.'

'And the old woman over there hasn't any nose at all. Wait, don't look round right away.'

Or else it was a group of sweaty-faced men trying to locate the empty-eyed face of some new concrete cube, and they pumped each other's hands, and they congratulated each other, CAMPBELL, THORNTON, after you, please, yes, W. C. ZIEGLER, really very interesting, PIENPONG SANG, magnificent enterprise, LEOPOLD, GALLI, PORTER, GEORGE F. DESTINY. Sometimes, too, there was a thin-faced, bright-eyed man who came running as far as the village and insisted on trying to embrace everyone within sight, men, women, old folk, children. And he held lovingly between his hands the deformed stumps blotched with white scabs, and there was something very ugly, a nasty sort of excitement smouldering in the depths of his eyes.

So much for that. Meanwhile, the shadow has slid a little farther toward the right. It has entered the concrete cabins and it can be seen swelling gently inside the empty orbits. The heat is grey and drab, like ash. Sleep will soon come, on this ship navigating its stationary voyage. Sleep will overcome the destroyed faces, one after the other, will lay the scarred bodies to rest on the ground. As everywhere else, there is no waiting here. Two children run barefoot over the soft ground, which retains strange prints from which the outlines of two or perhaps three toes are missing. A young woman has raised her head, and the two eyes in her flat, noseless, mouthless mask are perfectly tranquil. Her gaze reflects nothing beyond what she sees. The secret of the catastrophe is lost in time, it does not even exist any longer. Neither forgotten nor conquered, but the secret has become illegible upon the petrified flesh. The wound has closed its lips, and one can no longer see what had once been displayed for a brief moment. The body's sac. All these skin surfaces are tightly sealed, leaving no escape route for the blood.

Once upon a time, elsewhere, there had been this vision of crime, of war, of violence, against the human race. A gigantic foot shod with a gigantic slipper had slammed down on the earth, crushing everything. Then the insects had picked up their remains, preened their wings and legs, stretched their antennae. The monstrous foot had raised itself and vanished.

On the island, beauty continues to deal out blows. It strikes with its leaves, with its red and gold flowers, with its heat, its bird cries. Lizards run across the sandy clearings, rearing their rigid necks. Wasps skim the ground. The little patches of shadow gradually reunite, and night sets in from left to right. So much useless beauty, so much beauty, so much strength, so much

So many acrid perfumes rising from the ground, so much suppleness in the earth, so many colours, signs, names everywhere. Everything has come here to inscribe itself. Life's great spasms, its joys and memories. There was a day when a funnel sprouted up from this speck of the world, and every last ounce of power flowed down into it. How is it possible? How can the walls of this place stand the strain? It is possibly the final load to be carried within the swollen sides of the ark floating above the water. The boat is going nowhere. It has no destiny. It has simply risen higher than the mass of forgetfulness, with its cargo of leaves, earth, insects and men. Corrupt beauty, but the odour of corruption is itself a new beauty. Plenitude, danger, death everywhere, in each of these twigs, in each of these flowers. Concealed eyes spying on you when you pass, and these are not the eyes of self-awareness. They are life's millions of ocelli, all its quivering antennae, all its undeviating cells; here is surely the place to live, with a gnawed nose in one's face, and stumps in place of hands and feet. Inhabiting a concrete cube with a name inscribed above the door: George F. Destiny. It would be a way to become swept up in the world's fever, a way to bring one's flight to a halt. During the day one would sharpen pieces of wood with one's knife, and when evening came one would watch the sun setting over the muddy river.

And one would float all the time. Or else one would listen to the angry shrieks of the birds in the trees, one would watch ground-beetles exist. And all the time one would be the prisoner of the extraordinary beauty, the calm, the thrill of a kind of pleasure, everywhere one would sense the presence of the drama. And it would be like inhabiting a cemetery on an island, moving around among the tombs, reading the names, smoking cigarettes, proffering one's sweat for the flies to drink. There would be women and children, and the children's children, it would go on like that for ever. Life would pass very quickly, or else very slowly, impossible to tell. But it would pass, it would saunter along.

Everything was nearly over. Time now to leave the island, or the room; at the present moment, the shadow was smeared everywhere. Explosions of cries came from the trees' bushy tops, followed by silences. Above the doors the names gradually became illegible, then faded away altogether. The sky was hollow. One was thousands of miles from any-where, closed in, peaceful. Alone. It was a raft floating on one's memory, surrounded by the ramparts of the moist heat, or perhaps it was a volcano smoking in the centre of a plain. One did not leave. One turned back, one became lost in the corridor of time, and, right in the background, the white door became smaller and smaller.

Do you see it, now? A woman's head whose face has no features, whose two black eyes shine with a fixed stare, and this head is floating all by itself in the centre of a grey river, breathing through its open mouth, a mouth from which no word, no kind of cry or prayer or curse ever escapes, nothing but silence, silence, silence?

Travelling, always urged on by hatred. Today, I am advancing along the river. On the gliding boat, I am walking along the river. The water is very calm, the colour of metal, with great white reflections. I can hear, far behind me, the chugging of the engine. The water flows past the stem, sends out little ripples as it parts, shivers. The reeds sway aside as the boat glides between them. The sky's heat is reverberated on to the sheet of water, produces great flashes of lightning. The world is nothing but water now, water that is magical where the light strikes. I am walking along the endless mirror, watching the double image dance. I am in a stupor. The water washes the banks, washes the buffalos, washes the women's bodies. The water is stretched taut under the white sky, delicate as a spider's web, solid as marble. The heat is so fierce that it is as though a layer of cold had descended on everything. The air is motionless. Decayed things float in the river, drift with the boat. The water is full of snakes. The long lake is a flow of rubber, a cascade of spittle. Everything is crawling. The sounds come from far away, the sounds are sleeping curled up in a ball inside their shiny scales. There are millions of drowned men in the water, waiting expectantly for one to join them. The river descends toward the sea, it winds its way slowly across the green earth. Sometimes the loops join up, producing odd crescent-shaped puddles that evaporate in the sun.

Insects skim the surface, mosquitoes, dragonflies and solicitous spiders. The boat moves forward, caresses, moves forward. It glides into the middle of the invisible boiler and is swallowed up. There are islands, and capes. The water is a lens from a pair of dark glasses, impossible to see what is on the other side. The black raft drifts along this silvery river, with its white sky, its reflections, its chalky mists, the raft disappears among all this steel dust, all these drops of quicksilver. My features can just be made out in the light-dazzled snapshot, a few grey and black lines that will soon fade away.

I would like it so much if nothing were separate from me any longer, if estrangement were banished for ever.

Exoticism is a vice, because it is a way of forgetting the true aim of all quests, self-awareness. It is an invention of the white man, bound up with his mercantile conception of culture. This desire to possess is sterile. There can be no compromise: anyone who seeks to arrogate to himself the soul of a nation by nibbling away at it, by hoarding sensations or ideas, is incapable of knowing the world; is incapable of knowing himself. Reality is not to be won on those terms. It demands humility.

This country should be loved in another manner. It should be loved not because it is different, or distant (distant from what?) but because it is a country that does not allow itself to be possessed easily; because it is a country that defends itself against intrusion, because it is an inner truth that I shall doubtless never know. Because it is, like *my* country, a locality of this world, a moment of present time that is not reducible to theories and diagrams. There is no artifice in its makeup. Everything to be found there belongs to it. How can one fail to speak freely of a free country? How can one fail to be moved by so many natural contradictions that balance serenity with violence, dirtiness with beauty? These contradictions are real. The earth is neither fabulous nor paradisal. And therefore it is not hell.

No, what is interesting, what is refining, what finally dissolves the veil that separates each individual in this world from his fellows, is precisely a land such as this, an ancient land inhabited by men who speak the same language and work at the same things. Not a legendary land, but real soil supporting human beings with real faces, an ancient, always young people which has taken root slowly, and which has chosen this place for its own.

What invisible wall guards this people, what secret love unites these beings, what name defends them and protects them? Give me this name, if only for a single moment, so that I shall not forget it, I who am in full flight ... It is this same questioning that always reasserts itself, whether on the fringe of this flat, watery land, under this lowering sky, in the thick heat pouring down from the sun, or in the centre of the terrible anthill of this gigantic city. Diverted and obscured under the conditions of an existence based on aggression, this questioning receives a clear answer here. As though from the top of a lighthouse, one sees the vividly outlined spectacle, the astonishing destiny by which men are grouped and given affinities. One is there oneself, a speck among all the other specks, unessential, without remedy, a prisoner of one's language and one's race, a prisoner of one's time, and yet, at the same moment one is beyond all forms of expression, one is indefinitely FREE !

I would like, most of all, to talk about silence. A silence which is neither an absence of words nor a mental blockage. A silence which is an accession to a domain beyond the bounds of language, an animated silence, so to speak, a relationship of active equality between the world and man.

The botched universe of immediate significance, of useful words and actions, is no longer particularly important. What counts is this harmony of rhythms. One cannot forget this journey, this passage of thought into material existence.

In the centre of this flat countryside, on the Ayutthaya road, for example, when the terrible heat of noon holds sway. Steam rises from the scorching ground. I look around me. All I can see is the great expanse of earth moist with sweat, sweeping straight to the sky, with no horizon in between. There is no sound, and the light bounces back upon the huge puddle. There is no movement. The whole experience is indescribable. Then, quite naturally, without the slightest wrench, words, ideas and actions have all ceased to exist. All that remains is this prolongation of time over space. Somewhere, in this land of inherited wisdom, people are living, are working in the rice fields. Their thoughts and words are present, mingled with this soil and this water. It is as though, gently and smoothly, the veil separating me from reality had grown thinner, had worn away its texture, ready now to rip apart so that the great forces may pass through. It has become transparent, almost transparent. I can just make out, through its immobility, the blurred symbols of the replies that are about to flow forward. They are symbols of silence.

Or else, sitting in the bows of the boat, on the river. The heat glows on the metal-edged waves. Square-stemmed canoes plough upstream, through the bulging mass of water that flows between rows of wooden houses. Their motors screech. And that, too, is silence. For the weighty river is a voice; and what this voice says is more important and more beautiful than a poem.

In the hot night, cockroaches prowl. The booths of a fair have been set up inside the temple's courtyard. Men, women and children are squatting on the ground, in front of one of the booths, watching a play in which the masked actors are at this moment frozen in quivering poses, while music blares from the loudspeakers. The quickened rhythms of the *Auk Phassa*, the nasal songs of the *Rabam Dawadeung*, the intoned chants of the *Ramayana*. Old, violent tableaux under the neon lights, tableaux of a continuing life, music born of the sounds of the world, magic rhythms that one no longer hears, silence which demands that I should listen, that I should at last stop interrupting what is being ceaselessly communicated to me.

Rhythm of the day and the night, rhythm of the baths, rhythm of the Ja-Ké, rhythm of the pitch-accented language of Klong verses, of Kap and Klon verses. Rhythm of the light, of the rains, of the architectures whose roofs brandish claws. Rhythm of the wooden houses whose verandas slope gently downward so that the evening breeze can waft its way as far as the sleeping bodies inside. All these rhythms are silence, because they extinguish other rhythms in me, because they oblige me to be quiet.

This silence from beyond words is not apathetic. This peace is not a sleep. Together, they are a rampart built against the aggressions of the sun, of noise, of war. Pride and will-power are written on the naked face of this woman standing in the centre of her canoe. On her fixed mask, cast from the primordial matrix of her race, is written the text of the ancient deed whereby this people exchanged its soul with that of this piece of land. Every day, in the centre of the river, this face confronts the invisible enemy. She is not aware of the fact, no one really suspects it, but this combat is joined each day, each minute, and it is a mortal combat. Is she even aware that she is victorious? Is she aware of the strength and violence that animate her, when with her slow swaying movement she leans on the oar, propelling the fragile craft beneath her feet into the centre of the river? She is neither aware nor unaware, for she is she, and this river is she, and each of her gestures is noble because it is not gratuitous. She describes her destiny, her civilization.

Against the fearful noise that threatens every man, against hatred and anguish, she sets the harmony and peace of her silence. And at moments, beneath the enormous pressure of this sun, in the presence of this flat, waterlogged land bereft of horizon, or else in the face of the giddy swirl of this crowd with similar faces, similar thoughts, all moved by the same mysterious breeding instinct, this silence opens the way to a rare miracle that is the privilege of lands of self-awareness: the miracle of perceiving, through the fine net curtain separating us from reality, the exact design of the adventure.

These things happened not long ago, in Bangkok, in Bang-Pa-In, or in Djakarta.

THE FLUTE PLAYER AT ANGKOR

Hogan saw the little boy who was playing the flute, sitting on the ground among the ruins. There was this great dusty weed-covered amphitheatre, surrounded by the crumbling remains of walls and by stunted trees. It had not rained for a long time, and everything was dry and powdery. The time must have been about four in the afternoon: the sun was high in the sky, though it vanished, at regular intervals, behind globes of cirro-cumulus. Patches of grey shadow advanced across the ground like clouds of ash, glided noiselessly across the grass amphitheatre. The walls changed colour, became black, then red, then black again. In the hollows near the piles of stones, there must have been lots of lizards, all changing colour, too.

The little boy was sitting on the ground, in the centre of the amphitheatre's weeds and dust, paying no attention to the ruins. He was not exactly sitting: he was squatting on his heels, his naked legs doubled up, the top of his body leaning slightly forward. He was blowing into a long bamboo flute on which the craftsman had burned the image of a snake that wound itself round the tube. He blew into the flute without looking to the right or the left, expressionless, eyes staring straight ahead. His forearms were resting on his knees. Only his hands were moving. The brown fingers with their grimy nails raised and lowered themselves rapidly, without shifting position. The flute was pointed towards the ground, and the child's mouth was just touching the upper tip. From time to time the little boy stopped playing, to get his breath back. Then he placed his lips around the flute's mouthpiece, and his cheeks swelled, palpitating imperceptibly. The air descended the bamboo tube, creating odd kinds of invisible nodes, and clusters, and interferences. There was a series of holes running down the flute: seven along the top, one at the right-hand side, and another underneath. The holes were small and perfectly round, drilled through the wood, aligned behind each other, tiny bottomless wells. A red ribbon hung from the lower end of the flute.

The little boy played away tranquilly. When the sun was shining, he was playing his flute in the sun. His shadow squatted in the grass, right behind him.

When Hogan approached him, the child stopped playing and looked at him. His two hands lowered the flute to the ground, his fingers blocking all the holes. The child hesitated a moment, watched Hogan warily. Hogan squatted down in the grass, too, and lit a cigarette. In the blue sky, the cirro-cumulus clouds were very high, like grains of salt scattered at random. This meant that the sun was continually catching alight, then dying out again. The child looked at the sky to see what was happening. After that, he paid no more attention to Hogan than if the latter had been a dog that had come and sat down beside him. He lifted his flute and started to play once more.

The music was speaking all by itself in the centre of the circle of ruins, there on the dusty grass. It was always the same melody that emerged from the flute, a series of ascending notes, a hesitation, a new ascending series, a hesitation, then four or five low notes, a hesitation, a series of descending notes. But one immediately understood that it was an inexhaustible melody. Nothing began it, nothing could stop it. Or rather, one could stop it at any moment at all, in the middle of a hesitation, for instance, or else there, on that low trill, or again there, after that sequence of three semitone notes. The sound of the flute was very piercing, sharply defined, soaring straight into the dense air like a flight of birds, never wavering a fraction from its path. That, too, was something difficult, inaccessible, something beyond the mind's grasp.

Hogan was squatting in the grass, watching the little boy stare straight ahead as he played his flute. At one moment, he felt like getting up and asking the child what one had to do to play the flute like that. He felt like having a try at blowing into the flute, himself; he felt like using his fingers to stop up the nine holes along the bamboo tube, by placing his thumb over the hole underneath, his arched index over the hole at the side, and the middle and other fingers of his right hand over the first three of the seven holes along the top. And the snake engraved with a red-hot iron would have wound itself round as far as his mouth, and the red ribbon would have dangled between his knees. But a moment later, he did not think about it any longer, he just went on listening and watching.

There was no one in this grassy amphitheatre. On the other side of the ruined walls, tourists were strolling around and posing for photographs. They were reading books which explained all about bas-reliefs and *apsaras* and the invention of the movie camera. Women draped in long robes were selling bottles of mineral water. Thick-set men were running to and fro, waving paintings, proffering bits of pottery, bronze heads, key-rings.

The sound of the flute pierced the silence. It rose very high, with little sharp cries that vibrated intensely. It fell again quickly, sliding from note to note, and the ten fingers closed upon the tube. From time to time, the little boy slid his thumb down toward the base, and lifted his index finger: then the sound broke abruptly, and what emerged now was a sort of wailing very far away in space, a gentle rustling of leaves, an almost undetectable creaking sound. He stopped the lateral hole again, and the creaking became increasingly shrill, while the agile fingers released hundreds of quarter-tone notes, something like the cries of a bat, rising, descending, rising again, sweeping over the plain with their clumsy urgency. The flute was not confined to a single voice. It possessed several, dozens perhaps, all of them powerful: locomotive whistles, ships' sirens, whining of bullets, murmurs, doleful grating noises, squawks, hiccups, and various laughs, voices for gaining height rapidly, and voices for hovering, voices for imitating the voices of women, and voices for imitating the wind. But all this was achieved simply, unaffectedly, without any striving for virtuosity, without emotion. The flute did not want to make people emotional, or sad. It did not search the soul, it did not try to convince. It was there, there only when it had to be, an upsurge of wind and noise in the middle of the walls' silence, proclaiming nothing, awaiting nothing. The notes came and went, always the same, breaking off, dividing up, filling empty space for a fraction of a second. It was there like a blade of grass, or like a lizard; it had no will.

Hogan listened to the flute's music without daring to budge. When he had finished his cigarette, he stubbed it out under a clod of dry earth, between the weeds. He saw that the sun was a little lower in the sky, about half an inch lower. He saw that the clouds had crossed towards the right, the odd-looking balls of cirro-cumulus floating nearly four miles up in the air. At ground level, the stunted trees needed water. There were a few more ruined walls, scattered at random around the weed-filled plain, but no one was interested any longer. It was the flute's shrill music that had emptied everything in this way. It sucked things up from the world, dissolved them gently, made them disappear. The unique sound emerged from the bamboo tube between the little boy's hands, and wandered through space. Although it could not be seen, it travelled quickly, like a spreading crack, like a thin trickle of water down a slope.

It was the voice of a woman, perhaps, a flexible, firm voice with nasal intonations, with long clear syllables that reverberated in the silence. The voice, in a sense, of eternal woman, with her expressive face framing candid eyes, with her mouth and teeth, with her black hair, with her generous bosom and wide hips. She invaded space, she covered the earth. Wherever one looked, she was there ... She was dancing barefoot, stretching out her arms, splaying her fingers.

The music had ceased to be strange. It formed an integral part of everything, its sound issued clearly from the earth, the stunted trees, the old tumbledown walls. It gushed ceaselessly from the sky, floated along with the ball-shaped clouds, arrived at full speed with the light. There was no longer any reason to listen. Or to be far away. One no longer had ears. One was close, face to face with it. The music was long drawn out, no longer had an ending. It had never had a beginning. It was there, infinitely motionless, exactly like an arrow poised in mid-flight.

That is what the flute was saying, while the little boy squatted, blowing and moving his fingers. That is what it was seeing. The ductile notes had turned into a true gaze, a long gaze of awareness that lingered over the countryside. It came and went, it roamed over the blades of grass, it passed through the branches of bushes, through walls, through people's bodies. The calm gaze travelled as far as the most distant horizon, and then still farther, it soared into the transparent sky, it played over the cirro-cumulus four miles above the earth, it reached as far as the sun and the invisible stars, it visited all the island-universes fleeing through space. With a single leap it had attained the limits of the real world, had passed through existence like a shiver. The flute's keen gaze had seen everything. It had travelled effortlessly through human understanding, more rapidly than the millions of competing words, and it was still continuing its journey, farther than time, farther than knowledge, farther than the dizzy spiral in the process of boring its way into a madman's skull.

Hogan was far away, just now; he was sitting on his heels, in the weed-covered plain among the ruins, like a dog at the feet of his master; the heat and the light were harsh, unrelieved even by a breath of wind. Where was all this happening? What was he going to do? The clouds move lazily in the sky, the stunted trees need water. Are there enough words for each of us? There is great joy, joy in the notes that soar and swoop, in the soft hissing, in the sharp trills. There is great fear, too, the voluble fear that furnishes silence. The earth is far away, as though viewed through the wrong end of a telescope. Is one on this side or the other side of the mirror? The birds cry out, the horses cry out, the fish cry out, even the bugs cry out when the blood drains away, even the mouthless weeds. Everything is cold, everything is *inhabited*.

When the sun had reached about a quarter past four that afternoon, the little boy stopped playing. He got up without looking at Hogan and went away, walking barefoot through the grass. Then Hogan went away, too. He walked along a sort of causeway paved with worn flags, that crossed a canal. He saw a lot of people moving around with cameras, notebooks and sunglasses. And he had to make a great effort to remember even part of what he had understood.

The squatting posture:
in front of fire, in front of water
for urination, defecation, childbirth.
Uneasy repose
balance.
Posture favouring total concentration of the
being only the feet touch the ground
(being upright involves dispersion)
Posture for take-off
posture of vigilance
(being seated involves unconstraint)
Heedful peoples live in a squatting posture.
The compact shape of the man squatting in the
dust is repugnant to the civilized man.
CHILD SQUATTING IN FRONT OF THE WORLD
MAN SQUATTING AS HE EATS
WOMAN SQUATTING AS SHE WASHES IN THE
RIVER

'Those who follow ignorance enter into the darkness of
the blind, but those who seek only knowledge enter into an
even greater darkness.'

Īśa Upaniṣad

The question now is: one or several?

This is the big question, the only question one can hope to answer some day, with one's life, with one's life crammed full with words. I had been too busy fleeing to realize that. I just didn't see it. I didn't even suspect that such a question could exist. The only questions I used to ask myself were unimportant, irrelevant ones, like: Is there a God? What happens after death? And then: does the world have a purpose? Can one live without a moral code?

They were bad questions because it was obvious that I couldn't answer them.

They were questions, tremors of language, imperfections, the exposition of anassuaged desires in terms of the desirable. I was incapable of answering them because, like the others, I lacked the real means to do so. Language had blinded me with its daily mendacity. It had accustomed me to think in explicit terms, based upon linguistic justifications. What was there to say? There was the fact to be recorded, as usual, that thought was powerless to convince genuinely, to impose its laws on the universe. But that didn't matter. I wanted to know; I never imagined that one could escape from the narrow valley, look elsewhere, breathe elsewhere. But I know now that the true question is: the one or the several?

Yet at the same moment that the question assails me, overwhelms me, I know that I shall not answer it. That I shall have no vocabulary for it, since language is the one, whereas it is a matter of conceiving the several. I shall have no words for that. I shall have nothing but a few gestures, at a pinch, to light a fresh cigarette with my right hand, to squeeze the trigger of the camera that kills, or else to take a sheet of white paper and draw on it thousands of black dots:

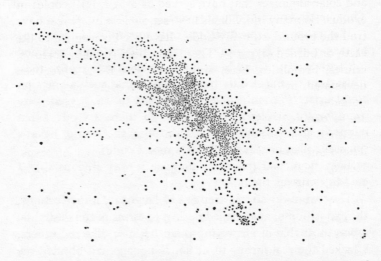

I shall have millions of gestures, from the beginning of my life right up to the end, and perhaps even beyond, and these millions of gestures will be my reply.

I shall have thousands of handwritings, cursive, script, slanting, back-handed, Tamil, Arabic, cuneiform. I shall have Mayan hieroglyphs, Chinese ideograms of A.D. 1000, Phoenician, Etruscan, Hebrew characters. I shall have Kuna pictographs, Maori tattoos, the notches in Magdalenian pebbles. Graffiti on the walls of London urinals. Tibetan mantras, the yellow daubs on the faces of *peyoteros*, display posters, Hongkong's illuminated signs, the incisions in Karaja dolls, the Guarayos' maze pictures.

I shall have highway codes, and the flashing signs at the side of expressways repeating their message, maintain speed! maintain speed! The signs of the Zodiac, runes, quipus, mosaics, tapestries, kites, knuckle-bones, all the tau crosses, all the *chalera* wheels, all the Totó flowers, all the rainbows and solar almanacs that have served as a path for peoples in exodus. So many individuals have set out! So many feet have trod the ground, so many bodies have been consigned to the earth or burned on pyres. There have been so many sorrows, crimes, brutalities, here, and there! The fields have been devastated, fields so vast that no one has ever seen their far boundaries. The ships have voyaged over the seas, and there are so many seas!

I shall also have those millions of bodies to help me reply. Those millions of ways of life, those millions of skins: Negro, Kabyle, Kirghiz, Sudanese, Indian, American Indian, half-breed, white, albino! Those millions of ages, give or take a few seconds, those millions of races, civilizations, tribes. To help me reply, I shall have the history of time, not history itself but the stories and adventures that have spanned time, that have inscribed themselves on the trunks of trees and the walls of caves.

I shall have the life of the peasant Aurelius, who tilled his field in Latium during the time of Claudius Niger. That of James Retherford, who shod horses at Canterbury in 1604. That of the settler Lipczick, whose wagon rolled across the plains of Wyoming in 1861. I shall have the life of Khabarov who has at last reached the banks of the river Love. The life of Cuauhtetzin, as he marches along in the sun, in the dust, surrounded by his band of slaves loaded down with cocoa, in the year One of Acatl.

I shall also have the life of a certain François Le Clézio, who, with his wife and daughter, has embarked for Mauritius, and I shall have written down on sheets of green paper:

Log of a voyage from Bordeaux to Mauritius
aboard the brig Le Courrier des Indes
Departed the 27 floreal Year 7
Arrived the 17 fructidor Year 7

this 29 floreal
The weather being foggy, our hearts were heavy,
our position being 44°26″ & 8°12″
This 30
At 7 in the morning we saw 2 ships, whereat we
went about.
at 44°33″ & 8°27″.
This 1st Prairial Year 7
At 3 in the afternoon we sighted 2 ships sailing on
opposite tacks to each other, whereat we went
about. at 44°53″ & 9°18″ longitude.
This 3 Pal 7th
At 8 in the morning, sighted a brig, whereat we
made ready for battle, but soon thereafter it made
off at 44°10″ & 11°17″.
This 6
At 2 in the morning, descried a sail on its
course.
At 1/2 past 4 sighted 3 frigates which gave chase
to us & in spite of all our efforts, they were 5
hrs & 1/2 a league distant from us : which obliged

us to stave in our water-casks which were on the bridge. At 7, seeing that they were gaining on us, we jettisoned 4 iron cannons and 6 wooden cannons with their mountings, and other objects, & in spite of all these precautions, we could draw away only a little. At 1/4 past 8, one of the frigates fired at us with a bow chaser. We made a new manoeuvre which gave us no more advantage then before. The nearest ship came within cannon range and fired upon us; a few balls fell right behind us; finally there was no course open to us but to strike our colours & to our great satisfaction we saw that the ships were French; they were the Franchise, the Concorde & the Médée, out of Rochefort the 27 fral, under the command of Cpn. Landolphe. We followed them at 41°39" & 19°42" longitude.

This 15 Pal Year 7

At 7 in the evening, 3 flying fish leaped on board & one of them flapped with some force into my face at 27°11" & 30°9".

This 17

At 6 in the morning, no sooner sighted a schooner sailing on the starboard tack than we gave chase. At 11 in the morning, having overtaken it, we fired a cannon-shot at it, & it at once struck its colours, and launched its dinghy & the Cpn climbed on board our ship. He chanced to be American, out of Cadiz whence he was transporting to Charlestown 35 passengers, among whom 6 Capuchin friars. The captain willingly yielded water to us, whereupon we parted our ways at 21°48" & 30°23".

This 26

At 10 in the morning, the sea almost calm, as a

mist lifted, descried a convoy which lay N.E. of us, at 2 leagues distance; at once went about, and shipped six sweeps to escape from a frigate and a brig which were giving chase to us. At noon we lost sight of them in a squall, but soon thereafter in calm weather though much rain at intervals, we saw them again still giving chase. At noon we became aware that they were losing the wind & that we were about to receive a squall from the N.W. We at once set our sails to receive it & we kept pulling together in good spirits.

At 1/2 past 3 the weather cleared & after 5 hours of arduous & general labour in the heat & under very abundant rains, at last hauled in our oars & saw the frigate that had abandoned the chase returning to rejoin the convoy. We counted 23 sails: it was an English convoy out of the East Indies & headed for Portsmouth.

5°48″ & 24°21″

This 26 Messidor

Saw an albatross, a bird four times greater than a turkey & having a wing span of between eight and fifteen feet: we hooked one of 10 feet: its plumage is very akin to that of the Swan.

29°42″ & 19°52″

22 to 23 Thermidor

During the afternoon, fresh south-westerly winds blowing true. The sea running high.

At 10 in the evening reefed the topsails; the sea running very high indeed, the Ship scudded before the wind under the mizzen and the fore-topsail, it proceeded at 10, 11 & even 12 knots with the

strength of the winds & the currents. Much thunder,
we shipped several heavy seas.

At one o'clock after midnight, shipped the heaviest
sea hitherto, we were awash from end to end; the
rudder failed to respond for about one minute; at
that moment we thought ourselves irretrievably
lost, the Ship being more and more down by the
head; but happily its buoyancy revived our spirits;
at this time the sea inundated our cabins, several
objects were swept off the bridge by the sea which
also deprived us of our last pig the loss of which
we regretted for several days thereafter. The
remainder of our hens were drowned, but we
contrived a fricassee two days later. This terrible
rush of water took place abeam of the Needles,
at 36°3″ & 24°14″

28
The winds almost calm, weather misty, sea rather
rough, occasional storms, at 34°14″ & 30°35″.
10 to 15
Fair weather, fair sea, fresh breezes at 21°55″ &
58°14″
16 fructidor Year 7
We have sighted the land of Mauritius, but because
of the night we lay off to the sea.

I shall have the life of Rudy Sanchez, sitting in the bar that
is made out of plastics, drinking beer and listening to strident
music. I shall have the life of Lena Borg, of Laurent Dufour,
of J. L. Quirichini, of Simone Chenu, of Troubetskoy, of
M. & Mme Bongiovanni, of Thanat Gojasevi. Or else I shall
have the life of Hoang Trung Thong and of Nguyen Ngoc
writing poems to win the war. And sometimes I shall have the

life of a certain Yarmayan, and I shall live in an odd kind of world of dazzling light, in towns full of steel and crystal, one day, in the year $10223\frac{1}{2}$.

All of that, then, will be my answer, although I shall never be able to learn it myself. And this answer will be of no importance because it will never be addressed to anyone but myself alone, like a secret letter.

There is no need to know this answer. All the other questions demanded an immediate answer. No matter what, provided it was given with words, in some language using words. They pounced, they were eager, indiscreet. They lacked patience.

Whereas my question is gentle; it demands nothing, almost nothing. It is not demanding. It is there, peacefully, hurting me, hollowing its tunnel in my body. I appease it with gestures and with time, with things that are either tremendous or insignificant. I fill it with reality. It is my worm, devouring my food as fast as I absorb it.

My question is delighted that I am in flight. It longs for still more movement, still more insecurity. The more I stay in motion, the stronger it becomes. Each time I am struck by a blow I feel it stirring in my depths, shivering with pleasure. Pain, enjoyment, desire, hatred, everything suits its purpose, which is to push me farther back, and so erase from my mind a little more than what I had learned. It is due to my question that I RETREAT all the time.

Always whittling away at the universe until nothing remains but an incomprehensible pulp.

Is there a thought process?

Is there an idea which remains true from one end of the world to the other, an idea which remains true for more than a second?

Is there a thought which is not attached to the object, like

174

slimy seaweed to the rock, a thought which is not carried away immediately in the sudden drop, down the drain which sucks things in noisily?

Or alternatively, and worse still, is it not all a lie, an utterly absurd, crazy lie, since thought's intention is not to disguise the real but to be one with it, to represent it, invent it?

Is there a thought which is not like a hair, a thought so great and so beautiful that in returning to the earth after a thousand centuries one would recognize it immediately? Is there a thought which my daughter could understand? Is there even a thought which I could capture on the wing, one day, after having abandoned it?

That is why I am going away. That is the reason why one day I am here, another day somewhere else. If I am off in all directions it is so as to escape from the evil spell which would like to turn me into a pillar of salt. Words are on the lookout. Behind the covers of books, on the façades of houses, in the mouths of women and children, they are after me. They are waiting for the instant of inattention, the weak moment when my glance wavers from their face: then they would pounce. Their tiny harpoons are ready. To them, I am a whale whose flanks are heavy with fat. Their solid cords want to coil themselves round my arms and legs, their spider's webs want to weave themselves over my head, smothering me under a mask of dust. They want to dress me. They want to draw down over my face the woollen hood that is already provided with imaginary nose, eyes and mouth. They want to give me the name, the mellifluous word of powerful syllables, that will cover me entirely. They want to call me simply Man, Young Man, Young Man H. All of them. And it is true that, in the depths of my being, room has already been set aside for these syllables, there is already the pain of the tattoo being pricked in.

What do they want to call me? They want to call me
THE ONE.

At one fell swoop they will drive me into the solid universe
with its square walls, its white ceiling from which the light
bulb hangs, its beautiful windows, universe without hope,
where everything makes sense. There will be no more fear, no
more misery. No more movement. There will be nothing but
stability, the extraordinary, abominable stability of falsehood.

If I say yes, what joy will radiate, what pride will shine in
the eyes of the rest of mankind. They are gathered around me,
great stone colossi with cruel eyes, and they are singing in
chorus

He has said yes, he has said yes, yes, yes

He has said yes, he has said yes, yes, yes

Young Man Hogan went out at five. He walked through the town, along an avenue that sloped gently downward. This was another huge town, set in a bay ringed by mountains, undulating across a series of hills. From high up, one could occasionally glimpse the town through the blocks of tall buildings, a sort of grey puddle made of roofs and walls. But once inside the town, one could no longer see anything at all. One walked down the sloping avenue that was lined on both sides by the frontages of low-built houses, shop windows, garages and gas stations. Cars bumped over the roadway's pitted surface, some going up, others coming down. Dilapidated old buses, full to overflowing, rattled along explosively, horns blasting.

Young walked along in the heavy air that reeked of exhaust fumes. He was making for the poor quarters, unhurriedly, paying little attention to the street scene around him. Hundreds of other people were walking along, too, skinny little men wearing thong sandals on their bare feet, fat women, children, dogs sniffing at bits of muck. At one moment he went into a dimly-lit shop to buy cigarettes. He was handed a yellowish pack bearing a design that represented the head of a smiling woman, with a ricefield in the background, and the words:

NEW PARADISE

or something like that. When he opened the pack he saw that they were American-style filter tips. They tasted rather peculiar, like burnt grass. Young went on down the boulevard, smoking.

The sun was invisible, hidden behind a grey haze. Heat rose from the ground, came out of the walls, a moist engine heat that penetrated people's clothes and glued their hair flat.

The boulevard descended like that for about a mile. Then it reached a bridge, and after crossing a miserable stream like a smear of spittle that trickled underneath, it led to an intersection from which a number of avenues radiated. Straight ahead lay the slum district, which could be entered only by narrow, dark streets burrowing their way between the blocks of houses. Young Man Hogan plunged into the warren. Walking along the alley, he felt a strange feeling of coolness come over him. It was not a soothing feeling, more like a sort of feverish shiver running down his spine, giving him gooseflesh.

The alley was unpaved, muddy patches alternating with the dusty surface as it wound its way through lines of grey brick hovels and the shells of tin shacks. As he progressed, Young began to see silhouettes appear. They loomed up suddenly from open doorways, ominous, stunted figures that vanished again immediately like ghosts. There was no noise, except for the occasional blare of music announcing some radio commercial, coming from transistors at the back of the shacks. And groups of children ran up and down the path, yelling, disappearing into invisible backyards. Young looked at the walls of the houses, the tin roofs. Sometimes an open window projected its blurred image towards him as he passed by: the floating shapes of two or three women eating round a table on which lay a naked child.

Or else, at the back of a cell-like dwelling so white that it seemed to have no roof, there was a brief glimpse of a young woman dressed in a long robe, combing her black hair with great, slow motions, from the crown of her head down to her hips; and for a few seconds, walking along the alley, Young Man Hogan could see nothing but that girl, that hair, so long that it covered her face and half her body, and that naked arm coming and going, sweeping downward, slowly, gravely, royally.

Somewhere in one of these shanties, under the corrugated tin roof where lizards scuttle, an old woman called Min was dying, lying on her side on a straw mat.

Farther away, a woman was in labour, in the corner of a room, her two hands gripping her sister's wrists, uttering cries of pain. But all that meant nothing, it was like dust, household dust or the grit on pathways.

Young Man Hogan turned right and walked along another alley. Then he turned left into yet another alley. And right, and left, and right again, and there were always more alleys ahead of him. The houses were never identical, there was always some minute difference, the shape of the bricks, for example, or the colour of the rusted sheets of tin, or else in the appearance of the pile of garbage beside the door.

After an hour, Young Man Hogan found himself in a slightly wider street, full of taverns. The doors in the brick walls were closed by canvas curtains, from behind which seeped a noise blended of music and upraised voices. Young dawdled past the fronts of the bars, trying to see what was going on inside. When he reached the end of the street, he saw a tavern on the opposite side, with its door curtain pulled back a little. He crossed over and looked inside. But the interior was pitch-dark. Music was blaring somewhere inside the building, and men were yelling drunkenly. He was about to go away when a man emerged, a skinny little man in a sweat-stained shirt, who whispered something into his ear. Young followed him inside the tavern. The man showed him to an iron table at the back of the room, and brought him a bottle of beer. When his eyes grew accustomed to the darkness, Young saw that there were not many other people in the room. A few drunks were asleep, with their heads slumped on table tops. The music was filled with the buzz of frantic flies, but the flies themselves could not be seen. Young drank straight from the bottle and listened to the music.

After a moment the skinny little man in the sweat-stained shirt returned and beckoned him to follow. Young crossed the room behind him. The skinny little man opened a door giving on to a kind of yard that had a row of wooden latrine huts down one side. On the opposite side, the little man stopped in front of a tin-roofed shed. He pushed the door open and beckoned Young to go in. When Young entered the shed he saw that it was a sort of a theatre, with a lot of people sitting on benches made from old crates. The shed was as dark as the bar-room had been, except at the far end where a wooden stage was lit by three big electric lamps. The skinny little man escorted Young to the fifth row and showed him his place. Before going, he demanded a few dollars which he promptly stuffed into his trouser pocket.

The shed echoed with the sound of the raucous music coming from a record player. In the room, the men waited, sitting on the benches, talking, smoking marijuana, drinking beer from cans. The air was heavy and sluggish. Little rays of daylight filtered through the boarded-up windows, and danced in the smoke. The heat was suffocating, and Young Man Hogan felt the sweat oozing from his back and armpits, trickling down his temples. The atmosphere was more oppressive than down a coalmine, 2,000 feet underground.

The air pressed down on the face and throat, crushed the lungs like a rubber ball, forced the eyelids to close over the eyes. One was the prisoner of an endless nightmare, but it was worse than a nightmare. The men sat listlessly on their benches, mopping the back of their necks with dirty handkerchiefs. Young saw their eyes glitter in the depths of their glowing faces. The music sputtered between the brick walls, a music made meaningless by the sheer din it was creating, the chief feature being a constant thunder of drumbeats. At the far end of the shed the three light bulbs threw their splashes of violent light like three drops of molten lead swimming in the air. Beneath them the stage was bare. At each side of the white rectangle the linen curtains were motionless. Young began to stare hard at the light, as though that had been the promised show; for several minutes on end he screwed up his eyes and studied the three sparkling stars. Then he tried smoking a cigarette, but he choked and had to stub it out on the ground after only one puff. From time to time the music stopped and a terrible silence welled up inside the shed. Then someone invisible put the same record on again, and the screeching noises and heavy drumbeat recommenced.

Suddenly, the curtain to the right of the stage began to undulate, and all eyes turned in that direction. The music blared out even louder, the light bulbs sent out a dazzling blaze of light. The curtain was drawn aside and a heavily-built woman appeared. She walked barefoot over the floorboards that sagged under her weight, and up to the centre of the stage without looking at a soul. On the benches made from crates the men leaned forward, their dripping faces shining in the light. The music had reached a shattering crescendo, soaring up out of control. The air pressed down on the backs of people's necks, throwing bronze-coloured patches on to the floor of beaten earth. Layers of smoke wavered between the brick walls and swirled against the tin roof. The woman was motionless on the stage, and one could see the thick outlines of her body, her dress of flowered cotton, her pudgy arms, her flat-skulled head with its frizzy black hair. She did not move. The light from the three light bulbs illuminated her violently, reflecting back from her sweating brown skin. The music beat against her, too, great drumbeats on her head, frantic screeches hurling themselves at the red and green flowers of her dress. Her naked feet with splayed toes were set flatly, heavily on the floorboards. This scene lasted hours, there, underground, at the bottom of the coalmine, far from the sun and the free air, far from the sea, far from the bird-filled trees. It lasted months, like a motionless voyage in the bowels of the earth, like a dream where thought and desire have been obliterated. It remained fixed on the retina like the image of the young woman combing her long coal-black hair at the back of the roofless white cell. The men looked at the stout woman standing on the stage, they said nothing, and the sweat trickled down, making detours round their eyes. They looked at the cotton dress with its red and green flowers twisting round in spirals, they looked at the two naked feet on the floorboards, the pudgy arms dangling along the hips. They said nothing. No one said anything. The music said nothing: it shrieked its sounds so loudly that they were like heaps of bricks thudding on to the ground. The men went on looking, in the suffocating heat, and what they were looking for was perhaps simply air, great gulps of air to drink. In the sealed shed, everything had turned into desperate expectation, hatred of the time that refuses to come, hatred of the too-white light, criminal intent, perhaps, criminal intent against the stout, ugly woman who refused to move.

Then, all of a sudden, everything happened very quickly. Between two or three flashes from the light bulbs, between two or three palls of dingy smoke, the men sitting on the benches saw the stout woman lift her dress up over her head. The music grated, banged its drums, deafeningly. The stout woman bent forward, with her cotton dress around her head. She went down on all fours, on the floor. The light beat upon her hideous body. Now there is a huge Alsatian dog on the stage. It comes forward, barking, bounding over the boards that sag under its weight. It runs through the patch of sizzling light, and it cries:

'Haw! Haw! Haw!'

And the music shakes the shed to pieces while the dog hurls itself upon the kneeling woman and covers her with its rearing body. The obsessive image will remain fixed on the retina for a long time, while already the stout woman is getting up and pulling down her green and red flowered dress, and the same skinny little man comes to fetch the dog and lead it back toward the curtain beside the stage. The image of insanity and humiliation, the violence of the dazzling light, the loathsomeness of the moist flesh and the rapid beauty of the great dog with hard muscles. Now the stage is empty again. The men get up one after the other, try to shake off their torpor by pretending to laugh. But in their sunken eyes, on their foreheads dripping with sweat, there are ineluctable traces of something like a great unavowable fear.

All of a sudden the music has been cut off. Emptiness has entered the shed, has chased the crowd of spectators out by the door. Cigarettes are lit up, bottles of beer are tilted towards mouths. The night is very near, now. In the tavern's dark room one crosses the path of the crowd of men going to watch the next performance. Then one is again walking along the alleys, through the great hollow shantytown. Perhaps one has passed by the silent house where Min is in the throes of dying on her mat, coughing a lingering cough. Perhaps one has forgotten all one knew, and is empty, empty, empty. One has never been so far from the earth, and at the same time so utterly upon the earth. The fact is that there are not a thousand ways of being alive, there are not a thousand words to say one is alive.

There was nothing much more to do here. Young Man Hogan left this town as quickly as he could. The scene was Macao, or Manilla, or else Taipeh, during the year 1967. If my memory serves me.

SELF-CRITICISM

I wanted to write an adventure story, no, it's true, I really did. Well, too bad, I shall have failed, that's all. Adventures bore me. I have no idea how to talk about countries, how to make people wish they had been there. I am not a good travelling salesman. Countries? Where are they, whatever became of them?

When I was twelve I dreamed of Hongkong. That tedious, commonplace little provincial town! Shops sprouting from every nook and cranny! The Chinese junks pictured on the lids of chocolate boxes used to fascinate me. Junks: sort of chopped-off barges, where the housewives do all their cooking and washing on deck. They even have television. As for the Niagara Falls: water, nothing but water! A dam is more interesting; at least one can occasionally see a big crack at its base, and hope for some excitement.

When one travels, one sees nothing but hotels. Squalid rooms, with iron bedsteads, and a picture of some kind hanging on the wall from a rusty nail, a coloured print of London Bridge or the Eiffel Tower.

One also sees trains, lots of trains, and airports that look like restaurants, and restaurants that look like morgues. All the ports in the world are hemmed in by oil slicks and shabby customs buildings. In the streets of the towns, people keep to the sidewalks, cars stop at red lights. If only one occasionally arrived in a country where women are the colour of steel and men wear owls on their heads. But no, they are sensible, they all have black ties, partings to one side, brassières and stiletto heels. In all the restaurants, when one has finished eating one calls over the individual who has been prowling among the tables, and pays him with a promissory note. There are cigarettes everywhere! There are airplanes and automobiles everywhere!

I wanted to flee by going farther than myself. I wanted to visit countries where no one speaks, countries where it is the dogs that write novels, not men in horn-rimmed glasses. I wanted to get to know countries where the roads peter out voluntarily, where people are greater than thoughts, brand-new countries, lands of uncertainty where one could die without shame, without anyone noticing. I wanted places where fires blaze night and day for years on end, where the tide rises and never ebbs again, where the lakes empty out like enormous washbasins.

I wanted to write, too, to write in a single session some stirring tale, a woman's quest, for example, or the revolutionary struggle. That's what a real adventure story would have been, not this trembling, this additional agitation among so many, in the middle of the wobbling world.

I had worked out the plan, I had written it down with a pen on a sheet of paper:

The end of the world

POEM

Adventure story

Hogan is run out of town. He can no longer understand why people stay in the same place all their lives. What holds together all the inhabitants of a city?

Why is he fleeing? When did it all start off?

Crime? Shame? Love? Revolution?

The landscapes, constant change of landscape. Imaginary journey? If so, what difference? Or else: fixed route.

The obsession with INHABITING. (To be at home, to be comfortable ...) The dizziness of movement: dizziness of life. No stopping any longer. Like a speeding train, like ... To be out in the open. Dizziness of expansion. To fill a vacuum, to be bigger, to be everywhere. To live everywhere. To love everywhere. To be a part. Apart ...

The town has become unbearable. Hogan has to leave. Everything is hideous: buildings, bridges, highways and streets, stretches of old crumbling walls, roofs that have caved in, mean lights, mocking eyes, the indecent laughter of hyenas.

Got to flee, but where?
And how? In space, in time.
What boundary will set the limit?
The greatest, most ancient of all quests: of a habitat.
Find the place that will preserve one's peace of mind, keep one alive.
Walk quietly, calmly toward things.
Walk toward the most precise image of oneself.

In search of a landscape that should be a face. In search of the eyes, nose, mouth of a woman (LAURA); in search, yes, of a country that should be a body. America, Africa, Asia,

Australia, the Oceans: does all that exist? Can one even cross them? Farewell, territories, trees, faces. Leave. Yield to the secret summons that says: be off!

The person who obeys and goes, not to discover other places, not even to reach a better understanding of himself, but simply to flee from the one unendurable aspect of the vertical position: hatred of death.

Bare landscapes.
Cold earth under an empty sun.
Warmth, moistness, air pressure.
Delight of familiar retreats.
Smell of the seasons.
Sound of the sea.
Sound of crazed towns.
Roads, roads, all the roads.
Handwritings.
Ancient dream that one has not forgotten, that one cannot forget: crossing the horizon.
Dizziness of simple actions.
Nearing the far edge of the world.
Hatred of the loneliness of words. Words like iron nails, words that are habits.
Comprehension of the earth. The language of places, the itineraries.

Or: *the march toward the sun*

Everything begins (and ends)
in whiteness
the intense whiteness   The dialogue is established

of the light which strikes The world: a mishmash of language
the ground and the roofs   The small mouths
  with its silver-handled   of objects and of men
  whip   SITUATIONS
     ↓   ACTIONS

  Walk in the town in
  the cruel light   Disorganization of the
    ↙   ↘   novel
Leave somehow Seek out the   Breaking-off of the
               reasoning   narrative
or other   that keeps men   Postponement of the
               in check   rest of the epic poem.

A few places that resemble hell: LONDON,
    NEW YORK, NEW DELHI, NICE;
    BANGKOK, LIMA, MEXICO CITY

Hogan leaves the place where he is staying.
But flight for me too as the writer.
Flight from woman. Flight through eroticism.

→ Time → Place → Self-awareness →

Steady series of resignations.

Self-awareness: summons from self-awareness. Search.
Truth in ceaseless movement, in *distraction*. Unity condemns.
Plunged into disparity, in search of the *anonymous*.

                              ↓
                         Flight
                         escape
                         evasion
            The art of traps   runaway

189

                              fugitive
                              refugee
                              deserter
                              avoiding
                              shunning
                              dodging
                              running
                              route
                              wheel
                    the book of flights

          Mixture of chapters of fiction
          and poems. Free-ranging meditation
          (Reflections, notes, key words,
          signals, logbook)
          Beware of that yoke, system!

          Fascination of the modern world: *ugliness*. Fear.
          Violence. Beauty. Fleeing figure: from the
          singular to dozens of persons, then to the crowd,
          then to nothing.

          Or: scrap the idea of a plan.
          Write as it comes.
          Alternate.
          Let it run out of oneself.
          Poem! Tale! Thought! Dialogue!
          ETC.!

   That is more or less what I wanted to do. Now I can
gauge the distance separating me from my waking dream. I
see a desert, a misty plain, just where there should have
been a mountain peak, black against the silky sky. I must be

careful. I must stab the stupid butterflies to death with pins. I am not a cat, I do not want to purr. I refuse to surrender to mirages, I do not want to smile. Why do I never give the names of the places, or the people? What am I afraid of?

System, repulsive system is there, lying in wait for me. It wants to make me kneel down, or raise my fist. It wants to teach me to possess houses and cars and, of course, women. I want no part of it. I have nothing. So it wants to make me possess destitution. Watch out, there, for style, for words that sound well, for beautiful shock-imagery: it is nothing more than a collision between two motor-scooters! Watch out, there, for metaphysics, for symbols, for psychology! There are so many things to say, beautiful, stupid, interminable things! I would like to write for a thousand years. Watch out, there, for the gaze that begins to waver. If he relaxes, if he stops, for a split second even, everything will collapse. It is the world that will be looking at *him*.

I do not hate you. I simply want to understand you. I do not want to find truth. I simply want to tell you that you are not dead, yes, yes. If all that was needed to bring my flight to a halt was to go to Timbuctoo, I would go right away. If all that was needed to bring my flight, and yours, to a halt was to give you my passport photo, I would not only give it to you, I would have millions of copies of it scattered from airplanes.

Filthy, filthy writer, living off his feelings like a whore off her flesh.

I am saying all this out of spite!

Something is waiting.
Something is there, hidden behind the wallpaper, it
cannot be seen, no one knows what,
why, from where, but it is WAITING.
Something is there, quietly.
In silence, as though, everywhere, always,
an eternal night were approaching.
On the flat tabletop,
In the whiteness of the white paper that becomes smudged,
In the water, the sound of water,
the sound of the air,
something is waiting.
But nothing, of course.
Nothing, the old void, no doubt,
the void's moulting wing with its silent glide.
There is nothing behind the wallpaper.
It is myself, waiting.

The one who is fleeing does not know what he is fleeing
from. Once upon a time there had been this steel-fanged
monster behind him, making as if to devour him, but he has
forgotten that, too. Now he is running breathlessly, knees
knocking, belly knotted by fear. The one who is fleeing has
no time to smoke or laugh. He is sliding along the taut
rail, he is in motion, downward perhaps. The wind is
whistling in his ears like a whiplash, the wind is rushing

into his nostrils, pouring into his lungs. The wind of flight. When the moving wall of air passes over the cubes of the houses, it means that the entire town is now in flight. When imperceptible ripples begin to tremble on the surface of stagnant puddles, it means that the water has already gone.

Wars create strange suctions which sweep clean the shattered fields where columns of black smoke drift upward. Wars are blasts of air that scatter men's bodies recklessly. While the fireball, the red and yellow kernel of fierce heat, lights up the horizon, the wind begins to travel; slowly at first, then with ever-increasing speed and force, until not a single tree is left, not a roof, not an animal.

The wind has risen from the depths of my own self. It has gushed out of the black mouth that I carry at the back of my head. The icy, burning wind, the wind of red sand that lights up the walls of my room, the dry, rocky wind that blows and blows interminably. Here it comes now, along my throat's deep gully, perhaps. It is going to make a clean sweep. It is going to destroy the barriers that are set up inside me, here and there, like fringed whalebones. This wind that is stronger than myself will work its will with me. It will whirl round at enormous speed inside my head, that empty gourd rocking to and fro on its base of meat, and the axis of its invisible spinning-top will bore a well in the centre of my life.

The one who is fleeing is the wind, and does not know it. The one who is gliding on outstretched wings is the wind's bird, the crazed sparrowhawk of immobility at the centre of speed, stationary self-awareness driven mad with rage by the exhalation of mobile self-awareness.

To flee. To hurl one's body forward, so that it may smash doors down, so that it may shuck off its own weight.

How black is ink. The air is hard, so hard that a hammer

is needed in order to breathe. Particles of welded stone stir in the veins.

Those are my thoughts. Those are my thoughts in motion. They have dug themselves a deep pit somewhere, and I am left no choice but to fill it up.

There is never any silence.

Whiteness is black, and the vast throat is agape, ready for the beastly spasm of deglutition.

The chasm awaits; it has half opened its larynx, revealing a glimpse of its inflamed undulations. Flame that consumes, water that drowns, earth that asphyxiates by entering the mouth and nostrils.

Fear is a black star that rises in the night sky.

Knot of wool,

death's temptation, rupture,

door opening slowly on to solid air.

I quit.

I QUIT.

I abandon the familiar threshold, I make my way through the network of towns, I walk between the close-set poles of the forest of iron. I know, I know, I know perfectly well:
I SHALL NEVER ARRIVE!

Impossible to reach the mountain.

Impossible to touch the empty sky.

Impossible, ever to sample the sun's delights.

Impossible to live even a few inches outside one's own skin.

Mortal prison, bag, unnameable chain of my unknown name, yoke of my shoulders and mask of my face,

it is from you that I am fleeing,

and it is you whom I continually find at random among the millions of clouded mirrors that climb into the foliage of the trees.

What I lose, alas, I find.

At the end of the miles per second, at the end of the world, even on the opposite bank of the muddy Mekong, I am standing there like an idiot, and I AM WAITING FOR MYSELF!

ITINERARY

from Tokyo to Moscow
via Yokohama, Nakhodka, Khabarovsk, Irkutsk,
Cheliabinsk

Flight from reality, but also, always, flight from dreaming. No more imagining. No more delirious frenzy. Facts, now, names, places, figures. Maps. The sort of straightforward, lucid mentality that one possesses for only a short period of one's life, the cruel mentality that immediately precedes death. Precise writings, random jottings. Words with concrete meanings. All the words that are frightening, that one does not dare write down. The words for which people have invented symbols, mysteries, adjectives: desire, sex, hunger, thirst, evil, pleasure, fear, sickness, poverty, freezing cold, love, murder, beauty, air, sea, sun. Those words which shine, those words which sparkle in silence, which are cold, and burning hot, as distant as stars, and impossible not to see. The only true words. The only certainties. Those hard words launched into the future, pointed rockets rushing through space. To attain those words it is necessary to flee the other world. It is necessary to flee the grey spiral that wreathes upward inside the body, and makes the head with its dead eyes nod on its shoulders. It is necessary to flee sleep. To be alert all the time, ready to fight, muscles tense, mind crystal clear. For how long shall

I manage to keep fleeing? How much time left to remain wild, savage? Rally to me, my harpoon-words, no pity, death to the slothful, glutinous whale. Rally to me, my revolver-words. I grasp you in my hands and riddle everything that approaches. Words of steel, words of glass, words of black bakelite. Language which goes straight to the centre of the storms of circles.

TRAVEL CONDITIONS

The People's Republic of China is easily accessible, by air or by rail from Moscow, Pyongyang, Ulan Bator or Hanoi to Peking. Services by Pakistan International Airlines with direct flights from Karachi and Dacca to Shanghai and Canton. Garuda International Airways, services between Canton, Phnom Penh and Djakarta. Train services between Hongkong and inland China.

Entry by road (private car or motorcycle) not possible at the present time.

TARIFF OF RAIL FARES (Single) — in Yuan

International services

	Sleeper, de luxe	Couchette	Couchette, hard
Peking–Moscow			
via Manchuli	144.50	128.20	90.90
via Erlien	149.50	133.00	94.30
Peking–Hanoi		55.50	38.00
Peking–Ulan Bator	51.00	45.20	32.10

Peking–Pyongyang	37.60	26.70

Internal services

	Seats or couchettes
Shumchun–Canton	3.50
Canton–Shanghai	91.50
Canton–Wuhan	67.40
Canton–Peking	116.90
Canton–Hangchow	85.10
Shanghai–Hangchow	6.50
Shanghai–Nanking	11.50
Peking–Wuhan	71.80
Peking–Shanghai	83.20
Peking–Tientsin	5.30
Peking–Nanking	69.60

Hotels

Peking	Hsinchiao Hotel, Chienmen Hotel, Hôtel de la Paix
Tientsin	Grand Hôtel de Tientsin
Shanghai	Hôtel de la Paix, Overseas Chinese Hotel
Canton	Aichun Hotel, Yang Chen Hotel
Wuhan	Shuankong Hotel, Shengli Hotel, Kianghan Hotel
Hangchow	Hangchow Hotel
Suchow	Suchow Hotel
Wusih	Lake Tai Hotel
Nanchang	Kiangsi Hotel
Chengchow	Chengchow Hotel
Loyang	Yuyi Hotel

At Lok Ma Chaw, the road runs through swampland, the sky is grey, the hills are motionless. Little bands of ducks are swimming in the pools along the paddy fields. The earth is full of little wrinkles, the trees are very tall, very black. In the steel coaches, peasants wedged together on wooden seats stare straight ahead of them as they smoke. Women with domed foreheads gossip together as they stand in front of the fields, distant, scarcely discernable.

After this, there is yet another town of steel and glass, on the other side of the Ocean. A town vaster than a lake, stretching out, unfurling its roads, counting out its blocks, its towers, its millions of inhabitants. The avenues, there, are eternal, the cars drive along them eternally. Bridges straddle the highways, but nothing has changed. At the airport, the paths of individual ants wind ahead. Each ant's brow juts out ahead of it, and within each brow is the humming of secret, invincible orders from outer space: Drive! Walk! Crush! Multiply! Be there! These words cannot be heard, but they are present everywhere. Up the escalators move lines of human beings, cans of living preserves. Three workmen in white overalls are cleaning the marble floor, frantically, calmly. They, too, have received their orders, and they never stop. The soft fringes of their mops absorb the dust, fold and unfold, glide over the white marble. I am there, then I am no longer there. What would be the point of staying? I no longer have enough words to express all the purity, the rapidity, the extraordinary reality contained within these human citadels. I mean: glass, glitter, neon, red plastics, white plastics, signals, electric voices, movements on almost silent tyres!

Glorious machines
Steel bodies, ball bearings, cogwheels,

Thumping pistons
Oil, oil everywhere!
Man is an infinitesimal sound.
Doing is nothing
What counts is being there.
Enough
Enough shouting
Enough display of feelings enough confessions
It's indecent.
From now on, no more talk of tears, ever again.
Machines are beautiful and clean-cut,
They have no griefs.
They lead lives that are as calm as trees
Lives of rock and water.
They never crumble away.
Man waiting around with
      his religions
      his desires
      his novels
      his poems
      his operatic airs
      his cigarettes
Pathetic braggart conceited ass
Man who has never possessed the jaguar's intelligence
or even the monkey's sharp teeth
has absent-mindedly created machines of silvery metal
that make great meticulous gestures
Gods alive at last, erect upon their plinths,
Who must be worshipped, do you hear, who must be
worshipped!

In the underground galleries of the University, men are
fighting. They are wearing long tunics and leather plastrons.

Their heads are covered by iron masks with slits for the eyes. They are squatting on the ground, in this great hall with its clammy walls. Then, two of them get up, and approach each other on the tips of their toes. They raise their right arms high in the air, and at the end of each arm is a fake sword with a wooden slat for a blade. When they are face to face, they halt, their swords still poised above their heads. Then suddenly they bring their arms down and strike, letting out a savage yell. The swords smack against head and shoulders, graze hands, withdraw, return to the attack. The cries of wild beasts echo through the underground room. Then the fight ends as abruptly as it had begun. The two men withdraw, unbuckle their plastrons and take off their masks. They go over and squat against the wall. Two others get up, tighten their belts, buckle on their leather protective pads, and walk towards each other on tiptoe, gliding forward on their naked feet. They brandish their swords. When it is all over, the men put on their grey suits and their ties once more, and disperse through the streets of the town. Their faces are as hard as fists.

Three young men are walking down the sloping street, in the sunshine. They stride straight through the crowd, and people draw aside hastily. They are wearing short, wide-sleeved white robes that are secured at the waist by a kind of black belt. Their smooth faces are brutal masks. Only their eyes move, under their bushy black eyebrows.

At the top of a flight of stairs there is a long hall. When night falls, it shines with hundreds of parallel neon rods. In this vast corridor, men and women are standing in front of machines that are attached to the walls. They are staring through the glass fronts at the little steel balls that are bouncing through a maze of nails, dancing downward along a path that is never the same. The spring-levers are released with a snap, and the little steel balls trickle endlessly down in hundreds of machines. Rapidly, without losing a moment, the little balls jump, fall back, collide, vanish, and the faces of the men and women have an odd sort of fixed expression that is serious, or mournful, or crazed, as they stare with eyes shaped like steel balls at the machines which are twitching with nervous tics.

Surrounded by the pitch-black night, a great tower rises in the centre of the town. At the tower's summit there is a revolving wheel. But it is a wheel with windows, for thousands of people are seated inside it, drinking, and watching the town circle round them.

Flight is precise. It never makes a mistake. What it rejects, it rejects for good. But what it takes, it keeps in the region of its heart, transforming it into blood and lymph, feeding on it.

One passes above things, in a precise dream. One makes a count of doors, all the doors that one will never open. The houses with paper walls stand motionless beside their gardens. The thick green tea froths to a boil in little pots. Then it passes from lip to lip, and that too is a kind of flight. The wooden sanctuaries stand rigid at the edge of their ponds, their floorboards biting cold to naked feet. Since far back in the centuries, those in flight have made their way there, astride speedy steeds, or else cleaving the waves in a stone boat. The gestures continue, the old needless gestures, the dull blows on the gongs, the kites, the grinning masks, the ritual wrestling matches, the snake-dances, the bowing and backing. Might not the world in fact be empty, might the world not be hollow, a vast mountain undermined by endless galleries? People swarm by their millions into the great concrete buildings. The cohorts march through the labyrinths of the banking houses, in the snow-white light.

In the streets the vehicles plough through the rain, and no one knows where they are going. Was there not a war, one day? Will there not come another day, like that one, when the lightning will strike the anthill, will bore its volcano into the mud and into the flesh, will mow down the shadows against the brick walls? Pitiless hardness and dryness waiting everywhere! Wriggling of insects, voracious mandibles that will strip the great animal's carcass down to the bone! Am I really here, is it really myself crossing this desert full of rooms? I am here, then elsewhere, then there again. I must try to remember: I have thrown pebbles. I have established my landmarks, I have made my notches in tree trunks. I have taken snapshots: a woman's face, a little red car wheeling along the expressway, a temple whose beauty makes it seem unreal, a restaurant where the customer chooses his fish live from a tank, a massive stone gateway from which there hangs, motionless, a paper lantern as big as a Montgolfier balloon. I have recorded on tape: sonorous words that rise and fall, that say Ga akarí no mawarí wo tónde irú. Kakitáku nái nára. Sakaná to góhan wo tabémashĭta. Taihén arigáto gozaimásŭ. Dō itashimáshite.

Groups of men wearing tight-fitting black vinyl jackets and trousers, riding high-powered motorcycles, are streaking down the broad highway that stretches as far as the eye can see. It is just a little gang of adventurers.

On its single rail going in a straight line to the horizon, the train called Streak of Lightning demolishes the air's barrier. At 170 miles an hour it glides above the blocks of houses, above the highways' broad rivers. It speeds effortlessly on, forsaking all the millions of humanity, and its white and red snout butts against the wind's taut sheets. There may be someone called Hogan in the car, sitting in one of the plastic-covered club chairs, someone looking through the big window and seeing a sort of volcano loom up through the clouds and pass by. That, too, is the direction that has to be taken, one movement more, so as to be always farther away, more unknown. At the end of the rail there will be a different station, and other streets. A woman's face, perhaps, with long black hair like seaweed, a bulging forehead, narrow eyes, lips firmly closed; she will be waiting, silently, and it will seem as though she had been there for centuries, standing there on the station's cold platform. There will be gardens, too, ornamental lakes covered with a layer of ice, towers of brown wood, houses that all look alike. Flight is not ruled by the clock, it never sleeps. When night comes, it continues through the dream, and when the sun rises one is still farther away, just a little bit farther away.

Masked race! I am not one of you. Intelligent faces! My features are more those of an animal, heavy and low-slung, with round eyes. Nara, Tokyo, Mishima, islands that float abandoned. Wooden theatres, fairs where blind soldiers beg, revulsive music, violence, intelligence of the sculptured gardens in which the trees are alternately large and small, to break the monotony. All that, tossing on the ocean, praying, crying out, lifting its poles towards the grey sky. Might not the earth be empty, by chance? Might not the airplanes be flying for no reason at all, might not the trains be torpedos, simply torpedos, is it not possible that the expressways and subway systems are carrying their clusters of anonymity round and round in an eternal circle? I have neither words nor signs to express what I know. What is to be is already here, it descended upon the world in this very spot. It has drawn its plan. I am ready, perfectly ready.

It is true that all roads lead to the stone garden. And yet that is, fatally, the garden of madness, not of wisdom. Its microcosms and schemata do not liberate human thought:

they spin it round until it sinks in giddy exhaustion, they drive it crazy with the blatant presence of their boundary walls. The thirteen rocks are floating among the evenly-patterned ripples of the ocean of sand. Shut up in the cage whose walls are mirrors, self-awareness does not cease to roam space; but what it encounters out there is precisely this shutting up, this human will, this language. It is impossible for self-awareness to get out of its cage, to escape into the boundless plains, despite its yearning to be free. Organization is not soothing, it is, on the contrary, a war against the rival organization, that of chaos, swarming, hatred. The moon is the symbol of hell, because it shows us just what the world is, in relation to the universe. The stars are deep pits of vengeance, being signals of impotence. I no longer want to see the earth. I no longer want to learn the pattern of history. I no longer want to find myself looking into my own eyes, I no longer want to acknowledge the existence of the old sphere of thought crammed with its prisoners. I no longer even want to imagine any longer this tiny desert suspended between its four walls; if I did think about it, it would be in the manner of a snail or a beetle. I want to crawl, to run over the featureless ground, to bump up against obstacles, to bleed over sharp pebbles, to disappear into deep valleys, to scale incomprehensible peaks. I refuse to be shown, ever again, this silence, this frozen light, this adventure cut off in mid-flight. Damnable garden of self-awareness! How could I possibly still face it, when I am incapable of looking at an apple, or a table, without immediately seeing the void's steep cliff? Garden that I know too well, I love it, and its gentleness and goodness enter me through my host of wounds. No, no, journeys do not end there. Impossible. Journeys go farther, still farther. They are swallowed up in the mist, and vanish, and there are more women's faces than there are grains of sand! I hate the absolute. I hate meditation I hate the monks of self-awareness. I hate all truths conquered from hell. I hate wisdom. Listen, I'll tell you what I'd really like: to be at the controls of a powerful bike, burning up the roads at 140 miles an hour.

Life of a tree
(1914 — 1966)

1914 The tree (umbrella pine) is born.

1919 The tree grows rapidly. Abundance of rain and sun during the spring and summer. The tree's rings are wide and regular.

1924 When it is ten years old, something has given the tree a jolt and made it lean (landslip? fall of a neighbouring tree?). The rings are now wider on the lower side, resulting from a *reaction by the wood* to help the tree support the extra weight.

1934 The tree grows straight upward, once more; but its neighbours are also growing, and their foliage and roots deprive the tree of part of its sun and water. The rings are narrower.

1937 The surrounding trees are pruned. The largest ones are cut down altogether, and there is once again plenty of food and sunshine. The tree grows rapidly.

1940 A fire sweeps the forest. Luckily, the tree is only lightly scorched. Each year, a new layer covers the burn scar.

1957 A new series of narrow rings, due perhaps

to an insect such as the larva of the sawfly, which feed on the leaves and buds of many conifers.

1966   Death of the tree, at the age of 52, cut down by an electric saw.

Enough of this 'I'! The person I want to talk about is *him*, is myself after becoming his friend. He is there. He has fled. He has moved forward against a background of crimes, hostile looks, wars. He has lived in all those places that people hurry through, in airport concourses, dance halls, hotels, ships, rafts, plastic-and-chrome bars. He has visited every derelict site. He has lugged bags and suitcases. He has burned up a lot of cigarette paper. He has drunk every kind of water, beer, rice wine. Why has he done all that? What was the point?

There wasn't any. No point at all.

The white-painted ship steams out of Yokohama. BAIKAL is written, in Cyrillic characters, along the bows, a word that floats upon the sea, that glides from one land mass to another. Why does it carry this name? There are all these names that are making weighty crossings, over a surface that is sometimes grey, sometimes blue, stirred by waves. ORSOVA, LILY OF LAGUNA, KISTNA, VIETNAM, EL NAVIGANTE, PROVIDENCE, CATAMARAN. The stems are tall, cleaving the waves, slicing through the drift ice. There is never enough sea for the ships' sharp faces. Mountains of water come from the end of the horizon, shrouded in mist, and are shattered against the stems. Sometimes the prow is extended by the figure of a woman carved out of wood and staring straight ahead. This means that there is a struggle going on and that its issue is in doubt. The hulls of rusting metal, covered with seaweed and parasites, follow the path beaten by the stems, plunge into the rows of troughs, rise to the top of the rows of slopes. The water is pure and full of bubbles. It squeezes the iron walls tightly, relaxes its grip, explodes, slides along with a creaking noise. It wants to enter, devour and digest, with its great open gullet. The wind is blowing sixty miles an hour, ripping the mist apart. And as for him, he is in the watertight box, the wooden deck is carrying him above the surface of the sea. Isn't that incredible? Isn't that an adventure, a true adventure involving a machine and a yawning chasm?

The sea stretches on and on. For days now, it has been breaking against the stem. Leaning over the railings at the stern, he can see the eddies spurting from the propeller, the black holes, the oil slicks, the dirty foam, the choppy wash. The horizon is curved, the universe is nothing more, now, than an immense drop of swollen water under the sky. In the airless cabins, women are sleeping, wrapped up in blankets. Inside the swaying saloons, men are talking, drinking, playing chess. Three men are seated near a porthole, smoking cigars.

'No, not communism, but ... '

'Comfort is not absolutely necessary, you know.'

'Our government wants to tackle the urgent tasks first, but after that, sure, we'll start thinking about cars, and individual luxuries.'

'Perhaps it would be a mistake ... '

'Why?'

'Well, because, I mean. You really don't appreciate just what the idea of revolution represents. I mean, yours is an absolute miracle for us, so now, if your country started behaving like all the others, you know, like, the educated minority working for the sake of a small house, a small car, a small holiday ... '

'You're looking at it from an intellectual point of view.'

'Yes, sure, but isn't that unavoidable? It's the idea of possessing things that has to be eliminated, first of all. The really extraordinary thing about any revolution is its capacity to make people want to live for something more than just earning money, to make them conceive of life in terms that go beyond the old mathematics of earning and spending.'

'But perhaps at the expense of freedom?'

'It's always the same. The freedom the West boasts about is based essentially on private property: smallholdings, at that. To have a small car, to have a small idea: it amounts to the same thing.'

'Would you say that about art, too?'

'Sure. You may not be aware of it, but what you are living through is perhaps the only true adventure, the only modern adventure. Freedom. But always for a minority. In the West, people imagine they are free because they can construct statues from melted ballpoint pens, or write novels full of incestuous relationships. But how can one be free so long as there are people dying of hunger at the gates of palaces, so long as there are people who are factory slaves, peeling chestnuts twelve hours a day for the price of a glass of beer, people who are ignorant, and sick, people who make war? To balance things, it's true that I have the right to shout long live the king or down with the reds, but what difference does it make?'

'You know, there are still a lot of mistakes being made in my country ... '

'Yes, perhaps, but it's still an adventure.'

'If only one could eliminate the whole concept of politics ... '

'The concept of possessing things ... '

Etc.

There would be many similar conversations going on in this iron coffin floating on the sea.

Then, the storm would rise. It would begin slowly, with the squeak of a violin and a few strokes on a gong. The high-pitched voice of a woman or a child would begin singing in the foreward saloon. That's exactly how it happens: the wind lifts up the heavy masses of the waves and crushes them against the ship's prow. The waves obliterate words as they are spoken, thrust ideas back into the darkness. The ground swoops upward and something faints away inside the body. The strident music rises, falls, and the drums groan. The metal walls crack, glasses roll around on the tables, and break. The sea is a herd of elephants trampling across the plain. By this time one has lost one's balance. One has been rolled along, ground to dust, pushed, struck, stamped on. One has had no more time to speak, or hope. One has thrown oneself on one's hard couch which does its best to rid itself of its burden. One has staggered along gangways that have gone insane, one has grabbed hold of everything that protruded and was made of iron. Violence has launched its wind in an assault on the ship, its wind that tears everything apart. The billows have scooped out their funnels of fury, have raised their walls high. The propellor thrashes in space, shuddering violently. There is so much anger here that ten million wars would be needed to expend it all. So much despair, so much beauty, and one simply floats upon them. Sea! Sea! Genius in action. Himalaya of water! ... Everything is sea: sky, water, wind, as well as the kind of can which contains human beings instead of luncheon meat. Everything has been transformed into long, dark whirlpools, into hard dunes that advance, roaring and sighing. The shrill music plays for hours, days, nights on end. It does not want earth, it never wants any kind of dry land.

What the music yearns for is this liquid vastness, this relent-
less animal that stretches out of sight in all directions, that
darts its countless tentacles, attempting to digest everything
within reach. Sea, tank of boiling blood, sea that covers
everything! The earth's true skin, its true face. Hammered,
tormented, with great shivering wrinkles, with countless
mouths and eyes. It is no longer a question of self-awareness
but of rage, sheer rage! Their snouts emerging from the very
depths of time, the cliffs of water slide forward on their
bases, stiff, invincible, with a thunderous din; and vanish
toward time's other end, out there where the sky is always
black. They rear up higher than the bridge and, as they
sweep by, strike the locked portholes with terrible blows.
The sea is the earth afraid. It is space that has melted, a
nasty diarrhoea. It is the coldness of empty space that has
filled the chasms to the brim with its bubbling liquid. He
who has seen that will never know peace again. He knows
where his flight must end, and that of all other men, and that
of the trees and birds. He knows only too well where time
ends up, and who swallows it.

A few moments later, at about three in the afternoon, he
would go up on to the bridge, and he would see in the offing,
over to the right, a broad, open bay. The smooth sea is
the colour of turquoise, and naked mountains are reflected
in it, conical mountains thrusting up out of the transparent
water, pointing straight at the blue sky. An icy wind is
blowing out of the north, the air is as sharp as a diamond.
The sun is sparkling in the west, but gives off no warmth.
This is the end of the world, as they say, one of the possible
destinations of the journey. Nakhodka Bay lies open to the
blue sea, with islands in the form of volcanoes, and hook-
shaped promontories covered with reddish soil. One swims
in a landscape drawn by a pen with fine strokes, a landscape

of vast silence. The ship's hull glides over the water, enters the calm zone; in the offing, the islands' cones slowly shift position. Everything is congealed in the cold, in the frigid light. The air is so pure that one can make out the smallest details along the coast, the striations of the rocks, the caves in which waves are boiling, the fishermen's homes, the boats moored by ropes. There is no smoke. The headlands advance, very black, across the open water. The mountains are blocks of sulphur, spines of sharp metal, the strange edge of a razor blade that has sliced through life. Thirty miles beyond the peninsula lies a taciturn city called Vladivostock. That is the place where everyone should really end up, sooner or later. People have so often posed the question to all the other people they have met on boats, in trains, in hotel lobbies:

'Have you ever been to Vladivostock?'

The deserted coast looms larger. It pricks up its sharp peaks. The islands drift along in water so blue as to be almost colourless. The mountains' crevasses appear, the landslides, the paths of trodden earth. The sun can rise and set a thousand times. Death can come, death with its silent pattern. There will always be this pageant of steel thread, these pure, clear lines, this wordless transparency, this truth transmuted into landscape.

After this, the train wheezes its way up as far as a brick-clad town called Khabarovsk. As far as a town called Irkutsk where there is a kind of lake. The giant airplane full of military personnel and their womenfolk flies for hours above regions of frost and ice. Nameless rivers flow along, their surfaces streaked with tiny needles of hoarfrost. But what possible difference can that make?

SELF-CRITICISM

I must make up my mind to adopt the following principles,
at long last:

   (a) Say everything I think
   (b) Stop using words that are merely agreeable
   (c) Do not try to do everything at the same time*
   (d) Stop being scared of names
   (e) Change the brand of ballpoint pen I use

* Unless it is a question, on the contrary, of saying everything simultaneously. In that case, may not literature (and, in particular, fiction) be
considered a desperate and permanently thwarted effort to produce a
unique form of expression? Something like a cry, perhaps, a cry that,
somehow, inexplicably contains all the millions of words that have ever
existed, anywhere, in any age. In contrast with the spoken word and its
classifying function, the purpose of writing seems, rather, to be a quest
for the egg, the seed, nothing more.

A little later on, Y. M. Hogan was in a town called New York. It was night-time. He was walking at a brisk pace down a very straight street full of traffic. The automobiles were long and wide. They sped along with headlamps blazing, and one could see them coming from far away, at the end of the horizon. They moved softly, their bodies skimming the road surface, their splayed tyres gripping the asphalt with a sucking noise. They sped past one, almost brushing against the sidewalk, twinkling and gleaming; through the smoked glass of the windows a seated silhouette could just be glimpsed.

Occasionally they came to a halt at a street crossing, and their hot engines throbbed slowly in the cold air. When the correct signal appeared in the air, a few horns were sounded and the vehicles shot off again into the distance. It was odd, walking around New York, as Y. M. Hogan was doing, watching it all happening. It was strange and yet familiar, a spectacle one had known and then forgotten, a dream, a flight in reverse. Perhaps one had always been there, in this town, perhaps one had been born there, had grown up there. Difficult to tell. So many things had happened since then.

Y. M. Hogan was surrounded, on the sidewalk, by a whole crowd of people walking in all directions. Men wearing raincoats, women swaying along on high heels. They sprang up from all sides, from the mouths of subway entrances, from out of movie houses, from doorways of apartment buildings, from the front doors of cars. They arrived, crossing the patches of darkness, surging up in the squares of red light; it was rather like a nervous, monotonous ballet, everyone stepping out with right foot and left hand forward. The walls were high, so high, sometimes, that their tops disappeared from view. Thousands of little windows were dotted about the walls, some lit, others dark. Iron stairways descended as far as the second floor and stayed there, uncompleted.

Y. M. Hogan studied the faces of the passers-by, the windows, and, from time to time, the cars' great shining headlamps.

Perhaps he really had been a child here, once upon a time. He had been born in a house in East 42nd Street, and his name had not been Young Man Hogan, then, but Daniel E. Langlois, Daniel Earl Langlois.

Daniel Earl Langlois was eleven and a half. One day, during the winter, he and his friend Tower went out of school together. They walked quite a long way down Fifth Avenue, watching the parade of black cars go by. Night was beginning to fall, and in the east the sky was already black. Everything glittered, the shop windows, the billboards, the red and white stripes of the neon signs. Daniel Earl Langlois and his friend Tower stopped for a moment at the entrance to a movie house, to look at the photos. It was a thriller, *55 Days at Peking*, or *A Fistful of Dollars*, or something like that. Then, since it was beginning to rain, they went into a café which sold sodas and ice-creams. Daniel Earl Langlois ordered a coke, and his friend Tower ordered an ice-cream soda which arrived in a tall glass. They took their drinks over to a table moulded from plastic, near the window, and sat there sipping them through straws and watching the street outside. When they had finished, Daniel Earl Langlois lit a cigarette. The waitress, a pretty redhead dressed in white, came over and stared down at them.

'Playing at being grown-up, eh?' she said, laughing derisively.

'OK, OK,' muttered Daniel Earl Langlois. He dropped the cigarette on the floor and crushed it under his foot. Then, feeling annoyed, he demanded the bill, paid it and left.

Some time later, Langlois and his friend Tower stopped at a canal that was flowing under a bridge. They leaned over the parapet and watched the water flowing along its concrete channel. It was quite dark by now. The cars that passed by all had their lights on, the streetlamps were glowing in the centre of drizzling haloes. It was getting cold. Daniel Earl Langlois offered a cigarette to his friend Tower, and they both smoked, and watched the canal flow under the bridge.

It was at that particular moment that Daniel Earl Langlois decided that the world was going to be ruled by twelve-year-olds. He explained to his friend Tower how they would put this plan into operation. They would visit all the Junior High Schools. They would organize mass meetings, and talk to all the kids. They would form an army, and there would be strikes, too, and demonstrations. And since there were more of them than there were grown-ups, they would easily win. Then they could condemn some of the grown-ups to death: their teachers, for example, and most cops. And they would pack the others off to jail. Then they would have elections, and instal a president. That might turn out to be him, of course, or his friend Tower, or perhaps Jimmy who was a whizz at maths. Or else Bernstein who was really good-looking, and made out all right with girls. Or Hal who knew how to drive. Easy as pie: just a question of getting started.

Tower agreed that it would be as easy as pie. Except, how about the army?

Daniel Earl Langlois flicked his cigarette butt into the canal, and remarked that the army was no problem. Everyone knew that grown-ups were no good at fighting. They were too heavy, for one thing, and couldn't run fast enough.

'But they've got the hydrogen bomb, haven't they,' said Tower.

Daniel Earl Langlois gave him a pitying glance.

'If they drop it on us, they automatically drop it on themselves as well, don't they! Ever think of that?'

Tower had to admit the truth of this argument.

'You see how easy it is,' said Langlois. 'And it's the same with the cops. They don't even begin to know how to run. You remember when Clayton forced open the vending machine outside that supermarket and stole all those cigarettes? He ran as far as the parking lot and wriggled under the cars. And those cops searched everywhere without finding him. They are too fat, you see. No idea how to run.'

'Yeah, but they have dogs,' said Tower.

'Ah, to heck with your dogs,' said Langlois. 'Any kid can drop a dog with the first shot of his catapult at twenty yards, can't he?'

Tower agreed that he was capable of doing that himself.

'Listen, Tower,' said Langlois, '*we* know what we're up to, and we know darn well who we can count on, but grown-ups just aren't wised up: they'll never expect this sort of thing. They're so sure that they can go on making us do everything they want, without us even answering back or anything. And then we live with them, so they won't be suspicious.'

He turned suddenly to face his friend Tower.

'You got the nerve to kill anyone?'

Tower made an effort to concentrate.

'Yeah, I guess so,' he said.

'You ever felt like killing someone?'

'Yeah.'

'Who?'

'Well, the history teacher, to start with. That day he called me a liar. And my father, too, when he punched me in the face. Just because I was late. How about you?'

'Me too. But, with me, it was a guy who lived next door to us. He killed my dog because it used to bark during the night. Once our war has got started, I'm going to pay a call on him and kill him.'

'And I've got another on my list. This guy who's always chasing my sister. Once, he forced her to kiss him. In the park. I saw it. He's a real creep. I told him, I told him I'd kill him. He just laughed. But it's true. I will kill him.'

Daniel Earl Langlois stared gloomily into the canal.

'You know, the important thing is that we should all agree on things. All the kids, including the girls. If we all get together, we'll be OK. We could really get going. You know what we'll do? We'll start by organizing a group. A real one. At school. We'll need to find a good name for it, something terrible to scare the grown-ups. The Black Panthers, for example.'

'Or the Vampires.'

'Or the Tentacles, perhaps.'

'The Red Wolves.'

'The Cobras.'

'Hey, how about the Scorpions?'

'The Sharks.'

'The Phantom Riders.'

'Hold on. There was this movie I saw last year, I think it all took place in India. Anyhow, there was this gang in it that stabbed folks to death while they were asleep. Right through their hammocks. They were called the Tongs.'

Daniel Earl Langlois looked at his friend Tower with shining eyes.

'That's it. Beginning tomorrow, we'll be the Terrible Tongs.'

And to seal the pact, he took a small knife out of his pocket and made a T-shaped cut in the palm of his friend's hand, and then in his own. Then they went away, walking back in the direction of Eighth Avenue.

Y. M. Hogan always felt slightly apprehensive, each time children passed by. He searched their eyes for signs of impending revolution, and tried to see whether maybe their closed fists concealed a scar in the shape of a T.

Some time around the middle of the night, Y. M. Hogan found himself in a slum area. The streets were full of potholes, and the houses leaned against each other as though in the aftermath of an earthquake. The windows had panes missing, the doors were covered with graffiti. Going down a very long street, with the wind blowing in his face, Y. M. Hogan found himself among men with black faces, among women who were drunk. These people had some things in common: their eyes smouldered in sunken sockets, and their hair was thick, slicked down, frizzy, brushed back, sometimes glistening with oil. Silhouettes fled quickly in the streetlamps' humid glow, feet echoed on the sidewalk. Here and there, clouds of steam seeped up from the middle of the black asphalt, and the cars slid through them. It was similar to a photo, shadowy patches and white blurs brought brutally into being, pinned to the ground. No sky was visible. It was also like a photo because of the silence.

Nothing expressed nothing. Movements that were the continuations of syncopated gesticulations passed each other slowly by. The buildings fled vertically, hurling their concrete ramps into the air. The street's sharp angles cut both the wind and the light. Hogan proceeded in silence from one street to another, crossing wide-open spaces by keeping close to the walls, then suddenly vanishing in the broad shadows. Where had he gone? He was no longer to be seen. Did he turn right, out of this street? Or did he venture into this concrete wasteland? Or enter one of the tall buildings through a black door? No, here he is again, walking past a streetlamp that haloes him with a blur of light. His shadow shrivels beneath his feet, moves ahead of him, divides up. What is he doing? He is waiting at the curb, while a car with raised fins speeds past. He crosses the street. He stumbles over a pothole. He mounts the opposite curb. Why did he cross over? The wall contains a lighted window. He passes in front of it, and becomes lighted, too. A man in an overcoat walks toward him. He walks toward the man. The man veers slightly to the left, while he simultaneously veers slightly to the right. They give each other a quick glance. What is the man in the overcoat thinking? What is Hogan thinking? They manoeuvre safely past each other, the man in the overcoat to the left, Hogan to the right. For a split second there is only a single silhouette to be seen, but it immediately separates, and the two parts draw away from each other. Who is the man in the overcoat? Who is Hogan? By now, he has moved so far up the black and white street that it is impossible to make out his features. A silhouette, merely an anonymous silhouette like all the others, strolling along the sidewalk. A group of men is coming toward him, and another group is overtaking him from the rear. Suddenly there is a knot of people on the sidewalk, a dozen blended silhouettes with arms, legs, heads. The knot surges to and fro. Then becomes untangled. Where is he? Where is Hogan? Is he the one over there who is walking quickly away from the spot? Or that second one? Or that third one? Is he the one who is crossing the street at an angle? Or is he perhaps the one who is retracing his steps, walking on the roadway so that he can get away faster? What does it matter? Let us assume that Hogan is *this* one here. He turns back and starts striding over the sidewalk's stone slabs. Then he stops. He lights a cigarette. He throws the match in the gutter. Wait a minute, though, Hogan had a lighter; yes, but maybe he has lost it, or sold it, or maybe he has bequeathed it to a woman called Ricky? He passes the lighted window again. Another silhouette walks towards him and joins him, and then, in a flash from the window, he is off again, retreating to the far end of the street. He is on the point of disappearing. He glides over the smooth sidewalk, he is no bigger than a dot. Then he walks back again, crosses over between two stationary vehicles, passes a group of people. He is part of the group, which is now walking back up the street, talking very loudly. Occasionally he comes to a halt, turns towards the others, waves his arms around and shouts. It is not very easy to hear what he is shouting, but it is something like: 'No! I tell you! No!'

A couple is walking down the street, holding hands. When he emerges from the other side of the group of men milling around on the sidewalk, it is Hogan who is holding the girl's hand. He is tending to pull her along, either because she is tired or because she cannot walk as fast as he can. They are swallowed up by a big patch of shadow and grow invisible. All that can be heard is the clicking of the girl's high heels on the ground. Then nothing more. Has he vanished for ever? No, no, something is emerging from the shadow and walking back up the street. The silhouette of a woman, moving rapidly and silently along the sidewalk. You don't mean to say that Hogan has turned into a woman? Why, yes, that's him all right, you can recognize him by the fact that he has two legs, two arms, and an indecipherable face. Man, woman, what difference does it make? Are they not all exactly the same, these little black insects with their rhythmic movements, the same eyes, the same thoughts? Hey presto! Man again, walking back down the street, quickly. Hey presto! Man crossing over, stopping to let a car go by. Hey presto! Man looking in the shop windows as he strolls along. Hey presto! Woman walking back, swinging her handbag. An interminable process that might very well go on for hours, days, years, longer even than that. Hogan came and went ceaselessly along that cold, motionless road resembling a photo, as he zigzagged, disappeared, reappeared again. Black, then white, then mottled, then woman, then man, then a woman. Mute insects with imponderable desires, praying mantises with wary gestures.

It was the place for exhilarating music, for sequences of identical sounds, with long monotonous slurs. It was the place for a song that repeats itself, and lulls people to sleep; for the strangled voice of the saxophone continually inventing the same phrase, losing it, picking it up again. The patches of shadow are the tremblings of the string-bass as it hesitates and gropes. Each repeated beat of the drums is a street, a street. The designs of the houses, the windows, the haloes round the streetlamps all ceaselessly trace the same thing, a voluble line that moves silently forward, mind and imagination soaring upward, inventing life where really nothing existed previously. And the adventures of the silhouettes, there, against the town's pattern! Adventures which one can no longer understand very well, useless adventures. Cubes of tall, elegant buildings, cubes of music! Town crisscrossed by dark canyons, town of music! Automobiles with dazzling headlamps, pounding, gliding, speeding towards the unknown. Jazz automobiles! Graceful bridges across the sea, all of them summonses! Vibrant, electric expressways, soaring and swooping! Deserted squares, black gardens where the trees are silent: it is not birds that you need, now, it is clarinets! Hogan, Earl Langlois, Tower, or alternatively Wasick, Wheeler, Rotrou, names that no longer exist, that have become meaningless. It is the blocks that exist, the tons of houses made of concrete and iron, the tunnelled mountains, the cast-iron statues standing around the islands, the tunnels of the subway system along which massive, blind cars lurch. Insects don't count. They are no longer to be seen. They pitter-patter in the cracks, they pullulate, ridiculous vermin, laughable army of long-legged aphides! Forgotten, forgotten! Never mention them again! No more sentiments at the level of aphides! We want sentiments as high-flown as twenty-five-storey buildings. Sentiments as lofty as towers, as broad as stadiums, as deep as tunnels.

Thinking! Thinking! The process should no longer be merely this feeble flurry of hailstones that raises a little dust. It should be something quite different. Thinking should be a terrifying process. When the earth thinks, whole towns crumble to the ground and thousands of people die.

Thinking: raising boulders, hollowing out valleys, preparing tidal waves out at sea. Thinking like a town, that's to say: eight million inhabitants, twelve million rats, nine million pints of carbon dioxide, two billion tons. Grey light. Cathedral of light. Din. Sudden flashes. Low-lying blanket of black cloud. Flat roofs. Fire alarms. Elevators. Streets. Eighteen thousand miles of streets. 145 million electric light bulbs.

Solitude: here the rampart of autonomy is breached. For instance, he who climbs up to the top of a tower, one night, and dares to survey this town, and all the other towns with it. The glance he gives is so cold that he becomes an integral part of the tower. Is he not even more distant than if he were surveying the earth from the outermost ends of space, through the porthole of a kind of armour-plated torpedo? Is what he sees not more beautiful and more moving than the frozen mass confronting the snout of an interplanetary capsule? What he sees is colder than the high plateaux of the Antarctic, brighter than salt lakes, vaster than the North Sea, fiercer than the Gila desert, lovelier than the Kamchatka, uglier than the mouth of the Orinoco. What he sees is so immeasurable that the bat can fly no longer and falls exhausted to the ground. What he sees is so precise that the mind becomes confused, he loses track of his thoughts and they evaporate. This is why there are guard-rails round the tops of all the towers, so that men should not climb up in droves, simply to throw themselves into space. This is why there are windows made of opaque glass, so that the terrible void should not lure them out, and devour them. This is why there are movie houses, paintings, picture postcards and books: to create walls, always more walls, protective ramparts.

Thought, infinite thought that longs to spread out and cover the whole of space. The mind is in flight. The mind escapes into the urban labyrinth. A single thought that has been allowed to circulate freely, and man is lost. Watches, calendars, rally to my side! Chronometers, help! Cigarettes, help, help! Houses, clothes, dictionaries, photographs, quick, quick, come to my rescue! Heap yourselves upon me! Money, cars, professions, quick, or it will be too late! Come and extract me from the tower, come and restore me to my rightful place among the insects. Come, mealtimes! Naked women, familiar obsessions, manias, do not delay! The void has already seized an arm, a leg, it is drawing me in. Hold your screen between my eyes and this gaze, or I shall topple!

At ground level, the little men and little women continue on their paths.

Y. M. Hogan found himself in a street where gangs of vagrants were stopping passing vehicles. One of them threw himself in front of the car's wheels, and when it came to a halt with a great squealing of brakes the others hurled themselves at it, making as though to smash the headlamps and windscreen. Then they hammered on the windows, and the driver hastily gave them some money.

In corridor-shaped bars, drunks were asleep, heads sprawled on tables.

A group of gigantic Negroes appeared on the sidewalk, striding forward in step, and staring straight ahead of them. Passers-by drew aside or flattened themselves against the wall, and the group of haughty, indifferent giants swept on.

Men with made-up faces and bleached hair minced along. From the corners of doorways, women whistled. A young man wearing tennis shoes, stretched out on the ground with his head in shadow, injected himself with a drug, then fell asleep.

At a bus stop, a fat woman with innocent eyes was holding

her handbag open against her stomach. She passed her right hand over the bag and slipped the fingertips inside the pocket of a man standing there, waiting for a bus. Her fingers emerged from the pocket holding a billfold which she dropped into the bag. She then walked off down the street, keeping an eye open for other bus stops in the vicinity.

At an intersection, there was a man gripping an iron bar. Every time a passing car came close enough, he lifted the bar and brought it down with all his might on the car's coachwork. Y. M. Hogan watched him doing this. The first two times, the cars accelerated and sped away, with a great dent in the boot. But the third time, Y. M. Hogan was not particularly surprised when the car stopped. Two men got out of it, without saying a word. The man raised his iron bar, meaning to strike them with it. But the two sprang forward, knocking him to the ground. For a whole minute Y. M. Hogan listened to the sound of the two pairs of fists smashing into the fallen man's face. The driver from the car stamped on the man's arm, forcing him to let go of the iron bar. Then, after gesturing his companion aside, he started hitting the man on the ground with the iron bar. The first stroke glanced off. The second crushed the man's skull, and a single brief little cry of 'Aah!' could be heard coming from the man's mouth. At the third stroke, the man was already dead, but the driver did not stop. He went on smashing the dead man's crushed head into a pulp, a process that produced a series of peculiar-sounding soft thuds. Cars whizzed by on either side, with their lights blazing. When he had had enough, the driver threw the iron bar on to the ground beside the body and he and his companion climbed back into their car. The car shot away, gliding up the street with its red rear lights gleaming. Then it turned down a side street and vanished. The man was sprawled on the roadway, beside the iron bar. Cars, beams of white light shining from their headlamps, continued to pass on either side of the corpse. One of them came so close that it was possible to hear, quite distinctly, its right-side tyres squelch in the pool of blood. Y. M. Hogan stayed a moment at the edge of the sidewalk, just to see whether some car would finally pass over the man's body. But people drive better than is generally supposed, and they all managed to swerve aside in time. So Y. M. Hogan went away. These were things that one could see going on in New York, or Baltimore, or maybe San Antonio, some time between 1965 and 1975.

My town is ill-famed: all along the seafront promenades, and in the streets where the night is lighting its lamps, hordes of pensive De Sades jostle and stare uncomprehendingly.

When these hordes surge from the glittering pane of the sun's downfall, passing through the tobacco smoke that moves like a footstep, all the shopkeepers are there, standing in front of their doors, and the eyes and mouths in their hard faces know only how to shout out the price of flesh, how to flash orders and angry words ...

They can be seen choosing cattle while dusk flickers like an eyelid.

Farther away, and nearer the sea, in the forests of curves and rounded forms, I have bought countless temptations!
I have allowed my harem to climb up around me; happier and randier than a lion, at last, I have been able to hear those soft, shuffling steps of theirs which carried me, which carried me away.

They can be seen choosing strange cattle while dusk trembles like a million flies.

Somewhere, a flight is under way; it has now reached cold climates, their own native lands in which I am a stranger. Their grave faces select and pay: I wince, jealous of their power — and yet, how this slave market reeks of sensual pleasure!

Emptiness of the sparkling stores with great red carpets trodden by women's stiletto heels. The music with its heavy beat revolves between the glass walls. I am in an empty place peopled by light. The women's naked legs move continually over the red carpet. Guitar music scratches the silence. Everything is beautiful. Everything is at peace. Everything is cunningly devised. Too bad that the owner of the store happens to be a gangster.

Animals possess something known as the flight reflex. It is a question of permanently maintaining sufficient distance between themselves and the world to permit escape. If you approach, you encroach upon this protective gap. The animal feels threatened, and automatically retreats slightly, to restore the necessary distance. It is the same with sleep. Sleep obliterates distance. The sleeper is so close that anyone may touch him. That is why animals never sleep.

But man? His legs are not made for running. He has no wings with which to soar away. His ears are not made for hearing sounds approach, his nose is not made for detecting odours. When he sleeps, he is stretched out on his back, offering his flabby belly to any foul blow. Set him down in a forest, alongside some famished tiger. He will not even see the claw that darts forward and rips him apart so easily.

Flies are a thousand times more agile than man. If flies were as adept at thinking as they are at avoiding man's slapping palm, they would reinvent all the scientific theories from Pythagoras to Einstein in just a few minutes.

Butterflies settle on flowers, and behold they too are flowers. Man does not know how to imitate anything, not even other men. Would he ever have thought of being striped among bamboos, or ocellate in foliage? Would he have been capable of becoming grey in sand, white in snow, black in the night? Would he even have had the idea of carrying on his back some owl's face with painted eyes, designed to frighten his enemies?

I flee, but my track is exposed, does not go right to the end, will never reach the destination. When danger swoops or springs up, it is already too late. I have known danger, lived through it. When I should have been thousands of miles away I am still stuck here, without having even lifted a finger.

The desperate slowness of man's flight! Flies, mosquitos, teach me to gather myself for the great leap that will outstrip the wind! Hares, teach me to twitch my ears! And you, leopards, jaguars, cougars, show me how you prowl in silence, placing your paws so that they do not even bruise a blade of grass!

I know, now, what I am fleeing from: emptiness.

I pass from one territory to another, I go from town to town, and I meet nothing.

Immense metropolises, immense highways. How is it that I never hear anything? Am I myself transporting emptiness wherever I go, like a deaf man for whom all other men are mutes? Sometimes I grow weary of so many images. If only the Plexiglass shell that holds me prisoner would open up. But there is no hope of that. Autonomy, cursed autonomy. I tell you, I am weary of being myself. To be someone, to be the one in relation to the others, could never suffice. I repudiate my name. Call me by your own first name.

Facial appearance of men and women, gestures, habits, occupations: all played out. The world is peopled by puppets, inhabited by robots. They laugh, they talk. But I see their eyes, and I know that there is nothing on the other side.

It is all that, perhaps, that I have now left behind. Hatred has enticed me into the very depths of space. I have taken all the paths: those which by-pass thought itself, those which lead to negative words.

I have stripped myself of my clothing. Walking, one day, with the sun in my eyes, along a street, East 37th, N. Y., for example, or Sherbrooke, Montreal, or Eglington W., Toronto, I have suddenly found that I was transparent. The warmthless light has pierced me, and I have glided along its rays, blinded, invisible, light-footed, my head floating far ahead of me, to be one, again, with the forty-four-rayed star.

I flee emptiness; in other words, I am attracted by it. The light has sunk its pit right at my feet, desiring me to fall, to fall! Yonder, at the very end of the tunnel, perhaps, lies paradise. Try to believe that: another earth, another town with parallel streets, another highway, other trees, other sparkling rivers. It is in that brand-new world that light resides. And is never extinguished. There, the plants have flowers that never wither. In that town without a name, whose streets have no numbers, great black automobiles glide along; their engines never stop, they keep running, day after day, with a soft throbbing noise. In the cafés, people are sitting in the sun, at spotless tables, eternally sipping the same water from the same glass. The music emerging from the loudspeakers is beautiful, stringing out its notes, one after the other, never forsaking mankind. In the movie houses, at the far end of dark halls as vast as cathedrals, the motion picture goes on and on. The faces appear and reappear upon the screen, their eyes open, their mouths uttering words, and everyone can decide for himself where the ending comes. It is a love story, perhaps, but one in which they never stop loving each other. For months on end, a man looks at a woman, then for months on end it is the woman looking at the man. They never sleep. They never leave each other. They continue to thrill with joy whenever their skins touch, and the man caresses the woman's right shoulder for a great deal longer than twenty-five years. They speak words, they say:

'Ah ... '
'Hm-hm ... '
'Yes?'
'Come ... '
'You've got a couple of blackheads there.'
'Do you like my hair like this?'
'Hm, yes, yes ... '

There are novels, too, on the frontages of business premises, novels that light up their words, from right to left, on the screen of electric light bulbs. These novels have no ending. They are not tragic novels. They are stories that are as simple as postcards, stories no sooner told than forgotten, stories that have nothing to do with death, war, victims of obsessions and suicide.

And perhaps there will be a woman waiting, over there, at the end of that road which stretches as far as the sun. And when, some day in the future, one is in that town and chances to pass her in the street, perhaps she will realize immediately that it is you for whom she has been waiting. She will come to a halt, there, on the edge of the sidewalk, and she will smile as she looks at you, and there will be this terrible word, this secret word which shatters cockpit windows and makes the casemate's old walls crumble into dust:

WELCOME!

That is what there is, in that far country which one may perhaps reach, one day. Meanwhile, I wander. Since I cannot grow as big as the world, as deep as the Pacific ocean, since I cannot think like Socrates or Lao-Tsü, since I cannot change men's lives as did Jesus Christ or Engels, since I shall never even know how to be myself, absolutely myself, myself to a pitch of ecstasy, there remains one course open to me: to slap the ground with my footsteps, to expand, to devour space, to absorb sights and entertainments, to watch names parade across the façades of stations, to get to know all sorts of extraordinary women, all sorts of men, all sorts of dogs.

The 1956-model Chevrolet speeds along the endless roads. The wind whistles past its windows. A sandstorm swirls across the road. The milestones arrive in a flash, one after the other, and wire fences wobble up and down.

The frontier towns are frozen in the middle of space. From time to time, their gates swing open to let caravans file out. In the waiting-rooms of bus stations, ragged Negroes are sleeping on benches. Workmen in dirty overalls are smoking, and watching television.

At MacAllen (Texas), the heat is so dry that the haze has the appearance of sand. Among the streets of dust, nothing but wooden shacks, tin huts, beer cans.

I pass by, I cross through. Towns are ever-growing refuse dumps; time no longer exists for them. When one travels the highways on foot one is more alone than the captain of a cargo vessel in mid-ocean. I am going farther, still farther. I am making for places that are new to me. I take trains that fritter away their time on their twin rails of solitude. I am seated in the buses of isolation, and the jolting of the wheels carries me away. Movement across the surface of the earth is not easy: it scrapes, it grates, it is an incurable disease. Everything that I have seen, I have forgotten immediately. I have not taken to the road so as to

draw maps or write books. I am not forging ahead so as to
know who I am, or where I am. No, I am on the move
quite simply so as not to be there, any longer, so as not to be
in your company any longer. If I really find out anything, I
will let you know.

Signed:

Juanito Holgazán

As the other fellow puts it:

I AM SO RESTLESS

The earth is filled with many noises, so many noises. People, everywhere, talk endlessly, and I can hear sounds rising from every cleft and gully: peculiar sorts of snarling, snuffling and yelping, followed by little twitterings, sighs, sniffs, belches, clicking of tongues and clacking of teeth. It is an immense aviary, chattering and shrieking away tirelessly, inflating the dome of the heavens with its gas. The echoes of vain words roll from one end of the world to the other, through the sky, in the wind, over the water. The noise rises, drops, breaks into waves, scrapes, crawls, bursts in billions of explosions that follow each other at intervals of a millionth of a second. There is no concord. There will never be harmony. Clocks never strike the same hour. Letters melting together, fierce swelling of the floods of words, adjectives, names, prepositions, numerals. Floods of slaver, of blood, of body-fluids, of gas tumbling through the breached barrage. I do not want to say anything. Rather, I cannot say anything. I am seated at my table, my hands resting on its surface, in front of me, and the waterspout sweeps past repeatedly, sucking up my tatters and my hair, tearing the branches off the trees. Water falls from the sky, the water of words, each drop shooting through the sky's space with the speed of light, then disappearing. Explosions, explosions, continual murmuring, cataract creating its wall of terror between myself and the others. The room is as vast as the earth, perhaps it is the earth, the so-called universe. There are so many people on the earth; this room alone is crammed with a dense, hideously noisy crowd. I am faced with an ocean of unattached words, a grey plain of language advancing, retreating, advancing, dancing up and down. My bubble is surrounded by a mountain of violet gelatine that trembles all over its nerveless flesh. And I am inside that mountain.

I have no respite. I do not want to pause. I do not want to dig my own grave. That is why I slip and slide away into the distance. The most detestable of all truths is the truth that confronts one when one pauses. That huge monstrosity scrabbling up the earth under its feet, puffing itself up: feeding on solitude. Hideous sheep urinating between its feet! I do not want to recognize myself. In recognizing myself I would have lost my reality. Danger. Danger of railroad stations, danger of peaceful gardens, danger of ports and airports. Everywhere, there is this face that lies in wait for me, plotting to become my own face. I shall tear out these eyes! Yes, I shall hack off this mouth, this nose, these ears! Yes, I shall smash in this skull with hammer blows! Who dared say that the others were myself? It is not true, the others are not myself. There are so many of the others, they are so powerful and so real that it is as though I were looking up at the night sky, at that half of its blackness where the stars are clustered. If the others were myself, knowing would be pointless. Even I am not myself! Where am I? What mirror will at last allow me to know my image, my true image? Narcissus was a liar, a dirty liar. It was not himself that he loved; it was his brother.

Intelligence never comes full circle. It is a line that goes forward, that goes through. Incapable of coming to a decision, because to do that it would have to stop emanating from itself, if only for a single second. And it never does stop. It sweats continually by way of its thinking-gland, and so achieves a pure freedom: continually free perspiration.

The earth is filled with many noises. Each emerging thought makes its distinctive noise. Everything, without exception, speaks, from the sea-slug to the leaves of water-lilies. Those who want to know themselves are either mad or just weak-minded. Those who want to watch themselves watching others are complaisant. They do not know what a real stare involves. They do not even suspect that their self-awareness is a terrible harpoon rending the air. I look at their round faces, with their eyes surmounted by eyelids, and nose pierced by two holes, and I see this: tiny lines spurting from their body, tails of comets, rays. These are their thoughts. I think, therefore the match's flame is. I think, therefore the antelope is. I think, therefore the great emperor-moth is.

I am always lagging behind my thoughts. I believed that I was here and they were with me, but they are already beyond the horizon. I believed that I recognized the glass ashtray, or else the sun's small disc, but I had already passed through. To be, is no longer to be there. When death comes, then perhaps ... Perhaps I will know at last what an ashtray is, or the moon, or the smell of grass. Meanwhile, I can only admit defeat. Do not expect me to grind out books full of definitions. I am not a good hunter. I will never bag any game. But if you enjoy wild chases, falls to the bottom of wells, railroad cars thundering along at eighty miles an hour, the agitations of armies of Argentinian ants around a sliver of cheese, then you will understand what I am trying to say.

Knowledge is never static. Even algebra is based upon infinity: is open, that is to say, in the direction of the unknown. No science is exact. Biology, etymology, aetiology and geology would give huge amusement to a dung-beetle, if their principles were explained to it. There are no systems: just imagine Confucius reading Pascal, imagine Pascal reading Marx. What a joke! Imagine Empedocles reading the Popol Vuh! What a face he would pull! There is no such thing as self-awareness. Imagine thought retreating into itself to think about itself. It would surely be easier to imagine a revolver bullet extracting itself from its victim's wound and re-entering the barrel. Yes, it would be easier to imagine the universe's explosion suddenly halting its outflow of energy, so that the galaxies congeal once more, and the millions of light-years of their flight through space are immediately annulled.

Now it is there, in the very depths of me. Not a certainty, but a desire, an appeal. I shall never know who I am. I shall never know anything. I shall do nothing but make my way, day in day out, toward the great masses of light, I shall dance toward everything that shines, I shall be the moth that dies searching for darkness.

The one who looked at himself was looking at nothingness. The one who wanted to love himself, to exhaust himself with love, was intoxicated. The one who talked to himself, or wanted to say something to the others, was a tongueless mute. Today, I realize this very well. It is the consequence of flight. I have at last opened reality's door and walked out. Its rooms are merely obscure spots that are too vast to contain knowledge and too small to contain the world. Nothing entered, there. The walls were heavy, sealed tight, hiding secrets rather than keeping them. The naked light bulb dangling from a cord was not a sun. The pieces of wooden furniture infested by larvæ were not mountains. The glass ashtray, in which the cigarette butts

239

live, had no truth other than its own. Hovering over him, hovering over the one whom I wanted to be myself, I saw nothing but glass, paper, ash. Look outside, now, just one good look, and tell me what you see. Do you see nothing more than an ashtray?

No, there is so much to see that one pair of eyes is not enough. Even if one had ten thousand eyes, it would still not be enough. One would have to be as quick as flies, as slow as trees, as big as whales, soar as high as vultures. And it would still not be enough. One would have to be as multiple as microbes, as heavy as osmium, as soft as earth, as cold as snow. One would have to be water like true water, fire like true fire. And I am just one single entity!

Multitudes of the earth, come to me! Lions, gnus, termites, snakes! And then, at my signal, off with you! Flee into the forests, the savanna, the mountain valleys. Sharks of the sea, troglodytes, parasites, explore your domains. Be my scouts. Find out all you can about this country. Tell me what is the night temperature there; tell me if the water there is good to drink, if there is salt to be mined there, or gold. Fleas, tell me which is better, the blood of the infant at its mother's breast, or the blood of the man making war. Black frogs of Darién, tell me how you distil poison from your skins. You, slow-worms, why have you chosen to imitate snakes? And you, white scorpions, tell me who has the power to frighten you.

Flight is not silence. It is, all of a sudden, an avalanche of noises compounded of rustlings, creakings, murmurs. Flight means talking, no longer with the aim of being understood, but so as to make a noise, one more noise among all the others.

Flight can never be solitude. Rather, it means finding oneself unexpectedly in the incredible crowd with its whirlwinds of movements. I think about rats, and at once I have eight billion brothers. I think about clouds, and there, outlined against the sky's sphere, I see all my aerial companions floating around me. I think about ants, and from that moment on, it is impossible to be lonely. I think about the grains of sand in the Mojave desert, and I immediately exist in each grain: if you know how many grains of sand there are in the Mojave desert, you will know exactly how many friends I have.

Meanwhile ... Hogan reached the coast of the Gulf of California, at a point where an island lay off shore. He scrutinized it, from where he was standing on the beach. On the horizon, the island floated tranquilly, like a big black fish, above the blue and white sea. The air was dry and harsh, and the wind blowing along the dunes sent sand into one's eyes. Hogan climbed back on to the road and started walking north. He occasionally passed American tourists in shorts, going fishing. On the outskirts of the village there was a brand-new motel with stuccoed walls, a bar, and air-conditioning units blowing scorching air out into the warm air. A little farther on, an old man wearing dirty linen trousers was repainting his delivery-truck blue. On the beach, a group of girls, their skins flushed from sunburn, were uttering piercing shrieks as they splashed about at the edge of the sea. Hogan had slept on the beach and felt tired. When he had woken up, he had seen the island rising there, above the sea, and had decided to go there. That is why he was walking along the beach, in the sun.

This island was called Shark Island. It had been inhabited for centuries by people called Kunkaaks. They had chosen this island because it was the wildest place around, and because the sea gave them additional protection from the marauding of other humans. It was a desert girdled by the sea, a mountain rising sheer out of the water, with just enough stunted shrubs and half-dried-up streams to make survival possible there. At low tide, the island is only a few cable-lengths from the coastline. But when the tide rises, great eddies cut it off as effectively as though a drawbridge had been raised.

There was this island, then, this black mountain with dry cliffs, grey beaches, and deep waters the colour of gasoline. The Kunkaaks lived on the island for part of the year, then went off on fishing expeditions for whole months on end, sailing away in their long, slim boats. When the fishing had been good they continued sailing northward, sometimes as far as the United States frontier, and sold their fish. Then they were away again as suddenly as they had arrived.

Nowadays, there are no more Kunkaaks on Shark Island. It was decided to create a game reserve on the island, for the benefit of millionaires and their high-powered rifles. It was decided to build motels made of concrete and glass, and cocktail bars, and beaches on which girls could get sunburned. The Kunkaaks have been expelled. They have evacuated their island in their long, slim boats, together with their women, their children, their dogs and their cats. But since it was their island, that they had once upon a time chosen for themselves, they have stayed on the coast, right opposite, where the land juts out into the sea and points at the island, and there they wait. They never stop gazing out over the water at the island. Since the Kunkaaks do not like concrete motels, or bars, they are in the process of dying. Not in-dividually, like everyone else: they are dying as a collectivity. They are gradually becoming extinct, untouched by calamities or epidemics or murders, simply fading away.

Hogan walked a long way along the coast, following a path in the sand. About midday, he found himself at the top of a hill, from which he could see the place called

Punta Chueco, framed between cacti and scrub. There, fields of dusty bushes slope down towards the sea. Right at the bottom is a sort of ill-defined beach that the sea laps hungrily. A grey sandspit juts out into the water, rather like a finger pointing at the open sea. At the tip of this finger, but separated from it by a blue platform, the island stands motionless. Hogan saw that the spit housed an encampment of tents made from torn sheets of sailcloth stretched over poles. The evidence of poverty, hunger and boredom became increasingly visible as he descended the path towards the village: rubbish littering the beach, rust-eaten food cans, rotted cartons, empty oil-drums, broken pots and pans, fish-heads, tangles of old rope.

The sand is not white. It is not made for the naked feet of young women in bright-coloured bikinis. It is a drab sand made of hard, coarse grains, a sand that yields an unwanted detritus, interspersed with thorny plants. Razor-like blades of grass cut through the salty deposits, and slant in the same direction that the wind blows. Dry rivulets have left their traces in the mud: thousands of furrows that signify old age, solitude and many things of that nature. Wind, rain, and spray from the hostile sea sweep over their patch of ground. The sun beats down upon it with evil rays when the desert wind blows through a cloudless sky. Here, beauty is not beautiful, but bitter and sad. The blueness has nothing gentle to say, has slammed its door on words. Here is what the world thinks and truth does not derive from men, neither from their speech, nor from their books, nor even from their religion. Truth does not derive from men, but from the world, the world. Truth derives from the light that radiates from the sky, the blue sea, the wind, great stretches of sand. The eyes of animals. Truth can be recognized: oscillating, shimmering, black island glowing on the horizon. Even the spoken word does not derive from men, it is in the vast, unendurable blue colour that covers the universe. Mountain-truth, harsh and profound truth, uniquely naked beauty, reign of the eternal verities, of all that touches directly without needing to use fingers.

As for the rest — men, words, ideas: lies, all lies.

In front of Hogan, now, stretches the opaque mass of the greenish water. Behind him, the mountains' jagged spines bristling with dry scrub. Above him, the naked sky, the weight of purplish-blue air. Nothing, here, offers repose, gentleness, maturity. It is a place that was born with the world itself, fierce and distrustful, a landscape toughened by solitude and aggressiveness.

Hogan began walking down the central alley. Men and women are squatting in the shelter of the rags of spread canvas. Fires are smouldering between piles of stones. Children are sprawling on the sand. Dogs are sniffing round piles of foul muck. A black pig, attached to a cord, goes round and round in a circle. Big boats are lying high and dry, as though resigned to their fate, all along the spit jutting into the open sea. The wind is blowing over the sand, raising invisible clouds that move horizontally and sting the face.

In front of Hogan, a man has risen to his feet and is walking along with great strides. His long black hair floats out behind him and flaps back against his face. Inside the tents, women are suckling babies, cooking food in earthen-ware pots, gnawing scraps, waiting, looking straight ahead. Dogs with arched backs are running around, their noses to the ground. The nasal sound of music from a transistor radio spurts from the dark depths of a tent set a little apart from the others. Then the music stops, and a man's voice begins speaking very fast in Spanish, talking about all sorts of things that no one can understand.

This is how the hours pass, each day, on the sandspit jutting out into the sea. The long, senseless hours and the shadows move in a regular rhythm over the grains of sand and over the thorny plants. Cormorants skim the water, skipping over the waves' rollers.

Along the sand, beside the beached boats, the men gaze at the sea. Right in front of their eyes, the heavy mass of the Isle of Sharks drifts without moving. The men and women have learned to decipher the form of each peak, the grey mark of each bay, the site of each tuft of grass. They have learned to see from afar what they had once touched with their own hands. They have learned not to desire any longer what they see. In the distance, the island sails over the sparkling water, truly inaccessible, truly unreal, like a steamboat about to cast off. The men are sitting on the beach, their long black hair floating on their backs. They have learned to remain seated beside their decaying boats, and wait for the sun to sink towards the island's summits.

The tides swell the sea, then drain it away into the Infernillo straits. But the sea never drains away sufficiently for the island suddenly to become attached to the tongue of sand stretched out towards it. The wind blows in from the open sea, the wind of the sea's desert. It never brings a twig or a speck of dust or an odour from the land that lies over there, on the other side.

Standing in front of his canvas house, in which his wife and his child are squatting, wrapped in blankets, the Kunkaak has drawn himself up to his full height. He looks at Hogan. The skin of his face is brown, almost black, and wrinkles radiate from his thick mouth. On his arched nose are perched a pair of dark glasses given him one day by a marauding German anthropologist. Behind the tinted lenses the narrow eyes stare at him intently. The wind ruffles the man's clothes, bends the rim of his broken hat. The thick jet-black hair is braided into two plaits which hang down his back, over his white shirt and as far as his belt; the ends of the plaits are tied with red ribbons.

When he speaks, his voice is hesitant, husky. He tells Hogan what life had been like on the island when the sea yielded great hauls of fish. He shows him the place where he used to get fresh water before going away for several weeks. Then he describes how policemen, armed with rifles, came and told them to go. He says: 'There, there, and there, they are going to make fine houses. Fine houses.' He walks down to the beach, stooping. Then he stands, facing the sea, and looks. His copper mask registers no emotion of any kind. The two eyes hidden by the sunglasses gaze without hatred, without sorrow. The wide mouth remains closed, the nostrils inhale regularly. There is neither sorrow nor desire. The wind beats against his shirt and his trousers, and the naked feet are planted on the cold sand like two chunks of stone. There is no more desire, no more future. The male Kunkaak looks at the island, over there, on the other side of the stretch of water. He sees the waves advancing, one behind the other, sending out reflections like ground glass, and he looks at them, too, because they come from the island. Then he looks once more at the enormous silhouette floating on the sea, at each detail of the outline that he learned by heart many years ago. More distant than a star, ugly, black, deserted, the island emerges from the waves like a steamboat riding at anchor, like a huge, shadowy animal filled with indifference and sadness.

A few days later, Hogan entered a town where automobiles reigned. This town was at the top of a mountain, in the bottom of a basin lost in the earth's silence, a vast city marked out by straight boulevards, and by row upon row of little square houses. Neither men, nor birds, nor trees were to be seen in this town: only streets, grey asphalt channels through which the automobiles sped at seventy miles an hour.

It had all happened suddenly: the vehicles had taken over the town, one day, and now they never stopped still for a moment. They hurtled down the forty-mile-long avenues, they vanished into tunnels, they crossed bridges, they went round traffic circles. Sometimes, in the middle of the boulevards, a red light glowed on top of a pylon, and all the vehicles obeyed. Human silhouettes hastened to cross over in front of the snarling bonnets. On the other side of the street, another long line of vehicles whizzed by, plunging between the rows of houses. Then, the red light suddenly went out and a green light glowed on top of the pylon; and it was as though some huge change had occurred in the world.

The vehicles had won their war. They were there, lording it over the country that they had conquered with their steel breastplates and rubber wheels. They passed between the houses, by thousands, making their grumbling noises. They were charged with menace. Hogan watched them as he strolled along the sidewalk; he knew quite well what they wanted. They wanted to kill him. One day, no doubt, they would finally achieve this aim. They were utterly ruthless. Old women, wrapped in their shawls, crossed the streets with short steps. And suddenly the steel bonnet snatched at them, broke their bones, dragged their shattered bodies along in the gutter.

Here, life revolved around these machines. Hogan walked along a dusty avenue that was divided down its centre by a raised strip in which willows grew. On each side, to the left and the right, lines of cars and trucks passed, whistling and yelling. Clouds of exhaust gas more terrible than clouds of flies floated down the avenue. As Hogan walked along, he looked at all the corpses of dogs that were rotting away on the centre strip of ground. There were hundreds of them, sprawled out on the yellowing grass, their bellies swollen, their stiff paws raised skyward. The vehicles felt a need to kill. It was their function. If they did not kill dogs, they would kill men. That is why, at night-time, the men amused themselves playing the game of dogs and trucks.

They sit by the side of the road, smoking cigarettes and drinking tequila out of a greasy tumbler. They hold a dog between their hands. And when a truck approaches, a gigantic truck with headlamps like balls of fire, racing along and making the ground tremble under its fourteen tyres, when the truck is almost there, just a few yards away, they hurl the dog into its path. Some dogs scramble to their feet and gallop along in front of the truck, howling with fright. Some just stand there, watching the dazzling headlamps grow enormous. Some see nothing; having landed sideways, they start investigating the shoulders of the road, to see what is going on there. The trucks' bonnets roar, their tyres flatten themselves against the ground with liquid noises.

The dogs have all sorts of different ways of dying. Some leap high into the air, their paws splayed out. Some open up like fruit, some squash flat like pancakes. Some emit piercing shrieks, while the bodies of others reverberate like drums. Some even escape death by crouching down as the rows of tyres pass on either side, and then scuttling off into some wasteland in the depths of the night.

Hogan tried to recognize the names of the vehicles as they passed. He recited them in a low voice, while their great, heavy, shining metal frames sped on down the avenue.

'1955 sky-blue Chevrolet'
'Dodge Dart'
'1960 wine-red Studebaker'
'Ford Mustang'
'Red Volkswagen'
'White Chevrolet Impala'

They were all names of the cuirass-clad soldiers who had, conquered the town. They had subdued it with their wheels, with their scorching engines and with their chrome-plated bumpers, and for the present the town belonged to them.

Hogan walked for a long time in the streets where the automobiles were swarming. He crossed streets between the bonnets, he listened to the terrifying din which rose and enveloped the houses and trees. He gazed at all the harsh reflections on the metal shells, he looked in all the shop windows, white or blue, that caught the sun's glare.

Buses passed, close in to the sidewalk, with screeching noises. They carried their engines at the back, in the open, and one could see everything, the cylinders, the fan, the leads. In the cabins with hot metal walls, people were jammed together in clusters, their arms hooked to the roof. The hanging clusters of people swayed to and fro each time the brakes were applied. Hogan stopped at a street corner and watched the buses come along. Some of them were very beautiful, square, with gleaming chrome plating and tinted windowpanes. Others were decrepit, with glassless windows, lurching along in the midst of a cloud of blue smoke, their metal panels wrenching apart at each jolt. One could climb into any one of these buses, adhere to the mass of arms and legs, and let oneself be carried away to unknown places. The wide-fronted machines permitted every kind of parasite to enter their body. They carried them without even noticing, too busy making their motors screech into the surrounding air, too busy banging with their tyres against the pot-holes in the roadway. They carried strange names, which were their own names, written above the windshield: RIO MIXCOAC, TLANEPANTLA, ZOCALO, OCOYOACAC, RIO ABAJO, COYOACAN, NET-ZAHUALCOYOTL. When a bus drew up, carrying the name NAUCALPAN, Hogan climbed into it.

At the end of all the streets dedicated to vehicles, after having changed buses twice, after having passed all those houses with closed shutters, after having seen all those faces, there was this terrible zone, this great area of silence and dust, where Hogan lived. He had decided to make his home there, for a little while, because there were no more roads or vehicles here, only paths gouged out by rainstorms, clay hills, gullies, and tin shacks. It was known as Shantytown.

For miles on end, as far as the eye could see, there was nothing but these dirt hillocks covered with huts, and silence weighed heavily over the scene. Now Hogan began climbing a path that rose steeply. He scaled the chunks of dried mud, the boulders, the stair treads hollowed out of the earth by feet. He found breathing difficult, perhaps because of the silence. The rest of the town stretched out behind him, right to the horizon, a grey sea in which, here and there, white skyscrapers glittered. He passed brick houses from which swarthy women glanced out at him furtively. He crossed fields of compressed dust. The path climbed to the top of the hill. All around him he could see other identical hills, with their cubes built of clay bricks and their corrugated iron roofs.

Perhaps it was a cemetery filled with many-coloured tombs. But the dead still lived: he could see them everywhere, walking along silently, crossing wasteland, jogging down steep slopes, climbing abrupt paths with buckets of water in their hands. It was a cemetery in which dogs roamed freely in search of bones and orange peel. Groups of dust-coloured children ran around between the tombs, piercing the silence with their shrill yells. Higher up, Hogan walked along a sort of terrace overhanging the dry bed of a stream. Casemates bristled everywhere, serried rows of them from which there was no hope of escaping. They had dug themselves into the earth with invisible claws, and nothing could tear them out. They had sprung up on every conceivable site: along the sides of the hills, on the slopes, on slight protuberances, in holes, on the edges of holes, on the sides of holes. Some were balanced precariously on the very edge of gullies, ready to crash down at the first tremor or the first rainstorm. Others were flattened out at the bottom of crevasses, imprisoned within a crater of dust. Yet others had sprouted on the faces of steep cliffs, and day by day leaned a little farther out into space. They were all similar, and yet never absolutely identical. There was always something intangible, some trifling little detail that was not apparent at first glance; the house's true identity was provided by a patch of rust on the roof, or else a bit of cardboard inscribed in red letters with a phrase such as GAS INC, or ATLANTIS, or perhaps an old crate, a green plastic door, a fuel-can for water, a truck tyre

being used as a seat by an old woman. These characteristics
served the same purpose as the bunch of flowers or the plastic
wreath on the tombstone, indicating that these walls har-
boured living people, people that had not stopped breathing
yet.

Hogan looked at the variegated warts that had sprung up on
the face of the earth; from the top of his hill he watched the
columns of smoke drifting skyward.

Then he stopped and sat down on a stone, and he too
created smoke, by means of a cigarette. And since he had
nothing to do, since he really had all the time in the world, he
sank into thought:

Thoughts by young Man Hogan
while surveying Barrio Colorado
the town just outside Naucalpan
that looked like a cemetery

'Maybe I'll stop there, you know. Maybe.
It's an extraordinary place, with lots of hills and
valleys. The most extraordinary thing of all is the
dust. It is fine and grey, you can't see it but it
covers everything. Even the water here must be
made of dust. The dust never stops sliding down
from the tops of the hills toward the town, it
floats through the air in very long streaks. It has
even replaced the clouds. It penetrates everywhere. It is in the food one eats and the water
one drinks. It lines the bottom of the throat when
one inhales. Isn't that extraordinary? Everything one tastes has the taste of dust. The
cigarettes one smokes are full of it. The other
day, I had bought a can of apricots in syrup,

because, after all, one still needs the occasional luxury. I opened the can: it was filled with dust. There is so much dust here that if vacuum cleaners had been invented yet they would be choked to death in a few seconds. This dust pays no attention to the wind. Whether there is any wind or not, it floats calmly, unhurriedly, in the air, settling down, then making off again. I think it must be alive. It is almost weightless: light, so very light. If one looked at it under a microscope, perhaps one would see that it has wings and legs. Or perhaps one would see that it does not exist, that it is simply in the imagination. Not everybody likes the dust. There are some people who wear things like handkerchiefs over their mouths when they are out of doors. But I'm really fond of the dust. I inhale as much of it as possible. I am never so happy as when I am coughing or sneezing. And then, the dust is a good thing. One is never alone when it's around. It is there, always drawing attention discreetly to the fact that it is there. It makes sure that one forgets nothing, that one remembers every second, that one always knows where one is, what one is doing. The dust is truly my friend. It does me so many good turns. For one thing, it swallows up the noises that I don't need. When there is a rather loud noise, a child's cry, an explosion, an alarm siren, the dust spreads over it and swallows it up. The noises become grey, then turn into ashes. And the dust swallows up the light that I don't need. It makes a pall in front of the sun and absorbs the fierce rays. Thanks to the dust, the sun is always like the glowing tip of a cigarette. Visible but harmless: an extraordinary object, an object made of dust. And at night-time, the night is never really black. It is grey. And when the weather turns cold, the dust makes an extra covering around me, it stops up all the holes in my skin. I can tell you all the extraordinary things that the dust knows how to do: it makes mirrors grow dim; it puts out small outbreaks of fire; it keeps the hair matted when the wind blows; it is nourishing, like flour; it slows up the mechanism of watches; it keeps mosquitoes away; it gives flavour to the water; it makes a carpet at the bottom of shoes; it polishes women's skin; it dirties the lenses of spectacles; it stops car engines; it conceals messes; it destroys cobwebs; it fills up cracks; it prevents people from looking at each other; it eats up old newspapers; it makes people want to die, or go to sleep; it wears away jagged boulders; it uproots useless weeds, brambles and trees; it hides the stars; it makes a halo round the moon; it wipes out footsteps; and so many more things besides.'

Hogan shifted his position on the rock he was sitting on, and stretched his legs out in front of him. He looked at the grey town, the millions of houses spread out before him. He thought:

'Maybe I'll stay on here, yes, for a very long time. I didn't tell you that from where I live one can see the sea. Not from the windows, there aren't any. But if you stand at the door, you can see the hill sloping down, in front of you, with its shacks made of planks and tin sheeting. And right at the end, you can see the sea. It is a great grey-blue sea with great white rocks sticking up vertically through its surface. In this sea, cars are speeding along straight roads with asphalt surfaces, although from where I am they are invisible. At sunrise and sunset, beautiful light-effects spread over the sea, red glints and violet patches. It is most impressive. I had always dreamed of having a house like that, with a view of the sea from the top of a hill. I can sit in front of the door and watch the sea while smoking a cigarette or drinking a cup of Nescafé, and I can hear the sound of the waves. It is a very distant noise, a continuous low rumbling coming from the sea and reaching the tops of the hills. If I feel like it, I can have conversations with people while looking at the sea and listening to it. Sometimes a procession of men and donkeys passes by my home. They are Otomis on their way back from market, returning to their mountains without a glance for anyone on the way. Their faces are closed like masks, and as they climb the path they urge their donkeys on by making peculiar noises with their mouths. The sky here is limpid and soft, because of the dust. Everything is so dry that time seems stationary. Everything is so quiet that it always seems to be the same hour. You, though, you can never have had those sensations. You live in a town which I do not know. You go to the movies. You are continually getting in and out of cars. You go off to work in offices filled with leather. Whereas, during all that time, I am living in a precise pattern. I have my hut, on top of a hill. I am not expecting anyone. I have my cube of dust. When night falls, the sea down there lights up with thousands of little lamps. Some of them move, the rest are stationary. It is marvellous to be able to see such extraordinary things without needing to leave one's own home.

That is what I have to think about: the idea of staying here, or in a similar place. The dust will never drive me out. When one lives in a cemetery, one doesn't have far to go to die. When a man comes into the world he is entitled to about 14,400 days and 14,400 nights. There are so many things to see, so many things to do, so many things to say, from the top of this hill, that it quite takes my breath away. And one can see so far beyond the mountains and the barriers of walls that emptiness can no longer possibly exist anywhere. Let us never again mention the indecent word *truth*. I talk about dust because I do not know how to talk about this man whom I met the other day. He, his wife and his three children had been walking for months, to get to this town. His handsome face was thin and intelligent. He was cradling their youngest child, a two-year-old boy, in his arms. He and the children were all barefoot. When I had given them something to eat, none of them said thank you. They ate quickly; even the two-year-old ate quickly. Then, since they were tired, they stretched out on the ground, just where they were, and went to sleep. The man smoked a cigarette before going to sleep. He said he was going to stay in the town to work. He told how they had been chased off their land and told to go to this town. He said he was going to stay here, in this cemetery-town. He had eyes that taught you something. Not eyes to kill you with a glance. But eyes that could teach you something. Now I know. Before saving the world, before becoming the spokesman of the poor, I want to stay here in this place, and live for 122 years so that I can understand.'

Y. M. H.

Stupid ugliness of scruffy towns spread over the ground! Loneliness of wretched streets, wretched wastelands! Casemates! Prisons made of red brick walls, leprous backyards, tin and cardboard shacks! Great heaps of filth! Nothing to be done about it, nothing to be done but look and suffer. The silent malady has taken hold. Malady of sadness and fear. It marks the skin with its big, brown blotches, it has left its trail of fever pustules and agues. Joyless cities, cities of the destitute in the cold air of five o'clock in the morning. Streets that no one has had time to tar, trees that have not had the time to grow, polluted rivers that have not had the time to obtain water! Patches of humiliation, drab spaces where the sunlight is merely an additional dullness. Nights without lamps! Each day they pour in: cowed men, women, children wearing woollen rags. They squat in the corners of huts, under the arches of bridges. They light fires with bits of broken crates. Then, first on one hill, then on others, they start building more mud huts, top them off with bits of metal sheeting, put stones around the edges of the roofs to stop

them from blowing away. Sleeping towns. Tapeworm
towns casting out their dead rings. The building sites are
frozen into immobility. The walls come to a halt. There are
mountains of sand, himalayas of black earth and scrap metal.
Great empty districts where people prowl rather than walk.
Razed tracts of ground, cold plains crossed only by the trains
and trucks. Evil places where the wind whistles and the dust
grates, places that are blotches of shadow, blotches of rust,
blotches of oil: innumerable blotches. Places where everything has been used and reused countless times! Battered
jalopies lie shipwrecked in broken-down sheds. And the
people sleep in their doorless, windowless shells, curled up
on their greasy mattresses. Ghost towns where one never
expects anything. The grey here is a murderous grey!
Square miles of gloomy silence, square miles of nothingness!
Towns where people do not wash! Towns where people do
not eat! Towns where people do not read or speak! Great
hollow cisterns in which nothing happens! These are places
where the adventures are called *ratadis*, croup, tuberculosis,
smallpox, nutritional deficiency, typhoid. There are no
hours. The mind is coiled up in a ball: it is neither asleep,
nor awake, simply elsewhere. Inexhaustible recitation of
solitudes, maladies, sadnesses: absence of location, location
that cannot be seen. There are these circles of emptiness
around the glittering towns, circles that have dug their
trenches, squeezed their rings tight. Everything might very
well topple into these gulfs and disappear. What the towns
reject is emptiness, and the excrements of emptiness pile up
around the towns, encircle them. Places fated to remain
perpetually foreign, places without nationality or language.
They are the rims of the crater. They are rings of jetsam, and
the traveller passes through them without noticing. Fringe of
dirty foam, soapy froth, rings of dirt. In the closed cabins,

the smoke spreads out and trickles through the cracks under the doors, the smoke of cold and hunger. Armies of rats race through the night. The living skeletons of dogs spin round and round in the vacant lots. Towns where people gnaw away! Sacks full of old papers, mounds of earth-coloured bones, black oil-drums. City of junkmen and ragpickers! Everything is lost, everything has been submerged beneath oblivion and hatred. The chimneys of the glowing factories manufacture smoke. In the centre of the grey deserts, the silver spaceships squat, without ever soaring away. These places are gasholders, oil tanks, cold metal reservoirs gleaming in the sun. Tubes traverse the air, electric cables sag. These places surely do not possess a word for hope, or for despair. Only a slow word for the waiting process, a word destined to last for centuries. Hunger gnaws at stomachs. Hunger is a third eye, a sort of pineal eye keeping watch from the summit of human brows. Sometimes, an unreal airplane glides along, high in the sky. Its shadow flies over the mud huts, makes the children blink, undulates along the tin roofs, and the harsh noise of its jet engines fills the emptiness. Concrete bridges span these dim zones, soaring over paths where the mud never dries. Thousands of vehicles stream over the bridges, and the wind buffets them as they speed away from the unsavoury environment. The important thing is to forget. To get away, right away. But is it possible? How to erase one's knowledge of all this? How to contrive a return to the sparkling shops, the movie houses, the bars, the churches gleaming with varnish? Committed, uncommitted: meaningless words. How to contrive an interest in abstract effigies, in language, in the reasoning of a thought process that feels no pangs of hunger? Is that really where flight is bound to find its goal? How to contrive to remain apart from all of this, now, so as to create revolutions out of flags and books, so as to believe in a God who is not ugly? Curse emanating from subterranean towns, towns that people hide away. One discovers them at random, one day, and knows one will never forget them. Each day, the brown blotches spread farther. They spread over dead skins, they slither backward, they drag away toward oblivion ... The grey blotches hurt, they squeeze, they sink their empty wells around human consciousness. All the blotches are silent. They make no noise. They ask for nothing more than space, sheet metal, mud, rats. They proclaim nothing. They do not march in the streets. They have no ideas, no words, no images. They are nothing but slabs of silence, trenches, tumbledown walls. Those who inhabit them are not trying to make conquests. They are merely children, there to people the emptiness, to multiply emptiness. They are foreigners. They speak languages that no one understands, they are hungry: not for a meal or a snack, but hungry for thousands, for millions of meals. They do not die: they disappear. They do not make love: they couple quickly, attaching no importance to the act. They do not breathe. They are not there. Poverty. Strained look that never penetrates but darts from one wall to another. The inhabitants of the blotches have faces like blotches, and eyes like pebbles. Airplanes were not made for them. The highways were not made for them. Neither electric wires, nor trees, nor underground drains were made for them. What really is made for them is rusty scrap metal, broken cartons, bits of glass, gashed tyres, the rain, the cold, the burning sun, the silence of wastelands. And also, dogs with protruding ribs, dust turning into mud, the odours of gas and garbage. And the trucks that drive over the bumpy road, stopping in front of each cube of tin and brick to sell cans of grimy water at prices that make watering a pot of geraniums more extravagant than owning a swimming-pool; water so expensive that after

people have brushed their teeth they wash their hands with
the water they have just spat out. Dead towns, cemetery
towns, towns in ruins even before you have been built, it is
your turn now! Go on, avenge yourselves! Avenge yourselves!

Grey sky
Grey town
All there, today, thousands of grey walls
Prison town, fortress town, town motionless
    under the sky
I know you:
I have nothing more to tell you
In the whole wide world there is only a single
    town
A single giant house
Four concrete walls
A zinc roof
Windows, doors

A woman is walking
Over the macadamized surface
Where can she be going?
Where can she be going?
With a measured pace that sets her hips swaying
There is nothing certain on her face
What one can read on her face
On the skin of her legs
Is:
WALLS

Town, O Towns that are never seen
Towns without contours
May I live in you?

City of the dead
Mighty palaces built for wars
Towns laden with artificial trees
Explorations by pigeons and rats

There are women
There are men
There are dogs which make their kennels in the
  holes of your walls

Towns, wait for me
I am coming, I am going to come, I may possibly
  come
I shall visit you

One cannot really talk of you, towns
O Nineveh
O Byzantium
O Tlaxcala, Pachacamac, Warsaw, Pitsanulok
O Tenóchtitlan
One cannot write words of love on your walls
Until you are dead.

SELF-CRITICISM

I wish I were able to write the way one speaks. I wish that, one day, the thin barrier of white paper that protects and isolates me might dissolve. What can there be behind this dazzling rectangle, what paradise or hell is hiding on the other side of this opaque window? Yes, how I wish I knew all that. The great hypocrisy of writing — and also this huge joy at the distance established, the gloves I put on in order to touch the world, to touch myself — resides precisely in this matter which interposes itself between me and myself, this circuitous route by means of which I address myself.

Those who claim that one cries out, those who want one to love or to hate, who want one to be oneself, just like that, directly and naturally: they are lying. There are no cries in literature, there can be neither voices nor gestures in literature. There is nothing but murmurs, sounds coming from very far away after having travelled for centuries from one end of the universe to the other.

When I write, I am he who does not speak.

My thought is abandoned throughout the vast, out-stretched night that separates my instant of self-awareness from the moment which liberates the word. My thought has fled, aimless, formless. Who speaks of the significant and the signified? Why analyse my spoken word so as to detach it from real movement? All of it false, all of it language about language. What remains true, and constant, is writing's abandonment of reality, loss of meaning, logical madness. Faced with the sight of a tiny fragment of the world, I conceive nothing, I invent nothing. I recite, following the ancient system that was bequeathed to me. The fact is that it really is a game, the cruellest, most nugatory of all games. To conceive on the basis of the norms of conception, to write on the basis of handwriting, to *be* on the basis of being. There is no table, chair, clenched hand, blue ballpoint pen with chewed end. There is no white paper, nor a twist of black paper that creeps forward by leapfrogging over itself. *None* of that exists. There is nothing but the fearful void which I measure ceaselessly, the infinite which I measure with my slide-rule in my hand. So, where is the world? Where is the square of sun and air, of steam, of sulphur, of metal hidden in the earth, of shadow, of perfume, of bitter or salty tastes? It is there, just there, behind the immaculate onion-skin lying flat on the wooden table. ('Leaf, be crumpled up!')

I wish I wrote the way one speaks. I wish I wrote the way one sings, or the way one yells, or simply the way one lights a cigarette with a match and smokes gently, thinking of unimportant things. But that is simply not done. So I write the way one writes, sitting on a straw-bottomed chair, head tilted slightly to the left, right forearm carrying at its end a hand resembling a tarantula in the process of paying out its path of entwined twigs and spittle. ('Leaf, be burned in the glass ashtray!')

Behind all the papers, behind all the photos, there is a universe which I know well but which I am never able to rediscover. Behind the glass wall of bottles, and beneath the plateaux of tables, there is a calm phantom which watches me wordlessly.

I peer in vain at the flimsy sheet, reading the words that

follow each other. I read in vain what is written between the
words, such as:

Hablar: ni, tlatoa
Habla: Tlatolli
H. en lengua extraña: Cecni tlatolli yc nitlatoa

I try in vain to see everything, my eyes can penetrate no
farther. Impossible to enter the kingdom. Impossible to travel
in the blurred photos full of large grey clouds floating in a
black sky. Impossible to pass through the glass door on
which is written:

('Leaf, be burned by the eyes' gaze!')

And in a word, I, frail spirit that I am, with my red-rimmed
eyes, constricted throat, itching hands, yes, it is true, I do
likewise. That is how I avenge myself, when, at night, I open
the door giving access to my warm, light-filled corridor, and
then (but who would really be likely to enter, since vision as it
reads constitutes a speedier flight even than that of the
telescope which takes the star that seems so close and thrusts
it thousands of light-years away?) bar the way.

I wish I wrote the way one sends postcards. But it cannot
be done. I cannot simply say: I went here, and then there,
and then I took the train for Penang, and one day, while I was
hugging the coast of Panama between Nargana island and
Tikantiki island, the engine broke down and I had to paddle.
Or that on the road to Oaxaca, a fat, moustachioed man in a
mauve Cadillac drew his revolver and aimed it at me, yelling:
'Que quieres?' I could have told all that very quickly, it
happened just like that, a few incidents from a glorious life,
brought impeccably to light. The time I smoked an Esfinge
cigarette, on Christmas Day, on the beach at San Juan del
Sur. The day I entered the dark shop at Saraburi, and said to
the man behind the counter:

'Khrung Thong mi maï kap?'

'Mi kap.'

Or the time I was in the smoke-filled room that reeked of beer, and said to Hastings:

'I used to be rather good, y'know, but now ... '

Or, on another occasion, to Mezcala:

'Quempatio?'

Or, that day, standing in front of the dog which had its ears cocked:

'Yap! Yap!'

All these languages that I have made use of, and all these faces in which the mobile mouth has opened for an instant to let strange, self-assured sounds emerge. I shall not forget them. I cannot forget them. But the fact remains that I could never translate them into other words, nor turn them into true and mildly adventurous stories. Nothing has happened. I know nothing. I was not capable of sending you the post-cards at the right moment.

So how could I possibly say what is meant by misery, or love, or fear? Perhaps people write novels simply because they do not know how to compose letters, or vice versa.

The Chilam Balam

The book of Enigmas
The sacred riddles
What is licked by the jaguar's tongue? Fire.
Iglukik legend of the man transformed into woman:
> A human being over here
> A penis over here.
> May the opening be wide
> and spacious.
> Opening, opening, opening!

The Walam Olum

But the journey must continue farther still, later still. I flee so that I shall no longer know anything about the future. Damnation take the years ahead, blind years! I no longer want to see the doors swing open. One must discard all the things that resemble reality and that are lies, nothing but lies. One must surrender oneself, like a sinking ship. One must search far away, in an upside-down world, one must rummage in the past. Find the father you never knew, the mother who never bore you. Concrete platforms, shop windows, you say: tomorrow! tomorrow! and men's eyes gleam with covetous desire. But I know what is lying in wait. This vision of the earth splitting apart, of mouths hollowing out their greedy whorls, is within me, horribly. I am in reverse. I am fleeing to be outside myself, to be bigger than myself. I do not want to know any countries. To know is to die. I do not want to know any women. To know women is to enter the scheme of mortal things.

I am nothing more than a wheel. I am empty of all thought, all imagination. I am empty of all fixed desire. Great highway of knowledge, slipstream, racetrack, prairie, cordillera of knowledge. I am continually exceeding limits. That is what one must do. Cross through the walls, smash the windowpanes, tear off the flowered wallpapers, break the horizon into little bits. It is time to leave the eternal room. It is time to find something else to say, something else to think, something else to see. I am free, I am probably free. Being free: does that not mean walking alone down the muddy streets of Huejuquilla, past the plaster houses? Being free: does that not mean riding up into the deserted mountains, under the blue sky which houses the sun? Movement is the only true self-awareness. Being free: does that not mean being large, lively, swift like oneself?

Time is immense. I see it everywhere, spread over the earth. It has huge masses of rock weighing tons, it has rivers that flow to the sea, it has innumerable trees, clouds, men. Time is there, on display in the open countryside, the mountains, the plains where towns have their being. It is not a dream. If time existed only in men's minds it would not be worth discussing. But it is there in front of me, absolutely real. It lacks nothing. Nothing has been forgotten. All the inexhaustible centuries are there, painted on the red earth, drawn on the limestone cliffs, stretched out over the sea. When I walk through the middle of this fabulous landscape, I am walking through time itself. I scale ravines, I cross forests of filaos, I drink water from pools full of leeches. All of that is a voyage through time's landscape. What I am fleeing from is mankind's future. But the hereafter, the universal advent is there, too, living all around me. It has no need of signs or symbols. It is whole. It breathes. It is known. It has the sky's air, the streams' water, the sharp peaks' rocks, the sun's heat, the frost's coldness. It has the emptiness of space, of the stars, of the galaxies. I will tell you what my flight entails: going from one end of time to the other, at a greater speed than light. Or alternatively, lying on my back in the dry grass, one day, looking up at the motionless sky which carries a detailed drawing of everything that has happened and everything that is going to happen.

Nothing is forgotten: so many men have died, without

anything changing in the world. In the fields, along the edges of roads, now, there are these little wooden crosses bearing neither name nor address; I flee through the middle of the forest of little crosses, and I remember everything.

It was yesterday. It was today. I have not forgotten their thin faces, their shining eyes, their quick, confident gestures. So many women have departed, too, women I still love despite the distance. They are still there. A close look is all that is needed. If one tilts the drawing a little askew, one will see the outline of their faces and bodies appear, there, traced by the lines of the foliage, by the horizon's hills, by the wings of the sparrow hawk or by the clouds' globes.

When I walk along like this, it is with them that I am walking. I follow the rhythm of their highlanders' pace, while they advance along the mule-path, under the blazing sun. I see their white costumes, their wide-brimmed hats, and the rifles that they carry slung across their backs. Cartridge-belts are draped around their hips, and a double bag and rolled blanket covers the left shoulder. They make quick progress, marching for days on end without resting. When evening comes, they light a fire and cook some corn-flour. They sleep rolled up in their blankets, their heads resting on their rifle butts. They never leave a trace behind them: they bury their excrements, and pile rocks over the dead fire to hide the scorched earth. I am one of them. I am always with them. I am fleeing along the same path that they are taking, stealthily across the mountains. I skirt great desert sierras where there is a red plant which is fatal to horses when eaten. I see the sun sparkling above the earth, the sun of eternity. My feet are gashed by flints, my limbs ache with weariness. Sometimes we are so thirsty that we chew bitter berries from trees. It is so cold at night that our bones are pierced through and through. We are afraid. We communicate in gestures, or whisper as we march. The mountains open up, always revealing new mountains. We all think and say the same things: the people of Mezquitic are traitors; the day before yesterday the federals hanged ten men and a child from the branches of a single tree. Among our company is a big, burly man whose red hair is cut short. Each morning, at dawn, he kneels on the ground and prays. Then he distributes the communion, the morsels of stale bread. Nothing has been forgotten. All the sufferings and deaths are alive in this landscape, inextricably mingled with its outspread beauty. Nothing has been of any use. But then the landscapes have not been of any use, either. They are there. They have time.

One day, we climbed up to a plateau covered with flat stones. That is what it is called. The Plateau of Stones. We skirted the walls that snake across the scrub. When the first rifle-shots rang out we could see nothing. The sun was high in the black-blue sky, the heat scorched the flat stones. We threw ourselves on the ground, and began firing at random. The battle lasted three days and two nights. The red-haired man gave orders. Occasionally, a prisoner was brought in. There was one who looked at us with eyes full of hatred. He said: 'You will die, all of you!' The red-haired man gave him absolution and made the sign of the cross; then he placed his revolver against the prisoner's temple and fired.

Nothing is effaced. Everything is always there, present in the pure air. It is that very essence that I inhale. By the third day we had realized that it was no longer possible to make our way out. The rifle reports had come closer and closer. Already, the dry ground had sprouted many little wooden crosses. The men were so thirsty that they sucked their own blood, and trembled with fever. They were so tired that they fell asleep like slabs of stone.

Then, around three in the afternoon, we heard the army

colonel shouting something. The hundred and fifty soldiers began racing towards the stone walls, the sounds of their running feet gradually converging. Bullets struck from all sides, the rattle of shots was continual now. The sun blazed in the centre of a sky that had turned even deeper blue, even deeper black. That is where we died, all of us, one after the other, our bodies riddled by dozens of bullets. All except one, who was just wounded. They hanged him the following day. We were not buried, and the vultures, wolves and ants ate us up.

And yet we are there, still. The dry mountains are there, too, and the Plateau of Stones, and the sun glittering in the black-blue sky. The flight leads from one end of time to the other, but it never goes outside the boundaries of the stone landscape. It destroys nothing. It sets nothing down in books, it fixes nothing in the yellowing photographs of hanged children. It is true, and precise, and living. Now is perhaps the right moment to set down the words of this nasal song, this deeply moving song:

> I am going to sing you a corrido
> About a friend of my country
> Called José Valentin
> Who was trapped and shot on the mountain
>
> And I want to recall
> That winter evening when
> As ill luck would have it
> Valentin fell into the hands of the Government
>
> The captain asked him
> What people were in command
> There are eight hundred soldiers who have occupied
> Olanda's farm

The colonel asked him
What people were acting as guides
There are eight hundred soldiers whom
Mariano Mejía is leading across the mountain

Valentin being a man
Refused to tell them anything
I am a true man one of those who devised
The Revolution

On the way to the hillside
Valentin felt like weeping
O Mother of Guadeloupe
Because of your religion they are going to kill me

Fly fly little dove
And tell what he told you
This is the ballad of a valiant man
Named Valentin

The flight leads in the direction of villages of mud huts with thatched roofs, clinging to the sides of mountains. It leads there at the end of long exhausting rides through forests and across the deserts of high plateaux. It involves crossing canyons more than a thousand feet deep. It involves descending endless paths, surrounded by silence, stubbing one's feet against the sharp pebbles embedded in the ground. It is a long, painful march that is a constant process of flinging towards the rear. The sun scorches the back of the neck, the empty sky is amorphous, the chunks of rock send out dazzling sparkles. There is so much power, so much light. It is words and rhythms that vanish backward, that are uprooted at each step. Emptiness enters slowly, stripping away, reducing to ashes, expelling. While the person known as Y. Man walks ahead of it, without ever pausing, the emptiness spreads out, penetrates everything. Movie houses, television sets, glossy magazines, jazz records, cafés, churches all disintegrate. The motionless sky strikes the head with terrible blows, demanding that one should be quiet at last. All the flights from reality, the books, photo albums, primers, all the songs and stories. Expelled, transformed into emptiness.

So, at the end, there is this circular village, inhabited by people who refuse. One day, around four in the afternoon, he enters the village along with a caravan of donkeys all loaded with cartons of beer. The rain is falling. He squats on the ground, under a tree, and waits. The tree is very big, and they are all able to shelter under its spreading branches. The donkeys and mules, relieved of their loads, graze in the rain. The others, those who refuse, are standing around the tree, arms crossed, watching. Nobody asks anybody anything.

Santa Catalina, under the tree.

It started raining as we entered.
The governor sent word that it was impossible to
give us lodging:
did others give *them* lodging when they went down
into the plain?
There was a tree, a very big tree
At least nine hundred years old.
Tree, tree,
living column with thousands of living leaves
tree with immense branches stretching towards
    the West,
the North, the South, and the East.
Sightless, voiceless, immobile tree,
Calm old tree
Indifferent
tree.
Perhaps it is you who taught me:
No truth
No truth!
You don't write
You stay put, you want nothing.
You never *give* anything.
Around the base
the masses of dead leaves made a carpet.

We slept on that carpet.
We lit a fire with the dead leaves,
and sat upon the roots protruding from the ground.
I made use of the tree,
but it did nothing for me in return.
Tree,
Tree haunted by hanged men
Tree with secret leaves
Tree smelling like a plant

Tree.
You are a giant vegetable
And I am a dwarfish man.

That is probably what he was thinking, just at that moment.
It is difficult to tell. Or maybe he was thinking:

'I renounce the Greco-Roman world! I am no longer its
son. I can no longer be a member of its race. I know nothing
about it any longer. Yesterday, no doubt, the world died
peacefully, sitting in its armchair. This man's eyes remained
as dry as pebbles. Filthy Latin world, you wanted to make a
slave out of me, so that I should kill, brand with a red-hot
iron, rape in your name. But I am a thoroughly ungrateful
son who bears no respect towards his dead father. Your wars
were useless, your laws were phony: I have no illusions on
that score. I am the bad son who laughs, and pisses on his
dead father's grave. Goodbye, farewell, I no longer have a
father, I no longer have a world.

'A civilization without secrets no longer has any surprises to
offer. The one thing left for me to learn is how to forget it.
Vast speechless landscapes, prairies, lakes, arid plateaux,
mosquito-infested lagoons! Come to my aid! Your silences are
welcome, because they kill men. I am nowhere. I have

left my world behind, and have not yet found another. That is the tragic adventure. I have departed, but not yet arrived. All the theories were false, all the inflated words that had been put into my head answered no purpose. It is easy to understand that: they were mute words, voiceless parrots. To doubt is to believe: I have slid beyond doubt. I am *stupefied*. I scarcely move. A step here, one step farther, a movement of the hand, a trembling of the eyelid. I can see what is happening all around my body. What I see, I know. What I know, is emptiness ... Let us wait. But for what? Watch out for what? Nothing comes. I am seized by the rocks, trees cover my face. That is all perfectly normal. Calm, calm. Did those who fed me, those who created me, know what they were doing? I am no longer a judge in any trial. I no longer want to give evidence. Did I really see the accident, see what happened? Was I THERE? No, I can no longer swear to anything. There must be moments when, despite willingness of body and habit of mind, I must have a peculiar air of being absent.

'I write that I do not know any longer. But when I write that, it is with the hand, the inspiration and the words of the white man. I say that I am no longer on this earth. But I say it while resting my weight upon this earth. Ancient trick of an ancient double-dealing people! I make use of negatives, but behind me, within me, is an imperceptible phantom nodding "yes".

'What men, then, are capable of teaching me something? The farther I advance in space, the farther men retreat. There are no Malays, or Laotians, or Chinese, or Maya Quichés, or Huichols. There is only the white man, everywhere, wearing tawdry fancy-dress to help him delude people more effectively. Miserable secret society that brings into the world and baptizes ... What I deny, I affirm twice over.

'Now, here is what other men can give me: the name of INTRUDER.'

The Indian? The Indian, the Arab, the Negrito, the Karen, the Burmese highlander. Those whom they do not kill, they turn into clowns. Accursed white race, to which I belong, and which wants nothing to change. Anthropologists, priests, merchants, philanthropists, travellers: all of them, soldiers in disguise.

But see: the Indian, diminutive though he may be, looks down on you. He will never forget; not he. He knows very well who you are. He has judged you since childhood. He knows very well what you are hiding.

You go forward to meet him, your hand outstretched, exuding your white man's coarse, smug frankness; and you say to him, in your coarse, smug voice: 'Kea Aco!', as though, in a flash, everything was going to be forgotten. But he turns his head away, refusing to look at you. He does not give a damn for your greeting. If he is feeling polite, if he is not particularly angry with you, he goes away without answering. But if he takes a dislike to you, then he turns brusquely, and there is a strange light glowing in his eyes which bodes you no good, no good at all. He thrusts his hand out in your direction, and spits out a single word, an order:

'Cigarillo!'

What alternative is there but to give him his cigarette?

Language: secret code. Food for thought, there, for ethnographers, anthropologists, linguists. All those who come along with their tape recorders and their notebooks, to manufacture dictionaries. They want to learn the native's language, so as to steal his secrets, so as to saddle him with theses. What impudence! Then they sit under a tree, at midday, and produce a book. A beautiful, fat book such as white men are so good at producing, six hundred close-set pages covered with little black signs. Text! With a fine abstract title such as civilized people are so good at producing. Something like WORDS AND THINGS. The Indian, naturally, is immediately distrustful. Following the letters with his finger, he reads the title on the cover:

'Vorreddess antt theengess.'

He laughs. Happy not to have understood. The sounds which his mouth has just pronounced are magic.

So now he has to be made to translate that. Into Spanish, first.

'Las palabras y las cosas.'

The boy laughs. He still does not understand. It has to be explained to him.

'Las palabras ... Y las cosas ... Es que dice.'

'Las palabras ... Y las cosas ... '

'Si! Ahora, como se dice en Huichol?'

The boy draws his face back. He is slightly scared, or ashamed. Now he is serious. He does not want to answer. Supposing it were a trap? Why should this fellow of a different race want to know all that? He hesitates, then, slowly and ironically, and with a note of alarm, too, utters the first phrase that every Indian learns, the phrase that he invariably brings out when he senses danger.

'Quien saaabe?'

A little later, when he has got used to the idea:

'Come now, how does one say that in Huichol?'

'That is not said.'

'What, that is not said?'

'No.'

'Look. Las palabras, what is the Huichol word for that?'
'I don't know.'
'Yes, look. Las palabras. When someone speaks, how does
one say that?'
'When one speaks?'
'Yes, to speak, like that, to speak, what is the Huichol for
that?'
'Quien saaabe?'
'How do you say to speak?'
'To speak?'
'Yes, to speak?'
'Niuki.'
'Niuki?'
'Niuki.'
'Good, niuki. And things, then, what is the Huichol word
for things?'
'Things?'
'Yes, things.'
'I don't know.'
'There is no word for things?'
'No ... '
'Things, I mean ... There is no word for trees, flowers,
houses, food, all that?'
'Food?'
'Yes, and shoes, cigarettes.'
'Everything?'
'All *things*, yes.'
'Perhaps, yes, who knows?'
'What is the word for that?'
'Pinné.'
'Peenay?'
'Pinné.'
'Pinné is things?'

'Yes, things in groups.'

'Good, now, Niuki, words, Pinné, things. How does one say and?'

'And?'

'Yes.'

'And? that is Tenga.'

'Tenga?'

'Tenga, tenga.'

'Good. So, niuki tenga pinné. Niuki tenga pinné. Words and things.'

And immediately, unexpectedly, peals of laughter ring out, laughter which means, though you will never realize it: what a clown, huh, what a donkey, that one trying to speak a language that doesn't belong to him ...

The fact is that, for the Huichol, and for all those who refuse, who are in flight, words and things are precisely what language does not speak about. Language is a natural act which implies belonging. He who exists, speaks. He who does not speak, does not exist. He has no place in the world. The Huichol language is Huichol to the same degree as the Huichol earth, the Huichol sky, religion, tattooing, dress, the *peyoteros*' hat. It is not enough to pronounce the syllables of the Huichol language to be Huichol. That is obvious.

Of course, in such circumstances, it is impossible to transpose and translate. The word has no equivalent because, fundamentally, it evokes nothing apart from what the community designates.

This closing-in of language is aggressive. It is a flight. But it is the very direction of language. Not everyone who wants, can speak. If a person can speak, it is because he has received, by birth, the implicit authorization of the speaking community. The antithesis is simple, and provides the proof of the intransgressible secret: those who do not speak Huichol are *mute*. Their foreign language is incapable of becoming another modality of the expressible; it is made of nothing but noises. Coherent noises, which correspond to certain exchange values, but noises all the same. The Huichol language is not a system of signification. It is a religious, political, family system. Like all true bonds, those of family or of faith, it cannot be acquired. It is magic.

Look of astonishment and distrust on the face of the Indian whom the white man or the half-breed addresses in his own language.

'Kea Aco!'

'Buenos dias,' says the Indian, and he is on the defensive. What kind of stranger is this, trying to steal words?

Face frozen immediately, irritated disdain.

'Kepettitewa?'

Face of stone. Mouth set tight, eyes narrowed, ears that do not want to hear.

'Kepawitaripahoca?'

Body of stone, too, man turned into statue, who does not want to, who does not want anything. Soul curled up in a ball. He has understood. It is perfectly clear that he has understood. But comprehension has come upon him like a moving wall, and has forced him to take refuge in inaccessible places. The words arrive, devoid of meaning. They come like projectiles, and so he shrinks back, withdraws into his shadow.

'Hawtya. Ac kixa neninakeriaga niuki? Jé?'

It is not a question of fear, it is a question of an intrusion, the most odious of all intrusions. Rather as though a dog were suddenly to raise its head and say to its master:

'I beg your pardon, but the whale is a mammal.'

Alternatively, he begins laughing, leaning his head a little to one side.

'No entendio. Quien sabe que dice?'

Is it my fault if I belong to the race of thieves? The white man has always stolen everything from everyone. From the Jews, Arabs, Hindus, Chinese, Negroes, Aztecs, Japanese, Balinese. When he has had his fill of stealing territories and slaves, the white man has begun stealing cultures. He has stolen religion from the Jews, science from the Arabs, literature from the Hindus. When he finished stealing the bodies of Negroes, he stole their music, their dances, their art. When the Christian religion, a religion that became contemptible, a religion for philistines, no longer satisfied him, he turned back toward the religion of India. In Mexico, the white man is first and foremost a stealer of lands. Then, in next to no time, because land itself was not enough, he develops into a stealer of souls. First he seizes the towns, then he razes the temples. And when the conquered people has nothing left, when the white man has despoiled and enslaved, when he has destroyed the people's language and faith, when he has evicted him from the best lands, when he has forced him to taste poverty, the real poverty of the white man; when he has ruined his race by stealing his women, when he has turned it into a tribe of servants at his beck and call, the white man still feels dissatisfied with his achievements. So what does he do? He steals the conquered people's past. In newspapers, books, lectures, on statues: 'Indian? Ah yes, Indian. I have Indian blood, myself. My ancestors, the Aztecs, Cuauhtemoc, Moctesuhzoma, Tlaloc, Cuauhcoatl, Tonatiuh. The Pyramids. Teotihuacan. Tezcoco, Mitla, Tlaxcala. That's what my ancestors did.' But if you draw him aside, you will immediately see hatred in his eyes, his ancient hatred for the vanquished. 'The Indians? Listen, the only solution is extermination. When there are no more Indians left, we might accomplish something around here.' The same thing when a young girl quarrels with a cab driver in the street. She searches her mind quickly for the worst, most comprehensive insult. She finds it suddenly: 'Indito!'

Then he had another thought:

'There they are, in the dense, humid forest, those who did not know how to refuse. Those whom the world is in the process of annihilating with its airplanes, tape recorders, Bibles and vaccines. They did not realize how ignoble it was to be Lacandon, in the eyes of people named Smith or Dupont. They did not realize that there were people thirsty for blood, watching for the right moment to pounce upon them, mummify them, palatalize them, analyse them to death!

Tourists, missionaries, explorers, journalists, prospectors, colonists, conquerors, sailors, prospectors for gold, peddlars of exoticism, trail-blazers, aviators, suntanned holiday-makers, hunters of precious stones, visitors of pagodas and museums, devotees of colour transparencies, the whole pack of you, incompetent philosophers of relativity, hunchbacked apostles of universalism, wily urbanists, economists, indigenists, messengers of peace and civilization in the style of soap salesmen, and you, cultural missions, embassies, Franco-Sudanese or Argentine-Khmer friendship societies, Goethe-&-Co.-type institutions, world experts, bushrangers, safari organizers, Alpinists, Indologists, Pygmy-lovers, Maori-worshippers, and you, comic opera revolutionaries, socialists imprisoned within the walls of your manifestoes, wreckers, and you too, drinkers of peyotl, chewers of hallucinogenic mushrooms whose jaws will grind out books about it, marauding drug-addicts, sharks, property owners, men who have only one god, and only one wife, cloud of locusts, army of rats intoxicated with everything unusual, I HATE YOU.'

Signed:

ISKUIR

During that time, Y. M. Hogan was travelling by pirogue along the Rio Chucunaque.

The Rio Chucunaque flowed slowly down to the sea. It went on flowing down, day after day, never stopping. At its mouth, it was wide and dirty, a muddy lake in which rotting tree trunks floated. Motorboats ploughed furrows through its moving mass. Higher up, the Rio Chucunaque was clear, narrower, with whirlpools, rapids, and oily shallows. Y. M. Hogan was seated in the front of the pirogue, peering closely into the sparkling water, and putting out his left or his right hand to give warning of dangers. Along the banks, among the trees, were the openings of other rivers, the Rio Chico, the Rio Tuquesa, the Rio Canglón, the Rio Ucurgantí, the Rio Mortí. Liquid branches never ceased sprouting from the main stem. During that time, Y. M. Hogan was paddling upstream along the Rio Chucunaque.

Rivers.

Rivers.

Roots of the sea.

THE FLUTE PLAYER AT CUZCO

One day, Hogan met the man who played a kind of flute at Cuzco. This happened in a big, deserted square surrounded by arcaded houses, at about eleven at night. It was cold. The sky was black, and the square shone dimly in the light of the street lamps. There was no noise. Even the cars were asleep. On one side of the square there was this big pointed building, with a portal that was open. As he passed by, Hogan had noticed this opening in the black walls, and deep inside, this sort of immense grotto glittering with gold. He had seen that image in a split second: in the centre of the house looking like a castle, the rain of yellow gold and rays of light. Women's knees were rubbing against the stone slabs. The gold crushed the men standing in the nave; the golden vault weighed on the women's shoulders. In the silent cavern, where the cold battled against body temperature the poor and wretched had all become children. He had seen that, too: the nervous gesture of fingers flying to the brow, the chest, then the mouth. In the castle's great hall, the kneeling men and women were engaged in touching the golden god.

A little farther on, under the arcades, Hogan had noticed the flute player. He was not playing at that moment. He was leaning against a wall, waiting. A few children were standing around, watching him. When Hogan stopped near one of the pillars, the man stepped forward one pace. Then he said, in an odd, husky voice:

'Now, the gringo's tango.'

And he began to sing a tango tune. At the same time, he danced. He raised his arms and spun round. He swayed to the left, then to the right, then spun round. Hogan and the children watched him without saying anything. The cold wind blew steadily along the corridor of the arcades, carrying bits of paper along with it. The man was wearing coarse linen trousers, scuffed shoes and a mouldy-coloured old sweater. His eyes were almost slits in his brown face, and his cheeks were wrinkled. His hands were red with cold.

When he had finished dancing, he rummaged in a bag propped against the wall. The first thing he took out of it was quite extraordinary: a sun cut out of a metal can with a pair of scissors. He fastened this to his forehead with a piece of string. He did this slowly, gravely, and the sun began shining on his forehead with the brightness of tin. The next thing he took out of the bag was a big, seven-tubed pan-pipe called an Arca. He blew into all the tubes, to try them out. Then he looked at Hogan and said:

'Virgen de Calakumo.'

Or something like that. He began playing.

From the first moment, Hogan realized that it was not music. The sounds coming out of the pipe's flutes were cries, not music. The harsh sounds tumbled out, rose, descended. They lacerated the silence with their breathy noises, they hesitated; it was not their nature to explain, or to construct. The raspings of loud breath grated against the walls of the house, pierced through the icy wind, bombarded the ears. They were sharp and rapid, and at the same time they exhaled heavily and dolefully.

The man wearing a tin sun on his forehead went on blowing into the pan-pipe's flutes. He was hunched over the reed tubes, blowing with all his might, his mouth darting to and fro. From time to time he paused to recover his breath, and one could hear the air whistle as it entered his lungs. Then the harsh sounds started up once more, hesitated, striking the silence one after the other. Around him, the square was almost deserted because of the cold, and the walls of the houses were like rocky cliffs, without doors or windows. The children did not move. Hogan did not move. Under their feet, the slabs of concrete sent out icy waves which crept up their clothes and settled in the region of the heart.

With his back against the wall, the man wearing the tin sun on his forehead began to move. Still bent over the outsize pan-pipe, he began to lurch. He lifted his legs high in the air, one after the other, then stamped his feet hard on the ground, so that the heels rang. He leant his head to one side, then threw it back, and the tin sun glittered on his black face. And all the time, the pipe's cries gushed and rasped. It was always the same thing that emerged from the seven attached flutes. Three ascending notes. Then three descending notes. It had no ending. The sounds of breathing hesitated, lurched; the grave, heavy voice, the voice that emerged from solitude and cold. The voice gasped, crept over the concrete ground, broke its way through the silence and the night. *What are the sad apertures through which the reeds cry out?*

On the bronze-hued forehead, the tin sun fastened with string rose and fell. In the dim passageway it shone with harsh reflections, like a car's headlamp.

That is what happened. The man played, kicking up his legs and swaying to and fro, and Hogan knew that music could never exist again. From now on, there would be nothing but these cries of birds, these stridulations of grasshoppers, this raucous breathing of a dying animal. From now on, there would be nothing but these efforts, this labouring over the pipe's tubes, indefatigably, these three notes rising, then falling, these six eternal tones which composed the world. The man had come from far away, crossing dusty mountains in ancient buses with broken windowpanes. He had left a place called Cojata, or perhaps even the high plateaux of Bolivia, to play his six notes on his pan-pipe. Each time he arrived in a town, he fastened the tin sun to his forehead, rested his back against a wall, at one side of a deserted square, at night, and blew. Sometimes people gave him food. And he danced heavily, making harrowing noises with his mouth as it glided along the reed tubes. Certainly, it did not mean anything, it demanded neither tears nor clicking of the fingers. It was a labour like any other, monotonous, a labouring of lungs and lips. It was like blowing down a long metal tube and watching the globule of glass swell and fill out. At first the glass is the colour of light, then it becomes red, then grey, and the glassblower whirls it round, above his head, to stretch it thinner.

It was the melody of a fugue relieved of all its useless noises. Become pure. Stripped of all the humming, become the simple breath of a man who has no desire to describe the world, who has no desire to imitate the wind or the rain, who no longer has anything to do with the real. True respiration which utters its little cries, which raises its taut stems in the transparent air, which is itself, magnificently itself, itself for itself, the essence of itself.

No houses, no towns, no spaces that have been reconnoitred, either on maps or in wars. But a sound that carries you away, a rhythm that sweeps you off the ground, a calm, unerring glide; and the sorrowful sound emerging from the reed tubes is the sound of a running engine.

Suddenly, the man stopped and lowered the pan-pipe from his mouth. He was exhausted, scarcely able to breathe.

Hogan could see the drops of sweat running down the man's cheeks, could hear the sound of the man's breath. Without saying anything, he placed a silver coin on the ground, and he saw that it shone with a very harsh glitter, like the tin sun on the man's forehead. Then he went away, crossing the square where the cold wind was still blowing.

The world is small. The world has become so small that, suddenly, one can hardly see it. The world has become just like a precious stone, a sort of alexandrite attached to a young woman's slender hand. Peculiar violet dot so small that the eye looking at it loses its way. Myriads of minuscule contracted rainbows reign inside the bevelled crystal. The world has become similar to a window always opening on to the same scene, a little herb garden, an old palm tree with fissured bark, two or three pots of dusty geraniums, a sky, a cloud, sometimes a live bird engaged in flying.

The world is narrow, today. One is balanced on its rim, like on the edge of a new Gillette blade. One progresses with gliding movements, sometimes cutting oneself, scarcely grazing the thin ground. One is on a blade of grass. The world has shrunk like that, in one or two nights, and no one has been able to discover how it happened. The world is a weight raised laboriously by the thoracic cage eager for air There is no air left. There is almost no water left. Just a few more drops, standing out in beads on the leaves of brambles, and it will all be over. The world is sweating like a sick stone. The world scarcely lasts longer than the phrase one writes, not even as long, scarcely as long as a quick cry such as 'Wa!' or 'Ho!'

The world is there, hidden at the back of the camera obscura, perceptible for the time it takes to press a button, when the terribly swift eyelid opens and closes again, while the star of light flashes above the lens.

World, snapped, stolen, tiny crumb of a world, flicking of fingers, synchronism of the machine-gun that perforates the circle of the airplane's propeller with a single streak of its lightning.

DEAD EVERLASTING END

> Don Aurelio watches the sun sink behind the mountains and says, simply: 'Suppose it never rises again?'

SELF-CRITICISM

Comedian! Ham actor! It is time to bring your pantomime to a halt. It is time to stop your mumbling, time for your muscles to reabsorb their tremors; for all your roads to take to the air like drawbridges. Nobody is taken in by the performance any longer. You pretend that you are not there, but you are, you are! You pretend to be bigger than you really are. You wear the masks of masters such as you will never be, you want to imitate the gestures which you yourself could never create. Incapable of conquering the world, you reject it. But the figure who really occupies your skin, deep inside you, is the court jester. Stop grinning and grimacing. It is time to put on an anonymous face, the face of the man who does not speak. It is time to assume your name.

Thought is so vast that no one will ever be able to identify it. Thought is so distant, gushes forth so fast and so vigorously that it can never be reduced to scribblings on paper or on walls. No more analysing, from now on. No more looking at things which should not be looked at. Come out from your warren! Come out into the light! Lose yourself! Just because you were acquainted with this and that, you would have liked to find that the world could be expressed in a few reveries. What an illusion! The wind blows across the centuries on to your words, and carries them away. The great storm that constitutes the universe does not care a rap for the screens you set up. It hurls at you its millions of miles per hour, crushes with all its light, with all its lives which are neither proofs nor explanations but miracles. You would have liked to find that death extinguishes the world; oh yes, you would. That the language of man is equally that of stones and cacti. You would have been delighted if there were never any children around. You would have liked so much to be able to turn into a table or an apple, as the mood took you, just so as to escape from your skin, to flee your prison. You would have been delighted if passions and feelings ceased to exist, thinking how much simpler things would be.

To go away and change completely. If only there had been lands where the people never died, where the women are always beautiful and always know how to love. Things would have been very simple. But there were no such lands. If only there had been some terrible catastrophe, one day, one that set the horizon ablaze from one end to the other, or perhaps a thousand year war, that would have arranged things nicely, would it not? But there were no wars, and the people who died suddenly, while working in their fields, never knew the reason. When steel-shelled automobiles shot off the expressway and crashed slowly into ditches, there was nothing else to say but: ugliness, ugliness.

In the rectangular, low-ceilinged room. Seated in the sort of balcony that surrounds it. Yellow light, grey shadow. Sounds of spoons, plates, glasses. Sounds of footsteps. Sounds of tongues chattering, jaws chewing, throats swallowing. In the centre of the room, illuminated heads, mirthful faces. Suddenly, the gaze settles on a point in the room, a red apparition trembling on the far horizon. This sun is setting, here, night is coming, the stars are beginning to stir. In the world's isolated grotto, inside the concrete fortress, like being in the centre of an impregnable blockhouse. Nothing can penetrate as far as this. Nor can anything slip through the stone walls and escape. It is the end of the world, here, its heart, its skull, its fist.

Or again, the ceiling is low, padded, its stifling surface covered with ventilation louvres puffing out air. On the tables, plastic flowers stuck into copper vases. There. That is all. The human forms move, eat, talk, think or simply do nothing. A young girl dressed in white passes by, carrying, as though it were a chalice, a tall glass filled with whipped cream and ice cream topped by a cherry. A cloud of cigar smoke mingled with words and laughter rises from a table set for a banquet.

There. It is nothing. That is all there is to it. The world has been locked up, yet again, in a concrete room, and the look that settles on no matter what point of the red wall, the look that wants to understand, is lost for ever. It has fled from reality, it has quit the photogenic world. No matter how efficient the men may be in their head waiter's costumes, or how demure the women may be in their white smocks, he who enters here is lost. It is like being deaf in downtown Chicago at midday, or blind at the ocean's edge. It is to come back to the tiny corner that one should never have left, to let truth glide along with its terrible serpentine motion, to forget all that one ever knew. The big room with its four thick walls —so thick that even a thousand years of nibbling away with the teeth and scratching away with the nails would not pierce them —is here, there, there too, everywhere throughout the world. The soft, whimpering music cannot help, nor can the rain falling outside, nor can the sun. Room lined with concrete and marble, room lined with padding and glass, room of light and shadow peopled with mysterious desires, this is my body, my skull, my sack of skin. It's me, only me. This being so, how could I still write to you, joy, gentleness, calm, peace, love. Since, in this place, it is WAR.

I no longer want to be this comedian who never knew when it was time to stop. I shall certainly have to renounce my pretensions, sooner or later. It had seemed to me that all these gestures were unassailable. I had not made them from habit, or unconsciously, but because I was afraid. I have acted my part, like the others. Now the stage is emptying. Who will applaud me? I did not want to recognize the true problem, the one that is not so easy to resolve:

Twelve children singing in a choir.

Are they twelve soloists?

The ineluctable presence of time, space, night, the incomprehensible: is it, then, true that I shut this presence in with me only at the moment when I found out there would always be something on the outside? Have I only been myself in contrast to others? And all the same, am I not the person that I am because I try to appropriate the world (and occasionally succeed)?

He who writes books that aim to convince is a comedian, too, just a comedian. What has he got to offer others, apart from chains, still more chains? Fiction never liberated anyone. No one ever brought anything back from voyages through dream worlds. But perhaps that is exactly what I have always aimed at, without knowing it: not to teach, never to teach any lesson at all?

I suppose I have no choice but to go along with this strained comedy for some time yet.

What really bores me stiff about writing is that it is too brief. When the sentence comes to an end, how many things have remained outside! Words have failed me. They did not move quickly enough. I did not have the time to strike out in all the necessary directions, I did not possess enough weapons. The world slipped away from me, under my very eyes, in a fraction of a second, and I would have needed millions of eyes to recover it, to see it again. Men make wretched hunters. Their language is a catapult at moments when it needs to be a machine gun. One second, just a single second, and I shall have written you books for eternity! The absolute is demoniacal. It taunts me, in the fleeting spectacle, it pulls faces at me, it zooms through the air like a fly, it plunges into the very depths of the ocean. I had fled in order to rediscover the world. I had rushed headlong down my path, in order to recapture time in action. But I found out that the world fled more quickly than I did.

I no sooner look at the wall of that twelve-storeyed building than it vanishes. I seek a face in the crowd, a true face amid that sea of mobile masks, a face, yes, just one face that will pause and offer itself to my contemplation. But everything is too rapid. There is too much of everything. And while I write, throngs of walls, mountains and human faces escape, carrying me away with their weight. They want to make me experience the genuine fall, that fatal drop down into oblivion and silence. I wanted to imagine, but it was impossible: one invents nothing. The most one achieves is to brush blindly against the outer fringes of the crowd. I wanted to describe, but it was a fraudulent attempt: one does not describe. One is described. Muffled blows dealt out by the world which jostles me, jolts delivered by life: it is from you that all thoughts and systems derive. Words lie. Words say what they had never hoped to say, what was decided for them at the last moment. Dialectic of what? Inventory, what inventory? No, no. Rather, darkness, illusion, stupid sensations always lagging behind the real, and garrulous feelings floating 20,000 feet above their point of birth. I have fled. I have claimed that I have fled. But it is not true. It is the world which has fled from me. It has drawn me along on its path, and I never attained freedom.

I wanted to say everything, I wanted to do everything. I saw something happening in front of me, one day, very long ago: it was life emerging from the spoken word, as sharply defined as a dream, applied flawlessly to reality. I saw the precise pattern of the space over which I must leap, and I thought that that leap could be accomplished. But it could not. I remained a laggard, overtaken by my own thinking, left behind by the thinking of the grasses and seaweeds, by the thinking of light and stars.

I thought that to get to know a desert it was enough to have been there. I thought that to have seen the dogs dying along the Cholula road, or to have seen the eyes of the lepers at Chiengmai gave me the right to talk about it. To have seen! To have been there! Rubbish! The world is not a book, it proves nothing. It gives nothing. The spaces one has crossed were dark corridors with closed doors. The faces of the women to whom one gave oneself up completely: did they speak for anyone but themselves? The cities of man are secret. One walks along their streets, one sees them shine under one's feet, but one is not there, one never enters them. The dusty fields inhabited by people who are hungry, who wait patiently, are paradises of luxury and nourishment; shining at a vast distance from intelligence, at a vast distance from reason. They are not to be subjugated.

Writer, comedian, eager for sensations, whipping out his little notebook and jotting down: 'Dry air. Clouds. Poverty. The *barriadas* of Lima. The dancer who has had painted on his chest a fair-haired Christ crucified in front of a blue sky in which a red sun shines. Violence. Earthquakes.' What does all that mean? If the world were a sum of experiences, it would all be so easy. But it is not like that at all. Palestine cannot be added to Nepal, or Arkansas to Japan. The woman Laura and the man Hogan convey no real idea of themselves. Flint has nothing in common with limestone. Man as intellectual, eager to get to know things so as to be able to construct his systems. Man as comedian, eager to forget the world so as to make a witty remark. But the world is not a sum. It is an inexhaustible enumeration in which each figure remains itself, in its variation and its flight, in which no one has rights over anyone else, in which unknown strength and desire and action all hold sway together. Which is not a logical fusion, but an indescribable intermingling of myriads of bonds, threads, fissures, branches and roots. Comedian, yes, a comedian because you were afraid of silence, and all your talking was to cover up that fear and to intoxicate yourself with the idea of your own materiality!

I could have told you about the sea which swells and subsides around the flat triangular rock. I could have told you about the Pachacamac desert which is rotting away, about the Mombacho volcano, or about the odour of fish at Lofoten. I could have told you about the colour of the sky at Khartoum, about the size of the mosquitoes in Mukkala, about the state of the weather in Calcutta. I could have told you, too, about the cry the jaguarundi utters to lure birds, and about the armoured eyes of the praying mantis. At a pinch, I could have told you something about the feelings which flutter through tender souls when a (handsome) (young) man meets a (beautiful) (young) girl. Then, about the hatred that produces clenched fists, the long, brooding hatred that produces dreams of crimes, of exploding cars hurtling over steep cliffs. About the loneliness that people assault savagely with kicks and blows, or electrocute with the lightning flashes of pleasure. But there it is. Writing is too brief a process, and I did not have the time. I did not choose what I have said. It arrived by chance, without my knowing why. It arrived back from the farthest point of the voyage towards consciousness; in the wink of an eye, it arrived, burst apart and scattered its 127,680 words through the air. Just the space of time required to press the stud that retracts the pen's ballpoint, and only three or four words were left. Applied thought, ponderous old beetle flapping about amid the flies' bright streaks! Thought that expresses itself, adrift in the middle of the vastness of liberated thought where all is speed, light, reality! One of these days, we shall have to find new ways of writing books: with electronic machines, with radar units, with the bubble-chambers of atomic laboratories.

CRITICISM OF THIS SELF-CRITICISM

And then, what is one to say of the writer who lies when he writes that he is lying?

And one day, inevitably, the same road passes through a village called Belisario Dominguez. The ramshackle buses leave early in the morning, at about six, and are off in a cloud of dust. They cross a succession of rock-strewn mountains, pass through fields of maize and valleys watered by mountain streams. The sky is blue, and the sun beats upon the sheet-iron roof, forcing its heat through the metal. The engine roars its way up hills, then makes the descents explosively. Sometimes the bus stops at the edge of a stagnant pool, and the driver pours buckets of water into the radiator. Finally, around two in the afternoon, from the top of a mountain, one catches one's first glimpse of the village in the distance, with its square houses and parallel streets. It is there, nestling in a fertile valley, a sort of blob the colour of dust and chalk.

That is how Young Man Hogan arrived in the village. He took a room in the hotel in the main square, and dropped his bag on the bed. Then he lay down beside the bag and slept for an hour. The room was dark, windowless. The folding doors gave on to a sort of inner courtyard where there were green plants, and children playing around. A copper tap was dripping into a basin. In the centre of the courtyard there was a fresh-water well. At the far end, a row of planks concealed latrines that swarmed with flies. Behind the latrines, three sleeping pigs were wallowing in mud and excrement.

When he had slept long enough, Young Man Hogan left the room. He washed his hands and face under the copper tap, and lit a cigar. Then he left the hotel and began walking around the square. He studied every detail of the large rectangle of dust surrounded by arcaded houses. The sun was very high in the sky, and the patches of white light lay motionless on the ground. There was a garden, too, in the centre of the square, and a cast-iron kiosk. A little farther away, on a pedestal, a black statue depicted a man on horseback brandishing a sword and a flag. There was no noise. Just faint sounds coming from somewhere far away: bells ringing, muffled explosions, tremors that passed through the sluggish air and faded away again, back in the same direction. The light burned the eyes, the nape of the neck, the chest. A slight wind lifted the dust.

Hogan crossed the square slowly. He saw that he was not alone. There were many women and children moving about in the bright light, carrying various loads. Men were sitting around on stone benches or with their backs against the trunks of trees. They were doing nothing. Round the statue, skinny old men were squatting on the ground, talking. Some young men were sitting on the steps of the kiosk, smoking silently.

A little farther on, Young Man Hogan walked through a market set up along the sidewalk. He stooped to pass under the awnings that were secured by strings, and stepped over the displays of vegetables and pottery. Women were sitting on their haunches under the stretched canvasses, waiting there in the dust. Hogan looked at the things they were offering for sale. He saw little piles of red chilis, little piles of lemons, little piles of seeds. He saw things that looked like bloated skins, and strips of boiled leather, and chunks of whitish fat set in the centre of green leaves. He saw flapjacks, and loaves, and cakes. All this was for sale, waiting there patiently. Up and down the corridor of flapping sails, the crowd jostled, peered, munched. The air was thick, glistening with dust and sweat, pulsating.

Before leaving the market, Young Man Hogan bought two oranges from a fat woman with plaits. He chose the fruit himself, paid for them, and carried them away in his hand.

Then he returned to the square and sat in the shade, between the columns of a house. He finished smoking his cigar and crushed it under his foot in the dust. In front of him, the square was white with light, and above his head the sky was blue. Young Man Hogan took his jack-knife out of his pocket and set about peeling the first orange. He cut thin strips off the peel and dropped them on to the ground in front of him. When he had removed the whole peel he picked away the white pith lining the skin of the fruit. Then he divided the orange into segments with his fingers, and ate them one after the other. The powerful odour rose slowly toward him, impregnating everything. The white square, the kiosk, the black statue, the sky and the dusty houses began to smell of orange. He swallowed the little sacs of pulp, and the acid taste flowed through his mouth. Perhaps it was the houses, the sky and the square that he was swallowing, now. There were one or two pips in each segment, and Y. M. Hogan spat them out in front of him, together with the bits of chewed skin. These fell on the ground and made little humid patches in the middle of the great dryness.

When he had finished eating the first orange, Y. M. Hogan shook the drops of juice off his fingers; then he ate the second orange.

It was good, eating these pieces of fruit, like this, while looking at the square as the sun beat down on it, and the silhouettes of the people crossing the sidewalk. That meant that there was not much farther to go, now. That he was quite close, just a few paces away, perhaps. Y. M. Hogan saw all the little patterns swarming in front of him, the tiny circles, the wrinkles, the fine lines engraved on the skin. The windowpane, the terrible glossy windowpane had vanished. The air was transparent, and weightless particles hovered in the light: midges, grains of wood and flour, seeds from trees. They danced above the ground, each detail clearly visible. Y. M. Hogan spat out the orange pips into the road in front of him. Then he studied them, and they gave an impression of certainty and immediacy, like immovable islands in the middle of a storm-tossed sea.

Y. M. Hogan chewed the orange's tender flesh, swallowed the spurts of juice. There would be no more hunger, ever again, no more thirst. There would be no more sadness or waiting, ever again. No more haste. The square occupied the centre of this village, which surrounded it with its houses made of dried mud. In the square, people were coming and going, dogs were sleeping curled up, the trees were indestructible. Someone was smoking a cigarette. Someone was fastening his sweat-soaked horse to a wooden post. Someone was sleeping in the shadow of a truck, his head hidden under a straw hat.

On this particular day, Y. M. Hogan was sitting in the centre of this village where peace reigned. He saw that in this place words had ceased to wound. Something had happened here, once upon a time, not so very long ago. Something had erased harshness, misery, crime. No one knew—no one knew yet—what that something was. Time had halted its damnable course, perhaps, and the years had rolled back. Or else space had entered his own body, abruptly shrinking its thousands of miles. The houses rested on their mud foundations, clouds of dust quivered in the wind, and the sun was high, hanging in the sky like an electric-light bulb.

Hogan was neither late, nor early. He was exactly there, clad in his linen trousers and white shirt, naked feet in dark brown thonged sandals. He ate the last remaining segment of the second orange, then snapped his knife shut and put it back in his pocket. He took out a big red handkerchief and wiped his fingers and mouth. Then he took another of the green, unidentified cigars from the breast-pocket of his shirt, and lit it with a match. He smoked the cigar with his eyes closed.

In front of his feet, the orange pips and chewed skins slowly aged. Farther away, a red house cast its shadow across the square, and the sun slipped backward. Swarms of flies buzzed around, then settled on the edge of the stone slab where Hogan was sitting, settled on the ground, on his linen trousers, on his hands. Flies with flattened bodies and outspread wings. Hairy flies. Flies with tiny blood-red heads.

It was *that* that needed to be said, before anything else: nothing killed. Nothing came out of the shadows, eyes gleaming with hatred, wielding sharp machetes like huge razor blades. Nothing sped along the vertiginous highways, any longer, headlamps and radiator grilles eager to commit murder. There were no shark-snouted airplanes in the sky. Men's boots did not seek for corpses to trample. The surrounding noises were not armed. The flashes of light were pure, gushing forth like springs from rock, clear, cold, innocent of evil. The people's eyes ... but I do not want to mention the people's eyes, yet.

And also: nothing went away for good. Y. M. H.'s wrist still had fastened to it a sort of circular machine with figures and pointers on it. And if he held it to his ear he could hear a very fast 'Tk! Tk! Tk! Tk!' But that no longer meant anything. Here, the time of day had stopped existing a long time ago. The springs of all the clocks had unwound their steel spirals right up to the tips, and now it did not matter one way or the other. The sun was here, then there, without anything having changed. In the centre of the square, the cast-iron kiosk swivelled its shadow slowly round, and then? Nothing went away for good.

The bricks of the walls were held together by cement; the air was a block of glass filled with little bubbles. Even the dust was faithful. Eddying gusts of wind scooped it up for a moment, then it sank back into place, each grain fitting exactly into its allotted hollow. The flies were no longer traitors: they always realighted on the hand that had shooed them away, or on the corner of the eyelid. They had their reasons for this faithfulness ... Happy the men whose wives are like these flies!

And also: nothing was dead. Nothing was rotten. The village was a little cemetery in the sun, with its neat rows of tombs painted pink and blue, and no one could disappear. Oblivion had stopped hovering menacingly in the depths of the empty sky. The intense dryness had hardened the surfaces of the walls and dusty roads. The kind of water that corrupts was infinitely absent. There was nothing but these flashes of light, this heat, these sharp shadows, these trees with leaves cut out of aluminium. No, one could not die, here. One could no longer be engulfed by the night, or crushed by the day. It was enough to be sitting, watching men's silhouettes walk through the white square. Nothing was alone any longer. No more walking along endless roads, listening to the intolerable clacking of heels against asphalt. No more swirling crowds, plunged into, then left behind. Those shop windows that were really made of steel, not glass, did not exist here. And all those figures and caricatures —grimaces of pain, grimaces of passion, grimaces of fear, grimaces of toothache —had disappeared. They had abated. The loneliness that encouraged one to flee, always farther, eternally opening and closing the doors of the great hospital; loneliness with doglike eyes; the loneliness of giants striding through the ocean of heads; that of dwarfs striding through forests of legs; the loneliness that makes a man cling to his woman, to any woman, like a leech. The curtain had risen, today, revealing the miracle of a scene full of warmth and light, almost within reach. Y. M. Hogan saw it stretching away before him, pulsating with life, the scene in which he figured, the scene that he was at last playing, with all the strength at his command. Suddenly he felt like laughing. He felt like lying on his back in the dust and laughing. Perhaps the world would have imitated him, and there would never have been any more wars again, anywhere.

It is still too early to tell you about Simulium, the coffee fly. So, for the moment, let us talk about dung-beetles. Young Man Hogan watched the dung-beetles pushing their balls of excrement across the square. They worked away with all their feet, tiny tanks advancing across the desert. Let us talk about the red cockroaches and the grey cockroaches that lie in wait in dark hollows. Let us talk about the white scorpions that hide under flat stones:

    Scorpions lead solitary lives.

    If you should see two together, it means that one

    of them is either courting or eating the other.

Let us talk about vultures, spiders, vampire bats, horned vipers. Y. M. Hogan felt a sense of disquiet growing in him. Something false and terrible seemed to be exerting menaces from very close at hand. A secret, perhaps, a horrible secret which should have been jealously guarded and never told to anyone. To fight this feeling, Y. M. Hogan started thinking to himself:

Thoughts by Y. M. Hogan
Belisario Dominguez
(State of Chiapas)
3.30 pm

'Laura, it is here, I have found it. I do not think I shall ever flee again. I have shaken off my enemies, once and for all. Al Capone, Custer, Mangin, MacNamara, Attila, Pizarro, De Soto, Bonaparte, you know, all my enemies. Not to mention Chevrolet, Panhard, Ford, Alfa Romeo. All those who were after me. They have lost track of me, I think. It is a miracle. And General Beautiful, Colonel Good, Field Marshal True. Admiral Evil. Major God, Captain Satan. All those who were on my trail. With their uniforms. With their swords. All my enemies in dark glasses, with their striped ties and slicked-down hair. And some women, too, Rimmel, Mascara, Garters. Those who were lying in wait for me behind the glossy pages of magazines, with their finely honed bodies, with their breasts, with the spears of their legs: the ones who had eyes of steel, black lashes, and coral-red lips. Those who set their disdainful traps for me, and laughed to see me stumble. The women called Love, the woman called Sweet, Beautiful. They will never get as far as this. Their skins could never stand the intense light that explodes everywhere. Their ears could never stand the silence. The gold and silver of their hair could never stand the dust. I am free, almost free! Come, now. I have kept a place for you beside me, on the stone step in the shade of the arcaded house. I have kept a place for you in the iron bed inside the windowless room. Come. Take boats, airplanes, trains and ramshackle buses, and get here! It is time. You could be here before the sun sets. Don't waste a moment! Get here! You will never again be far away. You will be finished with windowpanes, walls, clothes. You do not know what air is. You have no conception of a glass of water. Come, I will show you. Together, we shall discover so many things. We shall look inside houses, we shall climb up to the tops of mountains, we shall trace rivers back to their sources. There are herbs that one can eat, herbs to make the hair grow, herbs to produce delicious dreams. We shall follow the ant trails. We shall have nineteen children, whose names will be William, Henry, Maria, Jerome, Lourdès, Conception, Irene, David, Luz Elena, Yoloxochitl, Jésus, Suriwong, Bernard, James, Alice, Elzunka, Laura 1, Laura 2, Gabriel. We shall be so full of life that we shall need to use up 166 years before we can die. The sky will be so blue during the day, and so black at night, that words will fail us. The sun will be so hot that we shall become Negroes. Come, everything is ready. We shall eat oranges. We shall spit the pips out on the ground. We shall work all day in the coffee plantations, for a boss who will own a Rolls Royce and a jet plane. We shall drink coffee as thick as syrup out of stained glasses. We shall eat roots, and we shall talk to everybody. Come: the people here do not wear dark glasses. On the deserted road, at the entrance to the village, there is a big skeleton of a horse, standing upright and secured to a post by cords. Belisario Dominguez was a deputy. To take revenge on him, Victoriano Huerta imprisoned him, then had his tongue torn out. There are lots of things like that to tell you. Quick! Don't hesitate! I have some cigars for you, long cigars of green tobacco, that I buy by the hundred. I smoke them while watching the square shine in the sun. I exhale the acrid smoke through my nose and my mouth, and the smoke evaporates in the air. I am in the village. Here, absolute peace reigns. You will not be afraid of anyone because you will belong to the landscape. Isn't it marvellous? Isn't it?'

A little later, Y. M. Hogan got up. He crossed the square again, steering clear of the people who were groping their way along. He stopped at the outside counter of a grocery store and bought a small bottle full of a yellowish liquid. As he made his way back to the spot where he had been sitting, he noticed that his place had been taken. Someone had parked himself on the stone step in the shade of the colonnaded house. When he got closer, Y. M. Hogan saw that it was a young man, thirty years old at most, wearing linen trousers and a white shirt, his naked feet in thonged sandals. His thin face was the colour of terracotta, and he had very black hair. His face was covered with peculiar-looking grey patches containing clusters of little nodules: they were on his forehead, around his eyes, and on his cheeks. The tiny, flat flies flew ceaselessly around the man's face, making a halo of black dots. From time to time, the man shooed them away with his hand, but they returned immediately, swarming around the pustules.

Y. M. Hogan sat down beside the man. He greeted him. The man replied in a husky voice, without turning his head. When Y. M. Hogan prised the cap off the bottle with the blade of his knife, the man gave a start.

'It's nothing,' said Hogan, 'just a soda.'

'Ah,' said the man, reassured.

Hogan drank from the bottle. Then he held it out to the man.

'Would you care for some?' he asked.

'What?'

'The soda. Would you care for a drink?'

'Thanks,' said the man. And he held out his hand. He took three gulps of the soda and handed the bottle back. He wiped his mouth with his hand.

'Thanks a lot,' he said. 'You a stranger?'

'Yes,' said Hogan.

'Ah yes. Are you a doctor?'

'No,' Said Hogan.

The little black flies strolled around the man's eyes. Y. M. Hogan noticed that the eyes were swollen, red, gummed by tears.

'Pity,' said the man. 'We could certainly use one here.'

'What a terrible disease,' said Hogan.

'Yes,' the man answered, simply. His sharp profile was motionless in the shadow. Only the flies moved.

'It seems these filthy things are responsible,' said the man, sweeping his hand through the air.

'The flies?'

'Yes, these gnats.' He rubbed his eyes with his fingers.

'The gnats which infest the coffee plantations. They lay their eggs under a man's skin. Then he gets a fever. And since there is no doctor around, everybody catches it. You don't have this disease, yourself?'

'No,' said Hogan. 'Not yet.'

'And it hurts,' said the man. 'It burns the head, the eyes, the nostrils, everywhere. Your head feels like it's on fire.'

Y. M. Hogan fished out a cigar and gave it to the man.

'Smoke is good against the gnats,' he said.

He lit the man's cigar first, then his own.

'I could still see a little, ten days ago. Now, I'm finished. Nothing. Blackness.'

'You work on the plantation?'

'Yes, every day. Below the village.'

'How do you manage?'

'There are cords stretched right along the rows. You hold on to the cord with one hand, and pick with the other.'

The man blew a cloud of smoke in the air. The gnats scattered hastily. But Y. M. Hogan could see them dancing in the light, waiting. When the cigar was finished, they would come back.

'Feel better?'

'Yes,' said the man. 'Thanks for the cigar.'

'You from here?' asked Hogan.

'From here, yes. From Belisario.'

'You live alone?'

'No. With my family. Over there, near the plantation.'

He passed the glowing end of the cigar along his cheek, close to the skin.

'They say it's good for the pain,' he explained.

'So there's no doctor here?' said Hogan.

'No,' said the man. 'There was one who came, three

314

months ago. He said the first thing to do was spray DDT everywhere. But the boss refused. He said it would cost him the crop. Then the doctor went away. He said he would make a report. And we never heard any more of him.'

'And your wife?'

'What?'

'She ... Is she, has she, too?'

'My wife? Two years ago. My children have got it, too.'

'Do they work on the plantation?'

'The eldest one, yes. But my wife stays at home these days. She has a fever all the time.'

The man chewed the end of his cigar.

'It's funny, I'd never have thought,' he said. 'I'd never have thought that that could happen, just like that, to everyone. Perhaps it is God's curse upon us. Don't you think?'

'I don't know. Perhaps,' said Hogan.

'Perhaps the whole world will get to be like that. Perhaps the boss will get to be like that, and then you, and then the President, and then all the Russians and all the Chinese. Huh?'

Y. M. Hogan looked around him at the white square. He took another gulp of the soda and gave the bottle to the man. The man drank what was left, then handed back the empty bottle. He wiped his mouth with his hand once more, and said:

'Thanks. Thanks a lot, mister.'

Then he got up, leaning his weight on a stick made from a length of sugarcane. Hogan had not noticed that the man was carrying a stick. The man turned his head towards Hogan; it was puffy with the nodules that infested it. He put the cigar in his mouth and said:

'Thanks a lot for the cigar. I must get home now.'

'Goodbye,' said Hogan.
'Goodbye,' said the man.

There it is. The secret is out, now. The tragic mystery has risen suddenly to beauty's surface, forming its vile pustule. The secret has taken the shape of a gnat, this time. A minute black insect, half way between fly and mosquito, called Simulium. On the coffee plantations, the living clouds swirl into the air, then swoop down on the faces and hands of human beings, and suck their blood. Down the hollow needle of the insect's proboscis glide the parasites called *onchocerca caecutiens*: these invisible worms spread over the skin, raising fibrous nodules on the face and scalp, and around the eyes. The microfilariae multiply in the dermis. Then the human host scratches at his skin with his nails, opening abrasions through which the streptococci swarm. The result is tumefaction, erysipelas and fever. Pain has already started striking invisible blows that become increasingly agonizing. Finally, the microfilariae pierce the nodules round the eyes, and spread. Conjunctivitis inflames the eye. Keratitis and choroiditis make the eye opaque. There is the secret, then. Perhaps it would have been better not to tell it. Perhaps it would have been better to bypass it and forget it. By now, one would be far away. One would be on a beach of golden sand, stretched out in the sun, and one would be free to think about infinity, or to write a poem that the tide would wash out, while watching the sea's waves with their crests like the brows of bulls. Y. M. Hogan set off on a walk through the village where the people were blind. Around him, human figures were shuffling along, groping and tapping. He passed chains of men crossing the luminous square with linked arms. He saw an old woman striking the ground with the ferrule of her stick, and talking to herself as she went along. Near the black statue, two young men were sitting on the ground with bags at their feet. The glaucous eyes set deep in their ravaged faces were motionless and unseeing. Near the kiosk, a man was begging; but nobody could see him. Three women with long black hair were squatting on the ground, and above their heads there were these haloes of dots that moved like clouds. The square was full of men and women in motion. But it was a funnel of silence, really, a deep crater in which all movements were frozen still. Only the flies were active. They came and went in the transparent air, settling their delicate legs on faces, crawling along the rims of eyelids and the edges of lips. A blind woman was suckling a blind baby. In the dust, children were waving their arms around and yelling. But Hogan no longer heard anything. As he crossed the square, stepping over bodies, threading his way through the crowd in a zigzag movement, the tiny flies were already settling on him. Horror is not unimaginable, it has neither the face of a monster nor the bat-wings of a demon. It is calm and tranquil, and it is durable, lasting whole days and nights, months; years, perhaps. It is not mortal. It strikes at the eyes, only the eyes.

The blind population moves to and fro along the village's bright lanes. It gropes its way along walls, it enters the cool houses, it returns from the fields where the deep green plants grow. It sells, from the tents set up in the market, and it buys there, too. Behind the little mountains of pimentos, the hand reaches out and palpates. It takes a handful of the peppers and transfers them to the outstretched hand. Then it withdraws again, and the coin clinks as it falls into the tin box. Under the canvas awnings, the caravan advances, hand on shoulder. To the right, another caravan is moving in the opposite direction. In the impassive faces, the opaque eyes have closed up over the war that used to rage. But what has taken over is an insane peace, a peace worse than war. Tranquil suffering weighs down with all its weight upon the village. It is a cry which has been strangled in the throat and which has retreated within the body to ravage it.

Elsewhere in the world, on the other side of the encircling mountains, are the terrible countries where looks bulge out. But here, the looks are open mouths that suck in and swallow ceaselessly. Elsewhere, vicious windowpanes are shining. But here, the wind is blowing, sweeping down from the sky and into the depths of the extinguished sockets. What chance of standing up to such a hurricane? Where to hide, when the whole world has vanished into its hideaways? All round the rectangular square are groups of men feeling their way along the walls. When their hands come into contact with a window, they stop and turn the white eyes in their set faces towards the light. No one, in this village of termites and moles, ever arrives anywhere. One goes round and round in a circle, never stopping, one paces endlessly up and down the luminous square. The blue sky, above, is unendurable. It flays ruthlessly, it rains down its white arrows on to the dusty ground. It is of a purity that it has never attained elsewhere. When night falls, the stars shine frenziedly in the depths of empty space, and the moon is incomparably bigger than the sun. Somewhere in the village, a gasping generator is providing current for the electric lamps that light the unpaved streets. And it is as though all the lightning flashes in the world had packed themselves into these little glass bulbs. There is no time left, oh no, there is no time left. Who knows just how far the hours can travel inside sealed skulls? To the end of eternity, perhaps. The blind people move forward over the flat ground. Each fingers the other's clothes, brushes the other's face with his hands, before recognition comes. Hope rebounds from day to day with its repertory of slow gestures. In the dark café, where the metal tables are the flies' airports, the young girl sits patiently, listening to the music and the words that come from her transistor radio. When the loudspeaker vibrates with a quick tempo, she moves her right hand and whistles in rhythm with the tune. Her face has a delicately arched nose, and white teeth gleam between her parted lips; but the eyelids are stuck fast together. Her eyes will never again follow your movements as you pass to the right or the left. They will never again rise to look, miraculously, unwaveringly, straight into your own. They will never again flicker anxiously as they search for the mirrors that are everywhere. Who dared sew those lids together? Eyes, please open, just once. Look at me! I am here. I have come.

In the village filled with this atrocious peace, Young Man Hogan waited for the bus.

Real lives have no end. Real books have no end.

(To be continued.)